fourteen
summers

Quinn Anderson

RIPTIDE
PUBLISHING

Riptide Publishing
PO Box 1537
Burnsville, NC 28714
www.riptidepublishing.com

Fourteen Summers

Cover art: Melissa Liban, melissa-liban.squarespace.com
Editor: May Peterson, maypetersonbooks.com
Layout: L.C. Chase, lcchase.com/design.htm

ISBN: 978-1-62649-765-8

First edition
May, 2018

Also available in ebook:
ISBN: 978-1-62649-764-1

fourteen summers

Quinn Anderson

To my older siblings, whom I dubbed Bia and Seeester when I was too little to say their real names. Thank you for years of laughter, fighting over the front seat, advice, and epic prank wars. But most of all, thank you for giving me a childhood that helped me write this book, though we didn't know it at the time.

table of contents

Prologue: Aiden . . . .　1

Chapter One: Max . . . .　9

Chapter Two: Oliver . . . .　19

Chapter Three: Aiden . . . .　35

Chapter Four: Max . . . .　47

Chapter Five: Oliver . . . .　61

Chapter Six: Aiden . . . .　77

Chapter Seven: Max . . . .　91

Chapter Eight: Oliver 109

Chapter Nine: Aiden 129

Chapter Ten: Max 143

Chapter Eleven: Oliver 155

Chapter Twelve: Aiden 167

Chapter Thirteen: Max 183

Chapter Fourteen: Oliver 193

Epilogue: Aiden 205

prologue: Aiden

On a sunny afternoon in mid-March—when spring had finally asserted itself over the last vestiges of winter, and the frost had melted into grass the color of emeralds—Aiden Kingsman attended the wedding of his twin brother, Max.

Granted, they were six, and Aiden was officiating, but it was still a momentous occasion.

They were standing in their backyard beneath the shade of a mossy oak tree. The role of the bride was being played by their best friend and next-door neighbor, Oliver. Aiden had climbed on top of a plastic patio chair, the family Bible clutched in his pudgy, pink hands. He was pretending to read passages aloud, despite only recognizing a handful of the words.

Max had stolen one of their father's suit jackets from his closet. It was about six sizes too big, but he slung it over his shoulders and held it dutifully closed in the front. Oliver had pulled the white sheet off their parents' bed and wrapped it around himself. The pillowcase draped over his jet-black hair acted as a veil, and he had a fistful of yellow daisies clenched in his fingers.

Aiden did his best to act like Pastor Greenway—the man at their church who, by Aiden's estimation, was around one thousand years old—but he couldn't get his voice low and scratchy enough. He screwed up his face into what he hoped was an approximation of Pastor Greenway's scowl, and he made sure to clear his throat every few sentences with a barking cough.

Unfortunately, his imitation made the boys in front of him break out into giggles no matter how many times he shushed them.

"You sound silly." Max's eyes shined with mirth.

Aiden glared at him with bright-blue eyes identical to Max's. "Stop laughing. You're gonna upset your bride. Mom said that when you get a marriage, the bride has to get whatever they want."

Oliver lifted his makeshift bouquet to his nose and sniffed, batting his eyelashes. "Let Aiden finish, Max. As soon as he does, we can go play."

Oliver always knew just what to say to keep the peace.

Max stuck out his tongue but managed to school his face into a serious expression. For all of two seconds. Then a bee took an interest in Oliver's flowers, and the two of them dissolved into excited hooting until it flew away.

Aiden stamped his foot, and the plastic beneath him trembled. "Guys, stop it! If you don't get a marriage, then we can't all be brothers."

That shut them up.

Oliver elbowed Max into place and knuckled up on his flowers, looking like he was going to bat. "Get to the good part, then."

"Yeah," said Max. "The faster we get a marriage, the faster we get cake."

"There's no cake, Max. Mom said no."

Max's mouth popped open. "What a rip-off."

Ignoring him, as he often did, Aiden pulled out the piece of paper he'd tucked between the pages of the Bible. In crayon, he'd copied the vows he'd heard at their cousin's wedding a month ago. Or at least, as much of them as he could remember. And spell.

Attending that wedding had put the whole marriage idea into their heads. Since then, they'd hosted no fewer than a dozen mini ceremonies in their backyard, but Max and Oliver never made it to the end.

This time, however, Aiden was determined to see it through. Not only so Oliver could be their brother, but so Max could "settle down with a nice boy." According to Mom, that was what their cousin had done, and if Mom said it, it must be a good thing.

Aiden cleared his throat again and put on his most serious face. He held the crayon vows up to the dappled light and sounded out the first sentence. "Do you, Max Kingsman, promise to be good and true to Oliver for so long as you both shall live?" He glanced at Max.

Max stretched his mouth into a thin line and widened his eyes. "I swear." He was probably trying to look solemn, but he actually looked like a startled frog.

Oliver giggled, but Aiden cut him off with a glare. "It's 'I *do*,' Max."

"Okay. I do."

Satisfied, Aiden turned to Oliver. "And do you, Oliver . . ." He trailed off. "I don't remember your last name."

"Jones." Oliver frowned. "Or is it Kingsman now?"

Max whispered to him out of the corner of his mouth. "You don't have to change your name. I heard Mom say that was undated."

"*Out*dated," Aiden corrected. "Back to the vows. Do you, Oliver Jones, promise to be a good new brother and to play with us every day, forever and ever, until we croak?"

Oliver nodded, green eyes somber. "I do."

"And do you promise to share all your toys?"

He rubbed his chin like people did in movies when they were thinking. "Everything but my jigsaw puzzles. Max always loses a piece."

"I do not, Ollie!"

Before they could start arguing, Aiden interjected. "We can live with that." He squinted at the vows, which were sounding increasingly like a list of demands. "Do you promise to never hog the remote like *someone* always does." He glowered at Max.

Max made an affronted squawking noise, but Oliver answered, "I do."

"And will you make the special grilled cheese sandwiches your mom always makes?"

"I'm not allowed to use the stove."

"Hm." Aiden sucked on his bottom lip. "We're not allowed to either. Maybe we can get Mom to make them."

"Are we done yet?" Max whined. "I want to go play."

Aiden held up a finger. "One more. This is for both of you. Max and Oliver, do you both swear—cross your hearts and hope to die—that you will always, *always* be the very best of friends?"

They exchanged mischievous grins that were so identical, Aiden had to remind himself who was the twin here.

In unison, they said, "We do."

"Then by the power vest of me, in the state of New York, I here declare you . . . um, married, I think."

Oliver tossed his flowers into the air. "Woohoo!" Yellow petals floated down and landed in his soft black hair.

"We did it!" Max threw his arms out and fell straight backward, landing on the grass with a muted *thud*. Dad's suit jacket flew open to reveal Max's dirt-smudged play clothes. "Life as we know it will never be the same."

"What does that mean?" Aiden asked.

"I dunno. I heard it on TV."

Oliver sat cross-legged on the grass next to him, tossing a loose corner of his sheet-dress over his shoulder. "Do you think we'll be marriaged for real some day?"

Aiden jumped off the chair and landed with a wobble. He set the Bible on the seat with care. "Of course. How else can we all be brothers?"

Max twisted his mouth to the side in thought. "Maybe Mom and Dad can adopt Oliver."

Aiden waved him off. "That sounds hard. Marriage is much simpler."

"All right, then." Max propped himself up on his elbows. Little bits of grass were sticking out of his brown curls. "I'll marry Oliver so he can be our brother. But you"—he jabbed a finger at Aiden—"have to marry Chrissy Casen."

"Ew." Aiden wrinkled his nose. "Why would I marry her?"

"Because her parents have a pool."

"But she's a *girl*. I don't want to marry a *girl*."

"Yeah, but our seventh birthday could be a pool party."

Aiden paused. "Hm. Good point."

"I don't care who gets a marriage." Oliver was picking petals off one of his flowers and laying them in a pile on Max's chest. "So long as the three of us are friends."

"*Best* friends," Aiden corrected.

"No. *Brothers*." Max glared at him. "That's what we all said."

Aiden's little face grew hot. "It's the same thing."

"Is not."

"Is so!"

"Is not!"

"Is so times infinity!"

"*Is not times infinity, plus one!*"

Aiden pocketed the vows and—bellowing a wild war cry—launched himself at his brother. Max tried to roll to the side, but Aiden caught him right in the stomach. They hit the grass, grappling without mercy.

Oliver scooted out of the way, eyes wide and wary. "Um, guys? I don't think you should fight."

Aiden looked up at Oliver right as Max moved to shove him. Max ended up hitting him square in the face with all his six-year-old strength.

For a moment, Aiden was stunned. Then, he burst into tears. It didn't hurt that much, but the surprise of it was enough to wrench a tremulous wail from his throat.

Max was on his feet in an instant. "I'm sorry! I'm sorry!" He danced around Aiden. "Please don't tell Mom."

Aiden climbed to his feet without a word and headed for the house. He could see their mom through the sliding glass door leading into the kitchen. She was stirring a glass pitcher of lemonade with a wooden spoon, her pink mouth curled up into a smile. Her image blurred as his eyes filled with fresh tears.

Max chased after him, pleading with him not to tell, but Aiden ignored Max. By the time he got to the glass, his cries had quieted into whimpers punctuated by sniffling. He caught sight of their reflections, which were faint and dark like he needed a flashlight to see them. They had the same messy chestnut curls. Same round faces. Same blue eyes, except now Aiden's were red and puffy.

Just as he put his hand on the door, Oliver caught up to them. His cheeks were flushed with exertion, making his light eyes stand out in sharp contrast. "Don't tell your Mom, Aiden."

Because it was Oliver talking, Aiden stopped with his hand poised over the door handle. "Why not?"

"If Max gets in trouble, she'll send me home." He bit his lip. "I don't wanna go home."

Aiden's sobs evaporated. "Okay. I won't tell."

"Woohoo!" Max threw his hands up into the air. "My wife is the coolest!"

Mom must have heard him shout, because the glass slid open a second later. She poked her head out, smiling so wide her cheeks formed twin red apples in her face. "Are you boys ready to come in?"

"No," all three of them said at once.

Mom laughed. "I think it's time for you to get cleaned up. Dinner's almost ready, and Oliver's parents are here to pick him up." She caught sight of the grass stuck to Max's clothes and the now-stained sheet wrapped around Oliver. "Later, we're going to have a talk about what you're allowed to play with outside."

Aiden caught her hand and tugged on it. "Mom, can Oliver stay the night?"

"Not tonight, honey. His parents want him home for dinner."

"But he's our brother now," Max said.

Oliver elbowed Aiden in the side. "Lemme see the vows. I wanna read them to her."

"No way," Aiden whispered back. He shoved a chubby fist into his pocket and fingered the paper. "*I'm* gonna read them to her. Later. I bet she'll put them on the fridge."

Max plucked a petal out of Oliver's hair and held it up as if that proved something. "We got a marriage, and that means Oliver lives here now."

Mom covered her mouth with a hand, smothering laughter. "I see. Why wasn't I invited to my son's wedding?"

Max dropped the petal, looking stricken. "Uh-oh."

Mom ruffled his hair. "Much as I would love for Oliver to stay forever, you can't get married until you're eighteen. Besides, Oliver's parents would be heartbroken if he came to live with us. Oliver, you want to go home with your parents, don't you?"

Oliver didn't answer. His lips were pursed in a way Aiden had grown to recognize: he wanted to say no, but he was too polite to correct an adult.

Aiden answered for him. "He wants to stay here with us."

"I'm sure he does, but not today, okay? He can come over again tomorrow."

Max gave Aiden a sour look. "This is your fault. If you hadn't come up here to tell on me, she wouldn't be sending him home."

Mom's keen eyes darted between them. "Tell on you for what, Max?"

"Um," said Max.

"Well . . ." Aiden added.

Mr. and Mrs. Jones walked into the kitchen then, escorted by Dad. Mrs. Jones had dark hair and green eyes, same as Oliver, whereas Mr. Jones was tan all over: tan skin, tan hair, and eyes the color of raisins.

Aiden wasn't sure why, but he'd always thought there was something strange about Oliver's parents. They didn't laugh much. Mr. Jones's mouth was perpetually set into the same frown Max made when Mom forced him to eat peas. And unlike Mom and Dad, they never stood next to each other. In fact, the Joneses seemed to make an effort to stand as far apart as they could get.

Aiden didn't know what that meant, but it gave him a weird feeling in his stomach, like that time he'd accidentally swallowed an ice cube and he'd felt it slide all the way down.

He considered asking Oliver about it, but then Mom scooped him up and left big, noisy kisses on his cheek until he squealed. Max ran up to her and demanded to be picked up too, but he got Dad instead. Dad gave good kisses, but his face was scratchy. When their parents weren't watching, Aiden stuck his tongue out at Max.

"We've got to get going," Mr. Jones said. He looked down at his son. "Take that sheet off, Oliver. I'm sure the Kingsmans don't appreciate you ruining it."

"Don't worry about it." Dad tickled Max, making him shriek with joy. "Nothing a little white vinegar won't get out."

Oliver removed the sheet, handed it to Mom, and went to stand by Mrs. Jones. He shot Aiden a final, pleading look, but Aiden could only shrug.

"Thanks for having him," Mrs. Jones said. "You should come over for dinner at our house sometime."

"You bet." Mom smiled. "We'd love to."

The Joneses exited the kitchen, taking the odd ice-cube feeling with them. Oliver followed behind his parents, but right before they disappeared through the doorway, he turned back. Out of his pocket, he produced Aiden's crayon vows and waved them at him, as if he were taunting a bull with a red cape.

Aiden gasped, but by the time he'd gotten over the surprise, Oliver had disappeared. Aiden wasn't certain how he knew, but he had a feeling he wouldn't see those vows again for a long time.

Chapter 1: Max

Fourteen Years Later

"**M**ax? Max Kingsman? Is that you?"

At the sound of his name, Max looked up from the cantaloupe he was thumping and glanced around. Across the produce aisle, he spotted a young man with black hair staring at him as if he were wearing the cantaloupe like a hat.

For a second, Max stared back, a sea of faces sloshing around in his head. Then, a name he hadn't heard in years popped up and attached itself to the person in front of him. "Oliver?"

"Oh my God, it *is* you." Oliver transferred his basket to one hand, jogged over, and threw his free arm around Max.

Max hugged back as best he could with a five-pound melon clutched to his chest. "Oliver Jones. Holy shit. How are you? I haven't seen you in ..."

"Way too long." Oliver held Max at arm's length and studied him. "It's been at least a decade, for sure. Man, you're all grown-up now. You look good."

"So do you." It was true. Gone was the short, pretty-faced boy Max remembered from his childhood. Before him stood a man who'd shot up and filled out. Oliver's arms were corded with muscle, and his jawline could dice Max's cantaloupe. Max was comfortable enough with his sexuality to admit he wanted to whistle. "I'm so glad I ran into you. How'd you know it was me?"

Oliver blinked. "I know it's been a while, man, but there's no way I'd forget the face of one of my childhood best friends."

"No, I mean, how'd you know it was me and not my brother? Our own parents can't tell us apart sometimes."

"Oh, right." Oliver seemed to consider it. "I dunno. I could always tell you and Aiden apart when we were kids. I guess some things never change."

"Well, it's great to see you. What happened to you?" Max thought back. "You moved to the city the summer before middle school, right? I remember we were pen pals for a while, but then I think you moved again or something?"

"Kind of. My parents got divorced." Oliver ran a hand through his thick hair, which was as jet-black as Max remembered. "Apparently, they were waiting for me to finish elementary school before they made it official. They figured it'd make the transition easier for me, since I had to go to a new school regardless. My mom moved into the city while my dad moved out to California. I spent the school year with Mom and then summer and holidays with Dad. I was always bouncing back and forth."

Max gave in and whistled. "That explains why you're so damn tan. Been soaking up that Cali sunshine?"

"Nah, I think that's more the Italian in me. My friends on the East Coast used to joke I was the most 'stereotypical' New Yorker."

"So, if it's summer, why aren't you in California?"

"My dad moved back to Irvington not too long ago." He swept his free arm at the room around them. "Which means I got to come home sweet home."

"Well, fuck," Max said with all his trademark eloquence. "You should have dropped us a postcard or something. Aiden and I were half-convinced you'd been abducted by aliens."

"Aiden." Oliver's green eyes widened as if he'd realized something. "Is Aiden *here*? Like, is he with you? I'd love to see him."

"He's here, but just so you know, he pretty much looks like this." Max pointed at his face before cupping a hand over his mouth and yelling in the general direction of the next aisle. "Yo, Aiden! You're not gonna believe who I ran into!"

A voice sounded from over the shelves. "Who? And did Mom say she wanted multigrain or whole wheat?"

"Forget the bread. You're gonna freak."

A second later, Aiden rounded the corner and stopped a few feet from them, a loaf of nutty bread swinging in his grip. "I went with the multigrain, but—" His eyes latched on to Oliver and then popped out of his skull. "Oh my God. *Oliver*?"

"I know, right?" Max slapped Oliver on the shoulder. "Back from the dead."

He started to say something else but was shocked into silence when his brother dropped the loaf to the floor and pulled Oliver into a fierce hug.

Oliver hugged back, so tightly his shoulder muscles stood out beneath his blue T-shirt. "Good to see you too, buddy."

Max's eyes darted between them, eyebrows raised. He didn't know about Oliver, but Aiden wasn't one to show affection in public. When they were kids, he'd even refused to sit in Santa's lap, preferring instead to write him a polite letter.

After they released each other, Aiden seemed to realize what he'd done. He looked down at his shoes, blood rushing into his face. "Sorry. I didn't mean to pounce on you like that. I was just so shocked to see you. It's been *way* too long."

"No need to apologize." Oliver flashed a thousand-watt grin. "I wasn't expecting to run into you two either. Are you shopping?"

"Nah, we come in here every now and then to grope the produce." Max smirked. "Of course we're shopping. We came home for the summer, and the first thing Mom did was give us chores."

"She's cooking us a special dinner tonight," Aiden said with the air of a teacher correcting an errant pupil. "The least we could do was run to the store for her."

Max stuck out his tongue. "Suck-up."

"Delinquent."

"Ah." Oliver breathed in through his nose. "There's something I never thought I'd hear again. I dunno what it says about me, but I missed listening to the Kingsman twins' epic squabbling."

"There's plenty more where that came from." Max put the cantaloupe back into the pile and then held up their shopping basket.

"Mind if we walk and talk? I wanna catch up, but we've got to get this food to our mom."

"Oh, right." Oliver looked sheepish. "Listen, we can catch up later. I didn't mean to interrupt."

"Bullshit." Max punched him on the arm. "We gotta shop. You gotta shop. We might as well do it together. Isn't that right, Aiden?"

Aiden bent down to pick up the bread he'd dropped, face still pink as a rare steak. He tossed it into their basket and then shuffled his feet. "Right. Tell us everything you've been up to."

"Everything, huh? That might take a while."

Max led the way to the next aisle while Oliver and Aiden trailed behind him like ducklings. "Let's start simple. Are you in school?"

"I am, yeah." Oliver plucked something off a shelf and added it to his basket without stopping. "I go to NYU."

Max shot an impressed look over his shoulder. "Damn, that's a good school. You must be a genius, like my bro." He paused in the dairy aisle to peruse the fifty kinds of butter and butter-like substitutes the grocer offered.

Oliver glanced at Aiden. "Do you go to NYU too? I'll be so pissed at myself if we've been at the same school this whole time and I didn't know."

Aiden shook his head and opened his mouth, but all that came out was a garbled sound.

Max came to his rescue. "Nah. He got in to NYU, but we wanted to go to school together and stay close to home. We're both at Pace, the Westchester campus that's like twenty minutes from here. What are you majoring in?"

"Marketing. You?"

"Business," Max said.

Aiden regained control of his vocal chords. "Engineering."

"Very nice." Oliver grinned at Aiden, which for some reason made him flush red again. "It's cool that you guys go to school together."

"Yeah, it's fun." Max managed to locate some regular butter before moving on to the eggs next door. "We rented an apartment off campus. It's way cheaper than living in the dorms. Plus, I get to keep an eye on my precious baby brother." He winked at Aiden.

Aiden sighed in a long-suffering way. "You're older than me by five minutes, Max."

Max waggled his eyebrows. "Yeah, but that means I'll always have five more minutes of life experience than you."

"Not if I outlive you."

Oliver laughed. "Man, I really missed you guys. If I'd known you still lived in the area, I would have come by for a visit."

"What are you in town for?" Aiden asked.

"His dad moved back, and Oliver came with him," Max answered.

"Well, sort of." Oliver selected a gallon of milk and then adjusted his grip on his basket like it was starting to get heavy. "I'm only here for the summer, but my dad is once again a permanent resident of Irvington, New York. It's been a *nightmare*, to be honest."

"What, you're not happy to be back?"

"It's not that. It's just, my poor mom had to ferry me out here to my dad's new house because I don't have a car. Don't need one, when you live in the city."

"So? Is it that far of a drive?"

"No, but every time my parents are in the same room together, they fight. Or if they don't, you can *feel* how much they want to fight. Plus, my entire extended family decided to welcome my dad back. They're calling it a 'family reunion,' only there's no end date in sight. I got aunts and cousins and godparents I haven't seen since I was a baby crawling out of the woodwork, and they all want to know what I'm doing with my life."

Max groaned. "Oh man, I'm so glad our extended family doesn't live nearby."

"You have no idea. All my cousins are married with a million kids, and they run around screaming all the time."

"Your cousins or their kids?" Aiden asked.

"I'm not kidding when I say both. Plus, I miss my friends back in the city. I have a whole support network there that could get me through this, but there's only so much social media and Skype can do."

"Well, now you have us," Max said. "Summer break is gonna be a lot more exciting now that the Three Musketeers are back together."

"Yeah." Oliver looked at Aiden. "Much more exciting. I'll be right back, okay? I need something on aisle eight." Oliver disappeared down a row.

Max turned to his brother. "Fancy running into him here, huh? No homo, but he got *hot*. Must've shot up two feet and gained thirty pounds of pure muscle."

Aiden had been staring blankly at the spot where Oliver had disappeared, but at that he seemed to snap back to reality. "Max, don't say things like that."

"What? I'm being supportive. What's the point of having a gay brother if you can't talk about boys?"

"There's so much wrong with that question. And you shouldn't objectify our friend, you degenerate."

"I'm merely observing that puberty was kind to the guy. Don't act like you didn't notice. You may be a prude, but you're not blind."

Aiden shut his mouth with a click of teeth. Max added a tally to his side of the "won arguments" record he kept in his head.

Oliver reappeared with a fuller basket than he'd had a minute ago. "Who's blind?"

"No one," Max answered. "I was telling Aiden here that you look like you work out."

"Oh yeah, I joined crew over at NYU. The training is intense. Five days a week, and we have to wake up at the crack of dawn on Saturdays to do land exercises."

"No shit. I never took you for the team-sports type."

"Well, the last time you saw me, I was a skinny fifth grader. A lot has changed since then. Besides, the guys on my team are a lot of fun, and I love getting out onto the water."

Aiden piped up. "I'm on the lacrosse team at our school."

"No kidding?" Oliver smiled. "How do you like it?"

"I love it. I didn't expect to because I was never one for cardio, but being on a team is so much fun. And the matches are exhilarating. When I'm out on the field, I feel like I can do anything."

"You're telling me. I feel the same way when I'm rowing. You get into this rhythm, and even when your lungs are burning, you never want to stop."

"Yeah," Aiden said in a dreamy tone.

Feeling a little left out, Max searched for something to contribute. "Aiden shocked our parents half to death when he told them he'd taken up a sport. After all those years of sitting inside with his nose in a book, I think they'd given up on him."

Aiden glared at him. Max pretended he didn't see, though he couldn't stop his lips from twitching up.

Oliver looked at him sidelong. "And what about you? What's your sport of choice?"

Max frowned. "Well . . . I have a promising fantasy football league."

"Uh-huh." Oliver hefted his basket with ease. "I think I've got everything I need. I'm gonna get going, but let me get both your numbers so we can hang out."

Max dug in his pocket for his phone, but Aiden already had his in hand. "I think I found you on Facebook, actually. Is this you?"

Oliver peeked at the screen. "Yeah, that's me. I'm surprised you could tell, since my profile pic's a group shot."

Aiden had been blushing so hard for so long now, he had to be feeling woozy. "Oh, well, you stand out, I guess."

Oliver tapped the Add Friend button and then pulled out his phone to confirm the request. "Max, I'll add you off his page, okay? And I still want your numbers too."

Max and Aiden rattled off their phone numbers one at a time.

"Sweet. I'm sending you both a group text." Oliver pocketed his phone. "Lemme know what you're up to. Maybe we can plan something for tomorrow."

"Tomorrow?" Max put on his best affronted face. "Dude, we haven't seen each other in ten years. We gotta hang out *stat*. How about you come to dinner at our house tonight? I'm sure Mom and Dad would love to see you, and God knows we have enough food." He held up their overflowing basket as proof.

Oliver hesitated. "Well, I'm supposed to eat with my family tonight, but . . . I eat with them every night. And honestly, if I have to listen to my Great-aunt Berta drone on and on about 'the war' again, I'm gonna die. I can't tell which war she *means*."

"Then it's settled. You remember our old address?"

Oliver perked up. "You still live in the big blue house on Woodlark?"

"That's the one."

"Awesome. What time should I drop by?"

"Dinner's at seven, so come over at six. We can hang out beforehand."

"Perfect. See you then." He waved goodbye before heading off in the direction of the checkout lines.

Max watched him go, grinning widely. He'd planned on a summer vacation filled with Xbox and forcing Aiden to be fun, but now that the Three Musketeers were back together, he had a potential partner in crime.

He turned to Aiden with the intent of repeating this thought out loud but stopped short. His brother had a pained expression on his face. Max knew it well. It was the same one Aiden got before midterms, or when he had to make an important phone call. "Hey, what's wrong?"

Aiden shifted his weight from one foot to the other. "It's nothing."

"You can't lie to me, bro. We have that whole twin-telepathy thing going on. I can tell you're anxious about something."

That earned him an eye roll, which he accepted with glee because it meant Aiden wasn't frowning anymore. "It's nothing. I just ... I wish you hadn't invited him to dinner."

"What? Why? You don't want to hang out with Oliver?"

"No, I do." Aiden's tongue seemed to be tripping over words. "But we, um, didn't ask Mom if it was okay. It's our first night back. Maybe she wants dinner to be a family affair."

"Dude, no way. She's gonna flip. She and Dad always loved Oliver. I think they were as heartbroken when he moved as we were. Besides, we have the whole summer to spend family time together. She's not gonna care if we bring our long-lost childhood friend to dinner for one night."

Aiden wouldn't quite look at him. "I guess you're right. I don't know why I got so nervous."

Max wasn't the most perceptive person, but he knew when his brother was giving him the brush-off. He got the distinct impression he was missing something.

In his head, he shrugged. If Aiden wanted to tell him, he'd tell him. He switched their basket to his other hand and started walking again. "Come on. If we don't deliver some ingredients, dinner isn't going to happen at all."

Aiden shuffled next to him, eyes glazed as if he were lost in thought.

Max couldn't say what it was, but a strange feeling burrowed into his chest. It was hard to describe. If he were the poetic sort, he'd say he sensed a change in the wind, despite being indoors. The second Oliver had called his name, something had shifted, and he had no idea what it was.

He shook his head. That was ridiculous. Since when was he such a drama queen?

Since forever, taunted a voice in his head.

Max ignored it and slung an arm over Aiden's shoulders. "Don't worry, little bro. I'm calling it right here and now: this is going to be the best summer of our lives."

Chapter 2: Oliver

As Oliver loaded groceries into the trunk of his dad's beat-up green Camry, he replayed his conversation with the Kingsman twins over and over in his head.

He still couldn't believe he'd bumped into them after all this time, and right as he'd gotten back into town too. It was like fate. Or kismet. Something like that. He was a cynical New Yorker through and through; he didn't normally buy into such things, but running into his childhood best friends after more than ten years apart was enough to make a believer out of him.

He'd recognized Max the moment he'd laid eyes on him. Even though he and Aiden were identical, their energies were totally different. Ten years later, all Oliver had needed was to see his face to know it was him. Max was always grinning, like life was one big joke that he couldn't explain or else it wouldn't be funny anymore.

Then there was Aiden. Aiden was like . . . stone. In a good way. Solid. Steadfast. Stubborn, when it came to things that really mattered. When they were kids, their classmates had teased him for being quiet, but Oliver remembered a little boy who could go on and on and on about bugs and math long after everyone had stopped listening. Except for Oliver.

Seeing them again was like opening a time capsule, and Oliver was eager to dig through it. Since he'd arrived in Irvington last week, his life had been nothing but endless family gatherings, small talk, and obligations. Now he had something to look forward to. But first, he had to get out of dinner at Dad's house that night, a Herculean feat to say the least.

Just pulling into the driveway made dread bloom like mold in his stomach. He studied the plain beige face of the little house Dad had bought. The tiny windows and red door made it look like a beady-eyed man with his tongue lolling out.

The rest of the houses on the street were mammoths. Oliver remembered a time in which they'd all been smallish bungalows like Dad's, but the building market had expanded, and now cookie-cutter mansions had taken over like an invasive species. Dad's modest house looked like a dull pebble wedged between two hunkering boulders. Oliver couldn't imagine what had possessed his father to give up a condo in San Diego for this.

Not that Oliver wasn't grateful he'd moved back. Living on the same coast made it easier to see him.

There's your answer right there. He moved to be closer to you. Now, go in there and tell him you're ditching him tonight.

"This ought to be fun," he muttered to himself, resting his forehead on the steering wheel. It was so hot it cooked his skin, but he kept his head where it was, seeing how long he could take it. He gave up when he imagined he smelled sizzling bacon.

He exited the car, gathered the groceries out of the trunk, and trotted up to the front door. It wasn't locked—thank god; he was out of hands—and so he was able to open it with a well-placed elbow. As the door swung open, he was greeted by the ominous but familiar sound of raised voices.

Great. His parents were getting an early start.

Oliver stood in the empty foyer, debating turning right back around. The plan had been for Mom to drive him up to the suburbs and drop him off, but some of the family had insisted she stay for a few days and catch up.

Mom would have found a gentle way to refuse, but her favorite brother-in-law—Oliver's uncle—had died two weeks earlier, and work had forced her to miss the funeral. This was her one chance to pay her respects.

She'd ended up taking a week off to spend time with Uncle Ralph's widow and cook an alarming number of lasagnas for his children, all of whom were adults with kids of their own. At least she'd had the good sense to refuse Dad's offer to stay in the house, opting for a hotel room instead. Otherwise, Oliver was certain they'd have found a way to argue in their sleep.

He wasn't convinced it was worth the headache. He'd loved Uncle Ralph too. In fact, the two of them had exchanged letters in Oliver's youth. He would never forget Uncle Ralph's steady handwriting, each loopy letter formed with care and consideration. In ten years, Oliver had never seen a blot-out in one of his letters.

But the near-constant fighting made his stomach acid churn. After his parents had split up, he'd thought he would never have to listen to it again. No such luck. Every time there was a holiday or life event, Mom and Dad were thrown back together, and the screaming started up again like clockwork. It was hard not to feel like this was all his fault, considering he was their common denominator.

Oliver had been standing in the doorway for so long, the air had become a tepid mixture of air-conditioning and heat from outside. He sighed and kicked the door shut behind him. He supposed there was no avoiding it. At least Mom was heading back to the city tomorrow. If he could chin up until then . . .

Bracing himself, Oliver held the groceries in front of him like a shield and made his way through the living room to the rest of the house. With every step, the sound of yelling grew louder. By the time he walked into the kitchen, it was deafening. He wasn't the least bit surprised to find his parents standing next to the ancient stove, red-faced and screaming at the top of their lungs.

Mom's dark hair—thick as oil, same as Oliver's—was twisted up into a bun. It might have been his imagination, but Oliver thought it had twice as many gray streaks in it now. Dad looked presentable in pressed khakis and a collared shirt, but the effect was ruined by the frustration dripping from his lanky form.

Oliver skirted around them and set the groceries on the Formica counter next to the fridge. He unpacked them while reciting song lyrics in his head, like he'd done when he was a kid and the shouting had kept him awake at night.

As soon as Mom spotted him, she stopped yelling and plastered a smile on her face. It was so strained, it morphed into a rictus. "Oliver. There you are. I didn't hear you come in."

Yeah, I'll bet.

Out loud, he said, "They were out of fat-free yogurt, so I got low fat. I hope that's okay."

"That's fine, honey. Don't worry about it."

He focused on putting the groceries away, but he could feel the tension sparking between his parents behind him. It was like standing with his back to a heat lamp.

After an excruciating silence, Dad said, "Oliver, after dinner tonight, your uncles are coming over for a friendly poker match. You're welcome to join us if you'd like." His tone had a hint of challenge, and Oliver would have bet money he and Mom had been fighting about that very thing. And with good reason.

Uncle Charlie and Uncle Marcus were loud, aggressive drunks. Happy ones, for the most part, but undeniably raucous. Since Oliver had arrived last week, they'd done nothing but remark about how skinny he was—which was true, compared to their lumbering, red-faced girth—and make snide comments about his "fancy school."

The funny thing was, Oliver had fond memories of them from his childhood, but ever since he'd come out, it was like they didn't know how to act around him. Most of Dad's side of the family was like that, actually. They came from old-school Italian-Catholic roots, and as a result, Oliver was stuck fielding questions about his "lifestyle."

Oliver opened the fridge and added the yogurt, milk, and eggs to the collection of beer and condiments inside. "I would love to, Dad, but you're never going to guess who I ran into at the grocery store."

"Who?" Mom was still smiling, but her eyes kept darting toward Dad, as if she were itching to start up their fight again.

"The Kingsman twins. You remember Max and Aiden, right?"

Dad huffed. "Yeah, I remember. Nice kids, though I was always a bit put off by their parents. Nobody's marriage is that perfect."

Mom rolled her eyes. "You only think theirs was perfect because ours was so miserable."

Dad opened his mouth, purportedly to start arguing all over again, but Oliver interrupted. "Well, I was thrilled to see Max and Aiden again. We used to be close when we were kids. Best friends, in truth."

Dad nodded, though he didn't look happy about it. "Of course. You slept over there as often as you slept in your own bed."

Yeah, because listening to you and Mom screaming gave me nightmares.

"They invited me to have dinner with them. I'd like to, if that's all right. It'll give us a chance to catch up."

Dad's eyes narrowed. "Let me get this straight. You spend all year in the city with your mother, and then when I get my one measly summer with you, you'd rather have dinner with two virtual strangers?"

Despite the accusatory words, the anger melted off Dad's face and was replaced with genuine hurt. He looked away like he didn't want Oliver to see, but it was too late.

I'm a bad son.

Guilt formed a lump in Oliver's throat, making it difficult to breathe. He swallowed, but that sent it sliding into his gut like cold lead. A voice in his head demanded that he spend time with his dad, even if it meant missing out on a chance to reconnect with the Kingsmans. But another, oilier voice whispered what he wanted to hear: it was only one night. It was normal for him to want to spend time with old friends. Dad would survive.

The second voice won. "I'm sorry, Dad, but I haven't seen them in years, and I've had dinner with the family every night this week. I need a break, a chance to spend some time with people my age."

Dad's face flickered with guilt of his own, but the stiff set of his mouth said he wasn't convinced. "Some of your cousins are your age. I'd rather you had dinner with us tonight."

"Oliver is an adult, Don." Mom dug into the pocket of her capris. "If he wants to spend a couple of hours with some friends, he's allowed." She pulled out her keys. "I'll drive you, Ollie. I need to head back to my hotel anyway, and I'd love to pop in and say hi to Kim and Roger."

"That would be great. Thanks, Mom."

"Oh no you don't," Dad said.

Damn. So close.

But then he shocked Oliver by adding, "*I* will drive him."

Before Oliver could react, Mom pursed her lips. "You said you don't like the Kingsmans."

"I like them fine, and anyway, it's not about them. I want to spend some time with my son."

Oliver wanted to be flattered. His parents were fighting over who got to spend the most time with him, after all. But he knew the truth. Half of the reason Dad wanted to drive him was so Mom wouldn't get to. And Oliver was considering letting him, if it meant he got to go.

He couldn't do that to Mom. He had to stick up for her. "Dad, I appreciate the offer, but—"

Mom threw her hands up in exasperation. "Oh, *fine*. You take him. Deny me that on top of everything else. I'm out of here. Oliver, walk me to the front door." She grabbed Oliver's wrist and tugged him from the room, nose in the air.

Despite his confusion, Oliver allowed himself to be towed to the front of the house. Once there, he was about to ask what had happened when Mom turned to him and winked. "Is your dad easy or what?"

Oliver's jaw dropped to the tile floor. "You planned that?"

"Oh, come on. You think after all these years I don't know how to work your father?" She made a dismissive gesture with her hand. "Behold, your mother: the Oscar-worthy actress."

Oliver laughed. "Nice work. Though I have to admit, I feel kinda bad. You and Dad are fighting so much, and you wouldn't be here if it weren't for me."

She shushed him. "Honey, I'm a big girl. I made the decision to stay and see everyone. Besides, it's not your fault your father and I are fighting. We've been doing it since the day we met. I know you're an adult now, but you're still our boy. Leave the worrying to us, all right?"

"I guess. I hate the idea of you staying all by yourself in that hotel, though."

"What else could I do? Stay here and risk smothering your dad in his sleep? I can't resist a temptation that great." She patted his arm. "It's only for another night anyway, and then I'm headed back to the city. You, on the other hand, are stuck here all summer. You need to seize every opportunity you can to relax and have fun."

"I'll try my best."

"If it gets to be too much, you can always call me. I mean it. Say the word, and I'll drop everything and come get you."

"I appreciate that, but it's a two-hour drive roundtrip."

She pointed a finger at herself. "Is this the face of a mother who cares? Though I'd hate for you to miss out on time with your dad's side. They sure are a . . . colorful bunch. Remember Cousin Susie's wedding when you were eight? They got married in that dinky chapel out in the woods, only they didn't put up any directional signs, and everyone got lost? When the sun started to set, it was like the plot of a horror movie."

Oliver laughed. "Yup, I remember that."

"Good. If you repress everything, you'll have nothing to tell your therapist." She tossed her keys into the air and caught them neatly. "I'll see you tomorrow, honey. Make sure you wear something nice to dinner tonight. Seeing old friends for the first time in years is a perfect excuse to dress up."

"I will. Oh, and Mom?"

She'd taken a step toward the door, but she turned back. "Yes?"

"I love you."

"Love you too." Mom gave him a big kiss on the cheek and sashayed out the door.

Oliver shut it behind her. He considered going back into the kitchen, but he figured Dad needed time to cool off. Beyond that, he wanted to heed his mom's advice and pick out something sharp to wear. Good thing he'd had the foresight to pack a couple of dressier outfits, just in case.

His bedroom was to the left of the living room. Pushing his door open, he found the space exactly as he'd left it: barren and dusty with the stale smell all unoccupied rooms seemed to cultivate. Dad had made a few attempts to decorate, but the blue-and-white-striped walls and anchor pillows suggested he thought Oliver was still in his sailor phase. The sailor phase he'd gone through when he was five. It was a nice gesture, though.

His windows faced west, and so a healthy dose of afternoon sunlight set his white curtains ablaze. The pine furniture cast long shadows across the floor like spilled ink. He tossed himself onto his bed. The mattress—which he happened to know was the same one from their old house—squeaked beneath his weight as if protesting how much he'd grown during the school year.

Would this ever feel like home to him? Maybe by the end of the summer, right when he'd have to head back to the city. Then he'd get used to being there, only to come here again for Thanksgiving. Wash, rinse, repeat.

Oliver rolled over and tugged his phone out of his pants pocket. He had some Facebook notifications from friends back home, but he bypassed those in favor of checking out the two new names in his Contacts. Max and Aiden. The Kingsman twins, as they were often referred to. Talk about a blast from the past.

Though he'd recognized Max the second he'd spotted him, the brothers had changed a lot since they were all snot-nosed kids. They had the same brown curls, fair skin, and pale-blue eyes, but their faces, which had been soft and round in childhood, had sharpened into prominent cheekbones and strong jaws.

And as always . . . Aiden was somehow more handsome than his brother. Ever since they were kids, Oliver had thought they weren't really identical. Max was good-looking and all, but Aiden was downright gorgeous.

As it turned out, that was one thing that hadn't changed a bit over the years. Oliver's heart still beat like a drumline whenever Aiden Kingsman was around. It also didn't hurt that Aiden had gotten fit. Lacrosse had been good to him, sculpting his back and trimming his waist down to nothing. He still had that special something in his air, too. Oliver had never been able to describe it. It was soothing, like looking out through the rain and seeing everything soften into a gray haze.

Oliver hadn't thought about his massive crush on Aiden in years. He'd had no reason to. Absence made the heart forget. But now that he'd run into him again, it was like no time had passed. The torch he'd been carrying for Aiden blazed as bright as ever.

Not that Oliver could do anything about it. He'd just gotten back into town. The last thing he needed to do was make things awkward between his only potential friends in the area. Plus, he didn't know if Aiden liked him that way, or men in general.

There were bound to be things that'd changed in the past ten years. The twins were adults now. They must be different people. Oliver sure as hell wasn't the same sensitive kid who used to sneak over to their house and pretend he lived there. He'd wanted to become a Kingsman himself back then. He'd been relieved when his parents had announced they were getting divorced, but then they'd made him move away, and it'd shattered his little heart.

He remembered *begging* his mom not to move to the city, but he'd understood in his own youthful way that she needed to escape. This place had choked her like an airborne contaminant. And so, he'd done the whole tearful-goodbye thing with Max and Aiden.

They'd made a game of it, hatching scheme after scheme that would allow them to stay together. The brothers had offered to run away with him, or to keep him in the basement like a stray kitten. But in the end, Oliver had moved without a fuss, for his mom's sake.

He'd exchanged letters and phone calls with them at first, but with Oliver spending every holiday in California and the city being such a far drive, they never got to see each other. It was only a matter of time before they all made new friends and moved on. The letters stopped coming, and the phone calls dwindled. Before Oliver knew it, years had passed, and their friendship had become a distant childhood memory, no clearer than an old dream.

That was in the past, though. He had the opportunity to get to know them all over again, and he intended to take it. They might have nothing in common. They might not click at all. But if Oliver had to choose between them and hanging out with his invasive family, he'd pick stranger danger every time.

He rolled out of bed and shuffled over to his suitcase, which was lying open on the floor. He had a closet and a wardrobe, but he couldn't bring himself to unpack. Somehow, it felt like giving up.

Despite not being born in the city, he couldn't imagine living anywhere else. It'd only been a week, and he already missed it. The brightness of it. The life. The constant beat he could sense in the air, like a pulse. Or a proverbial New York minute ticking away. He doubted he could ever settle down somewhere like Irvington, with its manufactured lawns and HOA fees.

Out of his suitcase, he selected a green polo shirt and knee-length cutoffs. His dad would want him to wear slacks out of politeness, but they were in the midst of one of the worst heat waves in history. He'd burn to a crisp if he stepped foot outside in thick dress pants.

By the time he'd finished brushing his teeth, shaving, and styling his hair into soft peaks, it was time to leave. He walked out into the living room and was surprised to discover his uncles had arrived. Their hulking figures took up two spots at the folding card table they'd set up in the living room.

"Hey, Oliver," Uncle Charlie said, a stogie hanging from the corner of his mouth. "How's tricks?"

"Fine, thanks. Where's my dad?"

Uncle Marcus didn't look up from the chips he was counting. "He should be right back."

As if on cue, Dad drifted into the room. He eyed Oliver's outfit with a frown, but all he said was, "You ready to go?"

"Yeah." He turned to his uncles. "Sorry I can't join you guys tonight."

"We're sorry too," said Uncle Marcus, still sorting chips into colorful piles. "We heard you're ditching us to hang out with some friends."

Uncle Charlie took a sip of his beer. "You young people need to remember that blood is thicker than water."

Oliver swallowed a tart response and smiled. "I'll see you both tomorrow at breakfast?" *Assuming you're not too hungover.*

"Sure thing."

Dad led the way out of the house and to the car. He asked Oliver for the address, but otherwise they drove in silence. Oliver tried to pay attention to what was outside his window—this was his old neighborhood after all, and he hadn't had a chance to see what had changed—but his thoughts buzzed around his skull like a swarm. How much about him did the twins remember? Would their parents be happy to see him? He sure hoped so.

When they turned onto Woodlark Drive and the Kingsman house rose into view, Dad whistled. "Damn. It hasn't changed a bit."

It was true. In the white-gold light of the late-afternoon sun, all the familiar details stood out. It was like the house popped up— untouched—out of the depths of Oliver's memories. Same cheerful blue paint. Same white trim around the windows. Same azalea bushes lining the driveway, heavy with purple and pink flowers.

Dad pulled into the driveway and put the car into park. "Have fun tonight."

"You're not going to come in and say hi?"

"Nah, I'm not in the mood for small talk. Give them my best, and mind your manners, okay?"

"Will do. Thanks for driving me."

He gave his dad an awkward one-armed hug, got out, and strolled up to the front door without looking back. Tires scraped the driveway, and then the sound of the engine faded into the distance.

Oliver took a breath to calm the sudden tide of nerves rising in him. He patted his hair to make sure it was still in place, and knocked on the front door. It swung open before he'd put his hand down.

Mrs. Kingsman's bright smile greeted him like a lighthouse beacon. "Oliver! Oh, look at you." She held him by the shoulders and examined him at arm's length. "You're all grown-up!"

"Hello, Mrs. Kingsman." He smiled back and took her in. When he was little, he'd thought she was a giant, but now he had a good six inches on her. However, her warm brown eyes were exactly as he remembered. Like gingerbread.

"You're a young man now. Call me Kim." She squeezed one of his shoulders. "It's so good to see you. I was so sorry when you and the boys lost touch."

"Well, I'm here now, and I'm happy to be back. You still the best attorney in the state?"

She raised a thin eyebrow at him. "The *state*?"

"I'm so sorry. I meant the world." Oliver sniffed the air. "Something smells good."

"That's Roger's sauce. We made pizza doughs. Little individual ones, so everyone can pick their own toppings. I hope you're hungry." She paused. "And that you're not allergic to gluten or anything."

"Nope. Bring on the wheat."

"Excellent." She stepped back and opened the door wide. The interior was at once familiar and strange. They'd redecorated—which made sense, considering it'd been a decade—but he remembered the layout as if it were his own childhood home. He walked into a large living room with a formal dining room to the left and a hallway dead ahead.

He couldn't see them from here, but in the kitchen, he knew there were big, sliding glass doors that led out into the backyard. Oliver and the twins had spent many an afternoon out there, playing in the shade of the trees.

"Wow." He looked around. "It's like stepping into a memory."

Kim put a hand on his shoulder. "Welcome back, Ollie." She started toward the hallway and waved for him to follow. The closer they got to the kitchen, the stronger the smell. And the louder the voices. But instead of screaming, Oliver heard Max and Aiden having a lively debate about whether or not pineapple belonged on pizza.

Walking into the kitchen was like falling into a cloud of delicious food smells. Max and Aiden were nowhere in sight, but Mr. Kingsman (Roger) stood at the stove, stirring a saucepan filled with bubbling liquid. He glanced up when they walked in, and a crooked grin slid over his face. "Oliver! So glad you could join us." He dropped the wooden spoon he was holding and scooped Oliver into a hug.

Oliver returned it with enthusiasm. If he held on for a second too long, Roger didn't comment.

Kim sidled up next to her husband. "Hasn't Oliver gotten tall?"

Roger slid an arm around his wife's waist. "He sure has. I think you've got an inch on our boys, and they grew like weeds this past year."

Max and Aiden—who were one room over, judging by the sound of their muffled voices—popped into the kitchen as if summoned by their father's words.

"Oliver!" Max bounded over like an excited puppy. "When did you get here?"

"A sec ago. It's good to see you again." Oliver held out a hand to shake, but Max knocked it aside and pulled him into a hug instead. Oliver leaned into it. He was starting to suspect he might be a little affection-starved after hanging out with his macho uncles.

When Max let go, Aiden made a quieter but equally enthusiastic approach. "Hey." His curls were damp, like maybe he'd showered. Gulp.

"Hey, Aiden." Oliver cleared his throat. "For the record, I'm with you. Pineapple on pizza is *delicious*."

Max gasped and clutched a hand to his heart. "Et tu, Ollie? I might have expected this from Aiden—he's always been a bit odd— but not from *you*."

"Boys, there are plenty of toppings to choose from." Roger pointed to a series of small glass bowls laid out on the counter next to half a dozen stretched doughs. "Everything isn't quite ready yet, though. Why don't you take Oliver down to the game room while Mom and I finish up in here? We'll call you when they're ready to go in."

Oliver remembered his manners. "Thanks so much for dinner, Roger. And you too, Kim."

Max crinkled his nose. "Excuse you, their names are Mom and Dad. Now come on. The game room's in the basement." He bounced off.

Aiden followed after him at a slower pace.

Oliver started to do the same, but Roger caught his arm.

"It's wonderful to see you again, Ollie. We hope you won't be a stranger this summer."

"You're welcome here anytime," Kim added.

"Thank you." Oliver turned away before they could see his misty eyes. He couldn't remember the last time someone who wasn't a family member had been so happy to see him. Hell, half the time his actual relatives weren't that enthused.

The murmur of pleasant voices and Roger humming off-key followed him out of the kitchen. He walked into the family room and found Aiden waiting for him.

"This way." He waved toward a door in the far wall. "Max is already down there. No doubt firing up the Xbox."

Oliver belonged to the camp of people who thought basements were creepy, but he followed anyway. Aiden opened the door, and bright light spilled out into the family room.

Max was standing at the bottom of the wooden stairs. He grinned when they appeared and began their descent. "Check it out!" He spun around with his arms out. "Pretty cool, right?"

Oliver took in the room, whistling through his teeth. "Well, damn."

Instead of the dim lighting and cinder block walls he'd anticipated, the room looked like a windowless version of the living room upstairs. It'd been outfitted with hardwood floors, fresh paint, and overhead lights. There was a pool table off to one side, along with a dart board and an entertainment system that made Oliver salivate. The TV was the size of his closet, and inside the glass cabinets was every game console he could think of. And the games to go with them.

"Wow, this is incredible." He walked over and scanned some of the titles. "You guys are so lucky. If I had a room like this in my house, I'd never leave."

Aiden shifted from foot to foot. "This used to be the storage and laundry room, but Mom and Dad converted it after we left for college. I think they wanted to make sure we'd come home every break."

Max flopped onto a black sofa and held up a remote. "One of the many perks of having a lawyer and a dentist for parents. Wanna watch a movie or something?"

"Do we have time?" Oliver's stomach growled. "Food's gonna be ready soon, right? I'm starving."

Right on cue, the door opened, and Roger popped his head in. "You boys ready to make your pizzas? There's enough room in the oven for three at a time."

"You and Mom can go first," Max answered. "We want to spend some more time with 'Ollie olly oxen free.'"

"All right. They only take about fifteen minutes, so come up whenever you're ready." He left, shutting the door behind him.

Aiden sent his brother a sour look. "You could have asked us before answering. Oliver said he's starving."

"Hey, Dad spent all day slaving over a hot stove. He deserves to eat first. Same goes for Mom. Besides, old people need sustenance." He thumped his chest with a fist. "Us strong young men can survive without. At least, for a few minutes."

"You are so dramatic."

"I'm not dramatic. I'm—"

"Expressive. Yeah, I've heard that one before. Funny how it doesn't become truer the more you say it."

They dove headlong into a round of bickering while Oliver watched, caught between amusement and awkwardness. He'd thought their fighting was funny before, but now it highlighted something he'd been trying not to think about. Welcome as they'd made him feel, there was no doubt he was the outsider here. The Kingsmans were a family, and Max and Aiden were twins for Christ's sake. That was a bond he couldn't hope to touch.

At one point, the bickering took a surreal turn, and Max called Aiden a "soggy slice of bread." Oliver burst out laughing. Their matching faces turned to him in unison.

"Sorry, Oliver. We're being rude." Aiden perched on the arm of the sofa by his brother. "We invited you over so we could catch up, not ignore you. Tell us everything. What have you been up to?"

Oliver approached a set of oversized club chairs and flopped into one. "Honestly, not that much. I told you most of the exciting bits before. I go to NYU Stern, which is the business school. I'm majoring in marketing. I'm on the crew team." He tapped his chin. "Though I guess one thing has changed. I got this."

He lifted up his shirt, exposing his abdomen. To the right of his belly button, beneath his ribs, was a tattoo of detailed waves enclosed by a circle.

For some reason, Aiden's face turned the color of a ripe tomato. He jerked his eyes away. "That's, um, nice. Very cool. I like your placement choice."

Max, however, leaned forward and squinted at it. "Hell yeah! You got inked. I keep saying I'm going to get something. What's it mean?"

"Lots of different things. I've always loved the water. It also makes me think of my mom, and watching the sun set over the Hudson River. And of living in California. The waves there are so soothing to listen to. The roar and the rhythm of them. You know?"

"That's beautiful," Aiden said without looking at it.

Oliver lowered his shirt, wondering if he'd done something wrong. He changed the subject. "So, you guys said you go to the same school? And you live together, right? What's that like?"

Max shrugged. "Pretty much the same as when we lived together in this house for eighteen years. Our freshman year we were assigned to different dorms, but we both ended up hating our roommates. After that, we figured we'd stick together. The devil you know, and all that. Are you living in the dorms?"

"Nah. I live with my mom during the year. Her place isn't far from campus, and the city's *so* expensive. But it looks like I'll be spending summers here from now on. Or at least until I'm out of school."

Max whooped. "That's great! We can hang out whenever we're all in town."

"Yeah, definitely. Now that I have you guys, I might not die of boredom. This place is such a different speed from what I'm used to."

"Where in the city do you live?" Aiden asked.

"Queens. I know everyone thinks Manhattan is where it's at, but I love it. Everything's so busy all the time. You can walk everywhere. The only time I wish I had a car is when I'm late to class. NYU is great, but the campus is spread out all over."

"Do you have tons of friends back home?" Aiden was biting his nails. "Or a girlfriend or whatever?"

"Friends, yes. Girlfriend, no. I mostly hang out with the guys from my crew team, though my two best friends are Adam, a crew buddy, and this girl I met at freshman orientation, Christine. She's great, and a total genius." *And the first person I came out to.*

Max whistled in a suggestive way. "Christine, huh? Is she the reason you don't have a girlfriend? You're waiting for the right moment to make your move?"

Oliver winced. He'd hoped to avoid having this conversation right away, but he supposed it was inevitable. "Christine's wonderful, but she's not my type." He hesitated. "Adam would actually be my type, if he weren't such a stoner."

There was a pause. For once, it was Max who turned red. "Oh. *Oh.* Sorry, dude. I shouldn't have assumed."

Oliver held up a hand. "It's okay. I only came out this past year. It hasn't been easy, though. My parents were fine with it, but the rest of my family is another story. I don't think they're against it, per se, but they seem to have forgotten I'm the same person as before."

"Shit." Max wiped his mouth. "And you've been surrounded by them since you got back? That's gotta be rough."

"You have no idea. It's only for a while, though. Summer can't last forever, right?" Oliver peeked at Aiden for his reaction, but he was staring down at the floor.

Max seemed to notice his brother's lack of response as well. He elbowed him in the side. "Hey, what's with the vow of silence? I'd think you'd be thrilled to learn Oliver's gay."

Oliver raised an eyebrow. "Why would he be 'thrilled' about that?"

"Because—" Aiden finally looked up, his eyes cool as the ocean "—I'm gay too."

Chapter 3: Aiden

Aiden wasn't the praying sort, but that evening, when he took a seat at the dining room table between his parents and the boy he'd had a crush on for *years*, he begged anyone who was listening for mercy. If he could pull off a decent poker face this once, he swore he'd be charitable, altruistic, and that he'd stop stealing a handful of cashews out of the plastic bins at the grocery store.

He stared down at his pizza—which he'd loaded with pineapple while Max looked on with horror—and willed himself to eat. His mouth was so dry, however, he doubted he could swallow. He peeked across the table at Oliver for what had to be the hundredth time that night.

Oliver's attention was on Dad, who was telling some corny joke he'd heard from a patient. From this angle, Oliver's profile was in sharp relief: his smooth brow, full lips, and strong bone structure. His body language—from his easy smile to the relaxed set of his shoulders—said confident and comfortable.

It made Aiden *ache.*

He'd never been a demonstratively sexual person, but looking at Oliver now, he wanted to chew on some ice. What he wouldn't give to have Oliver's arms wrapped around him. Or maybe pinning him down, or—

Aiden took a deep breath and did long division in his head until the rising tide of his libido abated. What was wrong with him? Over the years, he'd had his fair share of crushes, but they didn't compare to what he was feeling now. It was like Oliver had his own gravitational field, and everything from Aiden's gaze to his thoughts kept getting sucked into it.

Admittedly, Aiden had thought about him less and less as time passed. But now, Oliver had waltzed back into their lives, bringing the heat of a New York summer with him. It seemed Aiden's puppy love had been waiting by the door for his return.

What would Oliver think if he knew Aiden was fantasizing about him? Would he be flattered, or would he find it wildly inappropriate? They didn't know each other anymore. He might think of Aiden as a total stranger, or worse, the scrawny little boy who used to talk his ear off about poison dart frogs and dung beetles.

Although, Oliver seemed to slot right back into their lives, like he'd never left. Finding out he was gay too made it hard not to hope.

Plus, the way Oliver had looked at him after he'd come out . . . Maybe it'd been Aiden's imagination, or some serious wishful thinking, but he swore something had crackled between them, like an electric charge. After years of pining, he might actually have a shot with the proverbial boy next door.

Stop it, Aiden. Your oldest friend is back in your life. Try being happy instead of hormonal.

He poured all of his energy into pretending to listen to Mom lecture Max on his lackluster study habits. If he kept staring at Oliver, someone was bound to notice. He couldn't decide who would be worse: Oliver or Max.

Oliver might be creeped out, but Max had an annoying ability to guess his thoughts as if they were plastered on his face. "Twin telepathy," Max called it. Aiden didn't believe in that, but he did believe Max was both perceptive and had known him every minute of his life. That was a dangerous combination.

Keep calm. We're all friends here. There's no reason for anyone to suspect your intentions aren't pure.

Aiden took another peek across the table. He sucked in a breath. Oliver was staring right at him. As if they'd choreographed it, they both looked away.

Aiden's heart pounded like he'd run the New York City marathon. *Is it just me, or did I see a spark of something in his eyes?*

His cheeks flamed up again. So much for his poker face. At this rate, he was going to set the house on fire.

"Aiden, you've been awfully quiet." Mom nudged him with her elbow. "You feeling all right?"

"Yeah, I'm great," Aiden squeaked. He took a bite of his pizza as if to prove it. Dad made phenomenal sauce, but right now it tasted like glue.

"It's because he put that disgusting fruit all over his pizza," Max joked. "It's inedible."

"Says the guy who'd eat a tire if someone deep-fried it."

"Boys," Mom said in the same warning tone Aiden had heard her use with uppity prosecutors. "Not in front of our guest."

"Oh, please," Max scoffed. "Ollie's seen us fight worse than this. Hey, Aiden, remember the time we went hunting for tadpoles, and I pushed you into the creek?"

"I think I remember that." Oliver shot Aiden a grin. "A fish swam up to you, and you cried."

Aiden gripped his pizza so hard, the crust snapped. *Please, God, no embarrassing childhood stories in front of my dream guy. I know Oliver was there, but he doesn't need reminding.*

It seemed no one heard his prayers, because Max continued. "Or what about that time I convinced you that five comes before four, and you got into an argument with your kindergarten teacher because of it?"

Aiden was going to have to remember this when Max's wedding day rolled around. He had his own arsenal of embarrassing stories, ready and waiting.

For now, however, he groped for another topic. "Speaking of fond memories, do you guys remember when we used to all go to the beach together? That was fun."

"Maybe for you." Max sniffed. "I never did learn to swim."

Oliver dropped the slice of pizza he'd been about to shove into his mouth, looking horrified. "What? How can you not know how to *swim*?"

"It's not like it's a necessary skill. When would I ever need to?"

"Oh my God." Oliver shook his head. "I don't know if we can be friends anymore. Half of my favorite recreational activities involve swimming."

Aiden barely kept the smirk off his face. *Revenge is sweet.*

Dad cut in before Max could say something acerbic. "I remember those cute fake weddings you boys used to host in the backyard."

Aiden's breath lodged in his throat like a rock. He remembered when they'd play "marriage" too, but he hadn't wanted to bring it up in case no one else did. Those memories had meant a lot to him when he'd gotten older and realized he was gay. They'd helped convince him his parents would support him.

He sneaked another look across the table. Max was pinching the bridge of his nose, but Oliver was grinning.

"Oh yeah, I *definitely* remember that." He elbowed Max in the side. "According to the laws of the playground, you and I have been married for fourteen years."

Max groaned. "Figures someone would bring this up just as I'd managed to repress it."

Aiden snorted. "Don't act all traumatized. You were always the first one to suggest we play marriage."

"Yeah, because I got to wear a suit. Proof that I've always had good taste."

"Especially in men." Oliver batted his eyelashes. "It's so wonderful to be reunited with my long-lost husband after all these years. How about a kiss, darling?"

Suddenly, Aiden didn't find this so funny anymore.

Oliver made kissy faces while Max groaned like a dying animal, and Aiden's lungs spasmed in his chest. It was ridiculous to feel jealous—Max was straight, and Oliver was obviously joking—but he did.

When they were kids, they'd all played together equally, but things were different now. No adults could force them to share. Aiden was quiet and awkward, and Max was extroverted and funny. What if Oliver ended up liking him better?

Stop it, Aiden. Oliver can like whoever he likes, and you shouldn't resent your own brother for it.

"If I'm going to be forced to relive my childhood, I need a drink." Max looked at their parents with big, dewy eyes. "Can we have some beer? I noticed a six-pack of that fancy craft stuff Mom likes in the fridge. We'll pay you back for it."

Aiden glanced at their parents, curious as to how they were going to react. Max and he didn't really drink, so they'd made it to adulthood without having the alcohol talk. But they were in college now, and libations were ubiquitous. It was bound to come up.

Mom and Dad exchanged a look.

"It *is* against the law," Mom said. "As a lawyer, I feel duty bound to mention that."

"They'll be twenty-one in November." Dad shrugged. "That's close enough for me. Besides, are we the sort of parents who pretend their adult children have never touched alcohol before?"

Mom sighed. "All right. But no one leaves this house. Oliver has to stay the night. I'm not sending him home to his parents smelling like a kegger."

Aiden's heart lurched as it tried to sink and soar at the same time. Oliver might sleep under the same roof as him. They might be drinking together. Surely that could only end well.

"And you have to remember your pre-bed routine," Dad added.

Oliver leaned toward Aiden, inadvertently setting his whole body on fire, and whispered, "'Pre-bed routine'?"

Aiden managed to mumble back an answer. "He means we have to remember to floss and brush our teeth. Getting a cavity in this house is like bringing home a failing grade."

"Ah." Oliver spoke to the whole table this time. "Well, my dad seemed like he wanted me to come home earlier, but by now, he'll be knee-deep in a poker game with my uncles. I bet he'd rather I stayed away so I won't see him lose his shirt. I'll call him and ask if I can spend the night."

Max pumped a fist in the air. "All right! Reunion sleepover. It's like old times."

Oliver excused himself from the table. Aiden watched him go, eyes lingering on his broad shoulders. He made a mental note to find out if he could somehow sponsor the NYU men's crew team.

When he turned back to the table, Max was watching him with narrowed eyes. Heat crept into Aiden's cheeks again. He needed to keep a tighter lid on his reactions. If he kept drooling, Max was bound to realize what was up.

Aiden had never told Max about his crush—they'd been kids, after all, and Oliver had moved away before it could amount to anything—and now was not the time for Max to find out. He'd think it was funny, and Aiden was embarrassed enough without having to endure his brother's heavy-handed humor.

Mom provided a ready distraction. "Isn't Oliver the sweetest?"

Max rolled his eyes. "You and Dad always did fawn over him, like he was the third son you never had."

"How could we not? He's so polite, and he obviously adores you boys." She tousled Max's curls. "Anyone who's good to my babies is all right in my book."

"*Mom*." Max swiped at his hair. "You're so embarrassing."

"Good," Dad joked. "That means she's doing it right."

At least Aiden knew his parents would approve if Oliver and he . . . He couldn't think it. He might jinx it or, worse, convince himself it could happen.

Oliver came back into the room and retook his seat at the table. "Dad said it's okay for me to stay over, so long as I get home in time for breakfast."

Max whooped. "Yeah! Party time. Bring on the beer."

Their mother bristled. Aiden shot Max a warning look. "Uh, Max? Try not to seem too excited about the underage drinking."

"Oh, right. Sorry." He pecked Mom on the cheek. "Don't worry. Three grown men splitting a six-pack? How much trouble can we get into with two beers each?"

That seemed to mollify her. "Promise me you'll keep the wild partying to the game room. There's a reason we had it soundproofed. You can make up the couch down there for Oliver. Unless one of you boys wants him to sleep with you."

Aiden choked on the sip of water he'd just taken and set his glass down hard. "No, I think the couch will be fine."

Max got up from the table, politely collected their parents' plates, and took them into the kitchen. When he reappeared, however, he had a six-pack of IPAs in his hand. "I'll be in the game room. See you guys down there."

Aiden rolled his eyes. "I'll get the rest of the plates, then."

"I'll help." Oliver stood and grabbed one in each hand, leaving Aiden with his own to take care of.

He struggled to keep his expression neutral as they scraped off the plates and loaded them into the dishwasher. Oliver was silent for his part. His furrowed brow suggested there was something on his mind, but Aiden didn't dare ask. When they were finished, they headed down to the basement, all without saying a word.

Well, this is off to a great start. Nothing like awkward silence to get a romance going.

Aiden had no idea how to flirt. He'd never had a boyfriend before, and Oliver wasn't some random guy Aiden found attractive. They'd known each other since the days of Spider-Man sheets and playing tag. There was a lot at stake here, and it would behoove Aiden to keep that in mind.

When they got downstairs, they found Max reclined on the sofa with his feet propped up on the coffee table and a beer already in hand.

"Gentlemen." He popped the tab, and the carbonation fizzled. "Come on in. The water's fine."

"Nice." Oliver took a beer and inspected the label. "This is an IPA, right? I hear those are strong."

"If you're going to consume illegal libations, you might as well do it properly." Max grinned. "That was my Aiden impression. Whatcha think?"

Oliver sent a smile Aiden's way as he took a seat next to Max. "Dead on."

Aiden frowned and snatched up a beer. "I don't sound like that."

"You kinda do, bro." Max leaned toward Oliver. "You should hear the things he says sometimes. He used the word 'anathema' the other day. In a regular conversation."

Aiden took a swig of his beer to hide his embarrassment and then moved over to a chair, careful to keep some distance between Oliver and him. "It's not my fault you're illiterate."

Max gasped. "You know very well our parents were married when they had us."

"That's 'illegitimate,' buddy," Oliver said.

"Oh." Max's brow knit together. "Yeah, sorry. I knew that."

Oliver shot Aiden a conspiratorial look, like they'd shared a private joke, and goose bumps popped up all over Aiden's arms.

Say something. Anything. Ask him about himself.

Oliver beat him to it. "So, Aiden, how do you like college?"

He cleared his throat. "I love it. It's so much more engaging than high school. My classes are hard, of course, but I love having control over my schedule."

"Which is hilarious, considering he picks nothing but hard classes, and they're always first thing in the morning." Max waved his beer. "Calculus. Physics. Organic something or other."

"Organic chemistry," Aiden said. "I have to take those classes to get my engineering degree, though Pace doesn't offer everything I need. I'll have to finish at Manhattan College."

Oliver perked up. "You're going to move to the city?"

"Yeah. The Bronx, to be specific. It's a Roman Catholic college, which is kind of rough for obvious reasons, but it's not like I'll have to go back into the closet. And it's only until I finish my degree."

Oliver seemed to hesitate and then looked down at his lap. "You're not going to leave behind a boyfriend or anything, are you?"

Before Aiden could get his heart started again, Max snorted. "Aiden? Boyfriend? Yeah right. He can't look at a guy without blushing, let alone talk to one."

Aiden glowered. "Thanks, brother dear."

"I'm teasing." He reached over and punched Aiden's arm. "It's gonna be rough being separated from you. Who's going to force you to go to parties and take you out for your first beer when we turn twenty-one?"

Aiden rolled his eyes. Trust his brother to make him sound like a friendless recluse in front of his crush. "Oh, I dunno. My *friends*. I'm sure I'll make plenty when you're not around to embarrass me."

"I don't have a ton of friends at NYU, I admit." Oliver rolled his beer between his palms. "Instead of a bunch of acquaintances, I have five or so close friends."

"Really?" Aiden asked. "I would think you'd know tons of people."

Oliver eyed him. "Why's that?"

Because you're handsome and smart and athletic and charming. "Well, it's such a big school, and the city is bigger. You must meet people everywhere you go."

"You would think, but campus is so spread out, and it's sure as hell not a college town. Plus, I can be kinda quiet."

"Oh, I remember that about you," Max said. "You never liked to talk in class. When we were in third grade, you had this whole formula worked out for how to be invisible. You'd sit in the third row, slightly off center, and you'd look at the teacher's nose instead of their eyes. It took Mrs. Dinehart a whole quarter to learn your name."

"Oh wow, I'd forgotten that," Oliver said. Aiden thought there might be some color in his cheeks. "That hasn't changed a bit. I still have palpitations every time my professors want to call on someone who 'hasn't spoken yet.'"

"Why do you suppose that is?" Max asked. "I mean, you're a smart guy and you have a lot going for you. Plus, you don't seem to have any trouble talking to us."

Oliver shrugged. "Well, yeah, but I know you guys. I'm not like this with everyone. Maybe it's because I'm an only child. I didn't have someone my own age to talk to before I was old enough for school. Or maybe it's because my parents were always fighting. If I didn't make myself scarce, they'd drag me into it. Staying quiet was the easiest way to not get noticed."

The energy in the room shifted as surely as if the lights had dimmed. Aiden felt like something cold and wet had touched the back of his neck. He sat there, fiddling with his empty beer can, and struggled to think of something to say.

For once, he was grateful when Max and his big mouth stepped in. "Well, as fun as this loaded silence is, I was thinking we could watch a movie."

Oliver looked relieved. "I'm down for that. What have you guys got?"

"It'd be easier for you to name some titles, and we'll tell you if we have them."

Max got up and opened the double cabinet full of DVDs, wafting a hand around them like a TV hostess showcasing a prize. Oliver called out titles while Max plucked them from the shelves.

Aiden observed, content to let them pick the movie. He didn't care what they watched, so long as he got to spend more time with Oliver. There was something calming about his presence, in spite of Aiden's nerves, and Oliver took the onus off of him to keep Max entertained.

Not that he normally minded. He was fortunate to have a brother who was also his best friend. He wasn't looking forward to leaving him next year to attend college by himself. They'd never been separated before. Although, ever since Oliver walked back into the picture, Aiden had found himself wishing that Max would leave so they could have some alone time.

I'm a bad brother.

Oliver and Max settled on some cheesy action movie. Max raved about it as he popped it into the DVD player. "Then the guy takes out like twelve cop cars with nothing but a handgun, and then this *helicopter* comes, and he—"

"Max," Aiden interrupted, "are we going to watch the movie, or are you going to do a dramatic reenactment for us?"

"Right, sorry. I'll get the lights."

He hit a switch by the stairs and then took his favorite spot on one side of the sofa. That forced Oliver to scooch over, and Aiden to sit beside him in order to see the screen. As the opening credits rolled, Aiden cracked open his second beer and took a sip. He was a shameless lightweight, and the IPAs were strong. He was already on the edge of being tipsy.

Without thinking, he glanced at Oliver out of the corner of his eye.

Oliver was watching him. When their eyes met, they both looked away, like they had at dinner.

Aiden's heart fluttered. *Perhaps it's not my imagination after all.*

Max's voice almost made Aiden jump out of his skin. "The beginning of this movie is so boring! I don't care about the couple and their broken-down car. One of them is gonna be dead soon anyway."

"Spoilers, dude," Oliver said without venom.

Aiden settled back in his seat and tried to focus on the screen, but it was impossible. He was hyperaware of Oliver sitting next to him, mere inches away. His presence was like the pull of a magnet, drawing Aiden's eyes back. This time, when he peeked, Oliver wasn't looking at him, but his gaze was trained so solidly ahead, it didn't seem natural.

Aiden looked away again, and the second he did, he thought he saw movement out of the corner of his eye. Was it the light from the TV playing tricks? Or were Oliver and he playing eye tag?

He's probably looking at you because you keep making moony eyes at him like a weirdo.

Between the beer and his self-flagellating inner commentary, Aiden found it impossible to concentrate. Minutes crawled by. Max was right: the movie started slow. Aiden couldn't use it to distract himself. He drained his beer in record time and plunged headlong into tipsiness.

By the light of the TV, he checked the ABV on the side of the can. Eight percent. That was twice as strong as the cheap, water-like swill they drank for free at parties. No wonder he was feeling it.

Don't do anything you'll regret. Keep your mouth shut and your eyes forward.

He had to be imagining the tension in the air. He whiled away another twenty minutes pretending to watch the film—which had gone from being a thriller to a gorefest in true genre-hopping fashion—but his attention never strayed from Oliver for long.

Scenes that had nothing to do with the movie floated into his head—memories that played as readily as if they were running on the big screen. He met Oliver in kindergarten. Some kids had been referring to Aiden as Max, and he was too embarrassed to correct them. Then, all of a sudden, the quiet kid who never spoke piped up. "That's Aiden."

Oliver had hidden under his desk for ten minutes afterward, but Aiden had never forgotten it. Max had been impressed too. Enough to force Oliver to talk to them no matter how much he resisted. After that, it was one memory after another. Sleepovers. Playing in the backyard. Calling themselves the Three Musketeers, though none of them had known what a Musketeer was.

Oliver had actually been present for some things that Max had missed, like that time in the fourth grade when Aiden had skipped a stone across a lake only to hit a duckling, killing it. He'd cried for *hours*, and Oliver had comforted him with a warm hand and whispered assurances that it was an accident. Aiden could picture the exact moment that Oliver had brushed the curls away from his eyes, and . . .

A noise to the left broke Aiden from his reverie. It sounded like a mix between a grunt and a growl. A second later, he heard it again. Aiden sighed. He'd know that sound anywhere.

Max was snoring.

His head had fallen against the back of the sofa, and his second beer lolled in his fingers. His lips were parted enough for dinosaur-esque noises to pour out.

For all the things Max and he *didn't* have in common, they had a mutual inability to hold their liquor.

Aiden debated with himself. He didn't want to wake Max up, but if neither of them were watching the movie anymore, they could pack it in for the night, if Oliver didn't mind. Aiden certainly wasn't interested in finishing it, and he'd love to wrap things up before he had a chance to make an alcohol-induced blunder. Then again, if Oliver wanted to hang out after, this was their chance to have that alone time Aiden had been praying for . . .

Aiden resolved to ask him. Oliver was the guest after all. They'd do whatever he wanted to do.

He turned to him, mouth already open to form the question, but he never got a chance. The breath was stolen from his lungs a moment later.

Oliver was staring at him with magnetic intensity. Even in the dim light, there was no question. The look in Oliver's eyes stopped Aiden's words in his throat. It was powerful, and almost . . . curious? As if Aiden was a puzzle he was trying to figure out.

Aiden didn't know what to make of it, but he didn't have long to think. Oliver's eyes swept down his face, lingering on his lips and throat, before dipping down his body. When they met Aiden's gaze once more, they were as dark as the shadows around them.

Aiden's heart was pounding so loudly, he could hear it in his ears. The movie might as well have stopped playing. Everything around him dissolved away until there was only Oliver and the raw electricity that had sprung up between them.

While Aiden was still struggling to process, Oliver hesitated, then moved one of his legs until his knee was pressing against Aiden's.

That single, warm touch sent a frisson up Aiden's spine. He swallowed hard, head spinning from more than the beer, and managed to say a single word. "Oliver?"

"So," Oliver said, breathy and low, "what should we do now?"

Chapter 4: Max

Max slept like a freaking baby. Or at least, he assumed he did. He didn't remember dreaming, or going to bed in the first place, which he took as evidence that he went down like a redwood.

At one point, the sunlight streaming through his window roused him, but when he glanced at his phone and saw that it was only ten, he grumbled, "Fuck that," rolled over, and went right back to sleep.

It wasn't until Aiden barged into his room—nattering on about sleep cycles or circadian rhythms or whatever geek shit was in his arsenal today—that Max finally sat up in bed and made a genuine effort to wake up.

He managed to crack one eye open and keep it that way, though the other remained glued shut. He focused on Aiden. "May I help you?"

"Have you heard a word I've said?" Aiden folded his arms over his chest and leaned against the doorframe. Instead of his usual sweats and a T-shirt, he was wearing new dark-wash jeans and a fitted red flannel with the sleeves rolled up to the elbows. If Max didn't know any better, he'd think Aiden had gotten dressed up.

"Sure I have, but the good news is, I'm too dumb to understand any of it."

"Max, for the umpteenth time, you're not dumb. We're *identical*, which means you're every bit as smart as I am. You could achieve all the same grades and accolades if you'd apply yourself."

"Ah yes. But see, the thing is: I don't want to." He yawned, stretching his arms above his head. "In all that nagging, did you happen to mention breakfast? Is Dad cooking?"

"He's at work, same as Mom. Just because we're free for the summer doesn't mean they are."

"They're working on a Sunday?"

"It's Tuesday, brother dear."

"Oh." He scratched his neck. "Damn. I guess when you're on vacation for long enough, you're bound to lose track of the days."

"It's been a week." Aiden rolled his eyes. "Anyway, if you want to eat, you should hurry up. Oliver's waiting for us."

At that, both of Max's eyes sprang open. "He's still here?"

"No, he had to go home for breakfast. He wants to hang out, though. I said we'd pick him up, since he doesn't have a car."

"Oh, okay." Max yawned again. "Did I miss anything good last night?"

That question made Aiden's eyes drop to the floor like stones for some reason. "Um, after you passed out last night—very dignified, by the way; it took both of us to haul you up the stairs—we, uh, went to sleep, and then I drove Oliver home this morning. You didn't miss anything at all. Anyway, he texted saying he's finished with his familial obligations."

Max checked his phone again. "I don't see anything in our group chat."

"He sent it to me."

Something slithered into the pit of Max's stomach and nested there. He couldn't quite put his finger on why, but the idea of Oliver and Aiden making plans without him left a bad taste in his mouth. Which was ridiculous, of course. It didn't matter which of them Oliver texted. They were always together. Contacting one of them was as good as contacting the other.

"Well, thanks so much for including me," he said for good measure. He swung his legs over the side of the bed and stumbled to his feet. "I'll throw some clothes on, and we can go."

"You need some aspirin or water or anything?"

That mollified him. Aiden could be so thoughtful when he wasn't being a giant nag. "Nah, I had two beers. If I was hungover from that, I'd have to drop out of college to avoid the shame."

"'If I *were*,'" Aiden corrected, smiling the smug smile that told Max he was being annoying on purpose. "I'll meet you in the kitchen."

He peeled himself off the doorframe and left, pulling the door closed behind him.

"Know-it-all!" Max shouted through the wall before shuffling over to the overflowing laundry basket by his closet. He sniff-tested several articles of clothing and dressed in a hurry: shorts and a green shirt with the cast of *The Goonies* print-screened on the front.

He ducked into the bathroom long enough to brush his teeth and peek in the mirror. His curls were even messier than usual, and his eyes were so bloodshot, the irises looked unnaturally blue, like monster eyes. He needed coffee.

When he'd finished, he trundled out to the kitchen. The sunlight pouring through the windows made him wince. Aiden was waiting for him, as promised, and miracle of miracles, he was sipping a mug of coffee. Without a word, he handed a second cup to Max.

"Precious baby brother," Max cooed, placing his hands over his heart. "For me? I love you so much." He made a big show of throwing his arms open for a hug.

Aiden tried to scramble away. "You're only five minutes older!"

Max was faster. He lifted Aiden up and squeezed him, singing a tuneless song he made up on the spot about fraternal love while Aiden squirmed like a puppy in his grip. Despite his protests, Aiden laughed so hard he wheezed.

When Max was satisfied he'd conveyed his gratefulness, he released Aiden and gulped down some coffee. Aiden straightened his clothes—seriously, since when was he so fussy about his appearance?—and complained about Max "manhandling" him. There was no acid behind his words, though.

"Did Oliver say what he wanted to do today?" Max finished his coffee and left the mug in the sink.

Aiden picked it up, rinsed it out, and loaded it into the dishwasher. "Remember that old arcade we used to love? Dr. Quirky's Good Time Emporium? Turns out, it's still in business."

"Oh, yeah! Man, I haven't thought about that place in years. How'd you come up with that?"

Aiden shifted his weight. "Oliver mentioned it. It was one of the last places we all went to together before he moved. We thought it might be fun to go back and see what's changed."

Something about that niggled at Max, but he brushed it off. Already, his head was filling with memories of the arcade: the smell of popcorn, the giant old-school video games, and the tacky blue carpeting that was somehow always sticky.

He bounced on his heels like a little kid. "Are you ready to go?"

Aiden extracted car keys from the pocket of his jeans. "Lead the way."

They locked up behind them, got into the car they shared, and drove to the address Oliver had provided. Once there, they pulled up to a small, dingy house that could have been a demonstration of the word *beige*. The lawn was green and freshly mowed, but the flowerbeds were in desperate need of weeding. The gravel driveway was so packed with cars, they couldn't pull in.

"Oliver's family must still be hanging around," Aiden muttered. He took out his phone. "I'll call him."

Before he could, Oliver's dark head appeared over the top of a minivan. Max reached across Aiden and honked the horn to get his attention.

Aiden smacked his hand away. "Don't."

It was too late. Oliver's head halted between two cars, mostly out of view.

At first, Max thought he'd startled Oliver into stopping, but then another head joined Oliver's. This one had lighter hair with noticeable gray. The two stood together for a prolonged moment before Oliver skirted around the car and jogged toward them. He opened the back door and dove in as if they were bank robbers making a getaway.

"Hey, guys." He was breathless, and his eyes were wild. "Let's get going."

"Oliver, what—" Max started to ask, but then Aiden gunned it.

They pulled away, but not before Max saw the other brown head break free of the cluster of cars. It belonged to a familiar-looking older man. It took Max a moment to place him, thanks to the sour expression on his face. Mr. Jones.

Max twisted around in the passenger seat to stare at Oliver. "Was that your dad?"

"No." Oliver's nonchalance fell short of convincing. "Well, yeah."

"Did you guys have a fight or something?"

"Something. Don't worry about it. He'll get over it."

Max wanted to ask more questions—especially about why Aiden didn't seem at all surprised by any of this—but for once, he shut his mouth. He turned back around in his seat and fiddled with the radio. "How 'bout some tunes? Oliver, what do you listen to?"

"Mostly pop, to be honest."

"Dude, you are breaking my heart."

The conversation veered into small-talk territory, punctuated by music and the occasional joke. Max noted some tension in the air, and it wasn't from the odd encounter with Oliver's dad. Aiden and Oliver managed to go the whole ride without addressing each other directly. When they spoke, it was to Max, as if he were a switchboard operator directing their calls.

Max didn't have long to think about it. They drove up to the arcade and vied for one of the few remaining parking spots.

As soon as the car stopped moving, Max jumped out and surveyed the area. "Damn, it's *packed.*"

"I thought that might be the case." Aiden locked the car and pocketed the keys. "School's out for everyone, not just us college kids. And with the heat wave, families must be searching for things to do indoors."

Oliver sauntered up to stand next to Aiden, hands stuffed in his pockets. "Well, I'm willing to battle some crowds if you guys are."

"Oh, I'm willing." Max was already striding toward the entrance: a giant clown's mouth worthy of a Stephen King novel. "I'm not going to let a bunch of kids ruin this place for me."

Aiden snorted. "You know this place is intended for children, right?"

"What? Says who?" Max waved him off. "Whatever. Whoever said that is wrong. You can't put an age limit on *fun.*"

As they approached the main building, Max swept his eyes over it, thinking to himself that it looked the same, yet so much smaller. And much, much more run-down. Dr. Quirky needed a facelift. The bright-yellow paint was peeling off the cinder block walls, and half of the light bulbs were out in the arch above the entrance. The creepy clown—Dr. Quirky himself—was the same, though: his giant red lips stretched into a smile for them to pass through.

Freud would have something to say about this, Max thought as he entered the clown's mouth. Talk about nightmare fuel.

Stepping through the front doors was like stepping ten years into the past. The interior of the arcade hadn't changed a lick. Same hulking arcade-style games lined up in the center of the room, same snack bar off to the right, and the same sticky carpet. Even the endless line for the bathroom that never seemed to get shorter was still there.

Max clapped his hands to his cheeks. "It's *beautiful*."

"It's something all right," Oliver said. "What should we hit first?"

"The snack bar," Max said at the same time that Aiden said, "Let's play Asteroids."

They glanced at each other.

Max faked a sniffle. "You want me to *starve*."

"It's not my fault you slept through breakfast."

"You could have woken me up sooner."

"You have an alarm on your phone, Max. Use it."

"If I may act as tie-breaker," Oliver piped up. "Breakfast was a couple of hours ago for me, and I ate light. The curly fries are calling my name."

Aiden went from unmovable boulder to pliant kitten in a blink. "Oh, okay. In that case, I guess I could go for a Coke."

"Oh, I see how it is," Max joked. "Oliver says he wants to go, so suddenly you do too?"

To his surprise, Oliver and Aiden both tensed.

Aiden's eyes dropped to the floor yet again, like they had a new summer home there. "It's not like that."

"He was . . . Um." Oliver bit his lip.

Max glanced between them. "Am I missing something here?"

"Yeah," Aiden said. "You're missing your chance to be first in line." He took off toward the snack bar at a dead sprint.

"Oh, you bastard!" Max raced after him, ignoring the affronted stares from nearby parents. Aiden's head start was too great, though, and he beat him to the end of the line by three seconds. Max skidded to a stop an inch shy of crashing into his brother and put his hands on his knees, panting. Aiden hadn't even broken a sweat, the jerk.

Oliver jogged up behind them, looking as unfazed by the exertion as Aiden did. "I'm not gonna lie, I could watch you two all day. Max, I especially liked when you stepped in that wad of gum and didn't slow down at all."

"What?" Max checked the bottom of one shoe and then the other. "Fuck."

"Stop cursing." Aiden peeked at their surroundings. "There are little kids everywhere."

"Sorry." Max had discovered in recent years that being a legal adult didn't mean he was too old for a scolding. He'd rather avoid that.

The line shuffled forward, and they shuffled with it. Aiden and Oliver started talking about something boring, like the weather or politics. Max half listened as he scoped out the crowd, searching for anyone their age that they might hang out with. Specifically, any ladies. Much as he loved his brother—and Oliver, to an extent—he didn't intend to spend the whole break glued to their sides. A little summer romance sounded right up his alley.

He spotted a group of college-age kids over by a row of claw machines. It was mixed-gender, and two of the guys were making a show of trying to win prizes for the girls. Max disregarded them. Too much competition.

Another nearby cluster was all girls, and as Max sized them up, a pretty brunette caught his eye and smiled.

Jackpot.

Max turned back to his companions at the same time they reached the front of the line. A bored-looking teenager with oily skin greeted them in a monotone. "Would you like to try an order of Quirky Fries?" His glassy eyes moved between Max and Aiden. "Hey, are you two, like, twins?"

"Either that or the grease has gotten to you." Max squinted at his name tag. "What are Quirky Fries . . . Dave?"

"Curly fries but dyed blue."

"Ugh. Gross. Why would anyone do that to perfectly good food?"

Aiden eyed him. "You're calling *fries* 'perfectly good'?"

"Hey, potatoes have kept the Irish alive for hundreds of years. That's good enough for me."

"Whatever. I'll take a small drink, and he"—Aiden jabbed his thumb at Oliver—"wants curly fries. Regular, non-blue ones."

"What size?"

Oliver popped his head over Aiden's shoulder. "Medium. That way we can share." He shifted his mouth toward Aiden's ear. "You'll eat some, right?"

Aiden turned as red as the ketchup dispenser. "Um, s-sure." He paid for them both.

"What, not gonna buy me anything?" Max asked.

Aiden's color stabilized, and he shot Max a wry look. "You owe me a fortune."

"I do not! What have you ever—"

"The limo we took to prom. The security deposit on our apartment. A countless number of tacos from the food truck by campus."

Max rubbed his chin. "Hm, I guess you got me there."

"If anything, you should be paying for all of us today."

That gave Max an idea. "Good point. Let me order, and I'll buy us some tokens." He turned back to Dave. "I'll take two corn dogs and a large soda."

"You don't have to buy us anything," Oliver said. "I have money."

"Don't worry about it. You're gonna pay me back in other ways."

Dave handed him his food, and Max inhaled one of his corn dogs before he even made it to the soda fountain.

"Disgusting," Aiden observed.

Max swallowed, choked a little bit, and washed his corn dog down with a healthy gulp of Mountain Dew. When his air passages were unclogged, he said, "Okay, so here's the plan. You see those girls over there?"

Oliver revolved in place, scanning the whole crowd. "You mean the ones hanging out by the tables?"

"Yeah. Have they noticed us?"

"Yup," Aiden confirmed. "They're watching you masticate that deep-fried carcass with what I can only call burgeoning horror."

"They're what?" Max jerked his head over, the other corn dog poised by his mouth like a lollipop. Sure enough, the girls were staring at him with expressions ranging from disgust to morbid curiosity. He whipped around, hiding his face. "Quick, do something charming! Smile! Or wave!"

"What?" Oliver asked.

"Just do it!"

Oliver waved, stiff as the Tin Man. "Why am I doing this?"

"Because we're going to flirt with those girls."

Aiden pursed his lips. "Brother dear, I know I promised I'd never tell you any gory details about being gay, but you do realize flirting with girls isn't my forte, right?"

"Or mine," Oliver said.

"No shit, guys. Give me some credit. You're not going to flirt with them for real. I need you to be my wingmen. You can help me charm them, and since you're no competition, I can take my time figuring out which one I like. Plus, straight girls love gay guys. You two are gonna be like catnip."

"That's stereotypical and offensive," Oliver said. "But since I don't think you have a chance in hell, if you buy us some tokens, I'll gladly watch you crash and burn."

"I dunno about this." Aiden shuffled his feet and glanced at Oliver. "I was kinda hoping we'd get to spend some time together."

Max sighed. "Bro, come on. We spend all day together. If we spent any more time bonding, we'd be *conjoined* twins."

"Actually, when I said 'we,' I meant—"

"We gotta move. We're losing daylight." Max finished his corn dog, downed his soda, and tossed the remains in the nearest trash can. "There's twenty bucks in it for you guys. I'll make it twenty bucks each if that pretty brunette gives me her phone number."

To broke college kids, that was a small fortune. Just as Max had predicted, Aiden and Oliver cracked like old sidewalks.

"Okay, we'll do it," Aiden said. "But we want the cash up front."

Max pulled his wallet out of his back pocket, removed a twenty, and handed it over. "Perfect. Now go talk to them."

Aiden nearly dropped the bill. "What? *Me?*"

"Yes, you. Walk over there, hold up the money, and ask where you can get some game tokens."

"Why can't you do it?"

"I can't pull off a line like that. It has to be you, little bro. You have an honest face."

"*We have the same face.*"

Oliver cut in. "What if I go with you? Safety in numbers."

Aiden's hackles lowered. "Okay."

Max frowned. *Damn, Oliver has some sort of magic touch. Maybe I can get him to ask Aiden if I can have his old iPad.*

Aiden and Oliver took off toward the girls. Max watched them go while pretending he wasn't watching at all. Easy as pie, they walked up to the group and started chatting. The girls enveloped them into their ranks like an amoeba.

"Gay guys have all the luck," Max muttered.

Before he could start talking to himself in earnest, Aiden waved him over. Max strolled over to his side, struggling to look casual while inside he was doing a little victory dance. He had the good sense to address Aiden first. "Did you find the tokens?"

"Oh my God," said one of the girls. "Are you guys *twins*?"

Having been a twin his whole life, Max would never understand people's fascination with it, but he was happy to reap the benefits.

He flashed his most debonair smile. "How astute of you to notice. I'm Max, and I assume you've already met my brother and our friend."

"Hey," the aforementioned pretty brunette greeted him. "I'm Danielle."

Max stuck his hand out. "Nice to meet you."

She made a serious face and shook his hand before dropping it with a giggle. She waved to her three friends. "This is Fabi, Evelyn, and Danesha."

The other girls said hi in unison.

"Hey there," Max said without taking his eyes off Danielle. "Are you ladies from around here?"

"We are." Fabi indicated herself and Danielle. "But Ev and Danesha are from Jersey."

"No wisecracks, please," Danesha said. "The whole state-rivalry thing is so played."

"Wouldn't dream of it. So, how are you liking the arcade?"

"We're kinda bored, honestly," Danielle said. "Or we were, until Aiden and Oliver walked up. Aiden mentioned he had a brother, but he didn't say you guys are twins."

Max nudged his brother with an elbow. "Did he tell you I'm the handsome one?"

Aiden made a pained noise, but he didn't speak.

Danielle laughed. "He didn't need to. I can see that for myself."

Max almost fell over. *Holy shit, I'm in love.*

Danesha said, "We were thinking about leaving, but now that you're here, maybe we'll stay." She eyed Oliver in a suggestive way.

Uh-oh. I guess they didn't lead with the whole gay thing. Makes sense.

While he debated what to do, Oliver came to his own rescue. "I hate to disappoint, but I'm actually gay."

"Same here," Aiden said.

The girls made interested oohing sounds.

Fabi asked, "Are you guys dating?"

Max snorted and was about to deny it when Oliver glanced at Aiden. "Sadly, no."

"Oliver." Aiden's face grew tense. His eyes darted toward Max as if gauging his reaction. "Don't joke around."

"Who's joking?" Oliver leaned toward the girls in a conspiratorial way. "We were reunited yesterday after ten years apart, so we're taking things slow."

"*Oliver.*" Aiden was a radioactive shade of red.

Max didn't get what Aiden was so upset about. It was a brilliant plan on Oliver's part: pretending there was something going on between them. It made it clear they weren't viable romantic partners while keeping the girls intrigued. Max was so going to write him a thank-you card.

He was about to crack a joke when he felt a tug on his sleeve. Danielle was standing next to him.

She brushed her hair aware from her big brown eyes. "I don't suppose you're gay too, are you? Because that's totally fine, of course, but I was kinda hoping . . ." She bit her lip, and Max wanted to cheer.

"No, I'm straight. Aiden and I are only identical on the surface."

"Oh, okay. Good. Well, not *good*. You know what I mean." She crinkled her nose. "Do you get asked that a lot, since you two have the same genes and all?"

"I wouldn't say a lot." Max did his absolute best Aiden impersonation. "Genetics are a complicated subject, after all, and Aiden and I have plenty of differences: our personalities, our hobbies, and our fingerprints."

"That's so interesting," Danielle said. "I'm studying biology at Columbia. I read an article once about the role that copy number variants play in twins with differing sexual orientations. Maybe we can grab a soda from the snack bar and talk about it?"

Jesus, she's a genius. Definitely smarter than me. I hit the jackpot!

Max offered his arm to her. "Allow me to escort you."

They spent the next hour or so talking, playing games, and talking some more. Their respective friends joined them for some of the team games, but otherwise they were left alone. It was like they were already having their first date.

Danielle was *amazing*. Smart and funny and playful. Max was starting to think she was made of stronger stuff than summer-fling material, like maybe girlfriend material. Columbia wasn't that far away, right?

After an epic round of whack-a-mole—which Danielle totally kicked his ass at—Fabi approached and said the others wanted to go somewhere else.

Danielle shot him an apologetic look. "I'm their ride, so if they want to leave, I gotta go."

"That's okay. I totally understand." Max was plucking up the nerve to ask for her phone number when she cupped his chin, stood up on her tiptoes, and kissed him.

Max was too surprised to kiss back. He barely registered her pushing a napkin into his hand and saying, "Call me." She strode off with a giggling Fabi by her side.

Slack-jawed, Max stared after them until they disappeared from view. Shit like that didn't happen to him in real life. Was he dreaming? He'd think so, if it weren't for the fact that he could taste her minty ChapStick on his lips.

What he'd said to Aiden the other day was so true: this was going to be the best summer vacation *ever*. He couldn't wait to share the good news. But first, he had to find his entourage.

He checked the tables where he'd last seen them, but they weren't there. What had Aiden said he wanted to do? Play Asteroids? Max glanced toward the rows of arcade games and spotted them standing at the far end. He made his way over, dodging squealing children and spilled popcorn as he went.

They didn't notice his approach. In fact, they seemed to be arguing, or at least having an intense discussion. Max frowned. What could they have to fight about? He slowed his approach and strained to hear what they were saying.

Aiden's face was tense. "I don't know what you were thinking, acting like that in front of—" Noise from the arcade games blotted out the end of his sentence.

Oliver shrugged. "It was a joke."

"Well, it wasn't funny. Especially not after . . ." Aiden trailed off, lips pressed hard together.

Max was only ten feet away now. They'd spot him any second. He almost called out to them, but then Oliver stepped closer to Aiden. *Way* closer. Closer than two bros should stand, in Max's humble opinion.

"Aiden, I already made my move. You're the one who—"

A pair of screaming kids whipped past Max. Goddamn it. He glanced back toward Aiden and Oliver, expecting them to have glanced over at the noise. But they were still focused on each other. It was like nothing else existed to them. Not the arcade. Not Max.

Aiden wrung his hands as if trying to pull them off. "My brother was right there, Oliver. And . . . I didn't know . . . I wasn't sure if you . . ."

Oliver took *another* step closer, obliterating the concept of personal space. Neither of them spoke, but their eyes said volumes. It was like they were memorizing each other's face.

Max had seen that before. It was how his parents looked at each other when they thought no one was watching. He made fun of them when they did it, but nothing about this struck him as funny.

It occurred to him, as if for the first time, that Aiden and Oliver were both gay. That fact, which had meant nothing to him before, filled his head like an expanding balloon, pushing all other thoughts out. Except for one.

Are they going to kiss?

Max's first instinct was to interrupt them before anything could happen, but that was ridiculous. They were *friends*. Their sexual orientation didn't mean anything. He had to be imagining things.

Before he could make a decision, Aiden glanced his way. When he spotted Max, he jumped away from Oliver as if he'd been shocked.

Well, that was subtle.

"Max!" Aiden turned a shade of white so pure, artists would fight over it. "I didn't see you there."

A dozen questions raced through Max's mind, each more awkward than the last. There was no way he was going to acknowledge what he'd seen. Or what he thought he'd seen. If he did, he'd have to acknowledge the changes he could already feel in the works.

He swallowed his questions down and asked a different one instead. "You guys ready to go?"

"Already?" Oliver grinned. "You don't want to go trolling for more girls with your gay entourage?"

"Nah." Max swallowed. "All of a sudden, I'm not in the mood for romance."

Chapter 5: Oliver

Oliver Jones was in hell.

When he'd first come home to Irvington, he'd expected a lot of boredom, family time, and headaches from the family time. It wasn't his idea of a perfect summer, but if it made his dad happy and gave him a chance to breathe some fresh air, he could survive anything.

He hadn't expected to run into his first love, and he certainly hadn't expected Aiden to turn out to be one of the most interesting, sexy, and all-around frustrating men he'd ever met. Oliver had been trying for days to figure out what was going on between them, to no avail.

Not for any lack of trying on both their parts. Every time they attempted to talk about what had happened between them—or rather, what had almost happened—they got interrupted. Max was always around, and if he wasn't, their parents were. They couldn't talk at home without company, and they couldn't talk in public without . . . well, the public.

It didn't help that Oliver kept having flashbacks to their encounter in the basement. Little sensory memories that taunted him with how *close* they'd been. Close to each other. Close to acknowledging the spark he was certain they could both feel. The scene played over and over in the quiet moments throughout his day.

Oliver's knee, pressed up against Aiden. Tension humming between them, tight as a wound spring. Aiden's eyes, bright and huge in the darkness.

For an entire, agonizing week, they'd been dancing around each other. Oliver refused to have this conversation through text, and it seemed Aiden did too. Thus, he was stuck in purgatory's waiting room, which in his head looked like his old orthodontist's office.

A handful of times, he started to convince himself he'd made the whole thing up, but then something would happen. He'd catch Aiden staring at him, or their fingers would brush, and it'd feel like a lightning strike. Plus, there was the fact that Aiden tended to blush like a good rosé whenever Oliver so much as said his name.

If they could spend some time alone, away from the constant interruptions, they could figure this out. Including what this *was*, exactly. A summer fling? Or the start of something more?

Oliver's body had moved of its own accord, shifting closer to Aiden. Despite the movie still blaring away, he'd heard Aiden's breath hitch as their lips got closer. It'd made his pulse race.

This was what happened when two introverts tried to flirt. They ended up with a lot of awkward silences and not-staring contests while they each waited to see if the other one was going to make a move. If Oliver gave Aiden one more lingering look from afar, he was going to become the protagonist of a YA novel.

Oliver could only wait for Aiden's response. It wasn't a position he was used to being in. He'd dated his fair share of men since he'd left for college, but they'd always pursued him. Now, things were the other way around.

And he *definitely* wanted to pursue Aiden. If there was the smallest chance of making something happen, he had to take it. Even if it meant risking his rekindled friendships with the Kingsman twins. Aiden had this way of breaking through his reservations that Oliver had never experienced before. It was like he . . . well, like he'd known Oliver his entire life.

At the last possible second, Aiden had jerked away. Muttered something about needing to put Max to bed, needing to think. A knife had twisted in Oliver's chest. He'd gone too far. He'd overstepped. But then, Aiden had reached out and brushed Oliver's hair away from his eyes, the warm fingers lingering with such . . . intent.

Damn. The memories were going to be the death of him.

There was no question. Whatever Aiden wanted, Oliver would give it to him, be it a summer fling or something more. It'd be worth it. Assuming, of course, that they ever got this thing off the ground.

Maybe he should be spontaneous and kiss Aiden the next time he saw him. Oh God, Oliver wanted to kiss him. The thought alone made him itch.

But he wasn't going to get relief anytime soon. Much as Oliver would love to camp out at the Kingsmans' for the rest of the summer, he had to go home sometime. Home, to his quarrelsome, drunken relatives. Awesome.

After yet another frustrating, exhilarating day with Aiden (et al.), he had the twins drop him off at his dad's house. It could be his imagination, but it looked dingier than usual. Brown and lifeless like a dead patch of grass.

For a moment, he stood in the driveway and let the afternoon sun bake into him. The sky was deep blue and dotted with fluffy clouds like dollops of frosting. It made him feel peaceful, but also oddly forlorn.

When sweat began to roll down his face, he worked up the motivation to trudge inside. It was quiet, for once, but all illusion of serenity shattered when he entered the kitchen and found his dad cleaning up a veritable Mount Doom of dirty dishes.

Oliver surveyed the trashed kitchen—from the discarded egg cartons to the spilled flour—in horror. "Jesus, Dad, what happened?"

Dad, who was standing at the sink, brandished a soapy saucepan at him. "Well, look who finally decided to come home. Long time no see, stranger. You missed breakfast."

"Did I miss breakfast or the apocalypse?"

"We had a little impromptu family brunch. We made pancakes. You'd know that if you were ever here these days."

Guilt clawed at Oliver's gut. He nodded at the dishes. "You need help with those?"

Dad considered him and then sighed. "No, I don't want to make you do dishes the second you walk through the door. I'll deal with these later."

"Why didn't anyone help you clean up?" He spotted some empty beer cans next to a pile of used napkins. "Were the uncles drinking again? It's the middle of the afternoon."

Dad immersed the saucepan into the water and suds. "Yeah, well. They work mornings, so their schedule isn't like ours."

Oliver debated with himself before deciding to focus on the bigger issue, for now. "You shouldn't keep cleaning up after our relatives. If they're going to spend so much time over here, they need to contribute. Or better yet, why don't we tell them this 'family reunion' has gone on long enough?"

Dad, to Oliver's surprise, chuckled. "There's no end to family, Oliver. They're going to be a part of our lives forever. That means we'll occasionally have to deal with them doing what family does best: being inconsiderate jerks. At the end of the day, we all still love each other."

You wouldn't be so forgiving if Mom had made this mess.

"I'd hoped things would be quieter around here now that Mom left."

Dad's face contorted with what looked like remorse. "About her, and all the fighting we did . . . I'm sorry. We swore we weren't going to do that around you anymore."

Oliver shrugged. "I don't see why you should stop now. I'm an adult. The damage is done."

"You shouldn't say things like that."

Oliver fell silent.

Dad started scouring a plate with superfluous force. "Let me try that apology again, all right? I'm sorry your mom and I can't keep things civil. We're going to make an effort, though, now that we're living in the same state again."

Oliver wanted to believe him, but his parents had been promising they'd get along for almost his whole life. He did appreciate the apology, though. Heavy-handed or not. "That's good. I suppose you can test it out when Mom comes to get me at the end of the summer."

"Speaking of which, she called for you. Said you weren't answering your phone."

He'd put it on silent during a movie. He checked it now, and sure enough, he had a missed call. "Whoops."

"Go call her back. I have to head in to work for a few hours. I expect you to show your face at dinner tonight. Your aunts are wondering where you've been."

Oliver restrained a sigh. "Okay. See you then."

He made his way to his room, noting the poker table still set up in the living room next to a pile of discarded toys. His cousins never picked up after their kids. This place would be a wreck if Dad weren't such a clean freak. He made a mental note to help around the house more. It wasn't fair for Dad to have to do everything.

When he reached his room, he shut the door behind him and flung himself on his bed. The stale, musty smell was starting to become familiar to him. He wasn't certain if he was relieved or alarmed.

He pulled his phone out, found Mom's name in his missed calls, and tapped on it. Two rings later, she answered.

"Ollie? Where have you been? My lunch break ended an hour ago."

"Sorry, Mom." He rolled onto his side and pressed the phone to his ear. "I was watching a movie. Want me to call back when you're off work?"

"No, it's all right. I'm driving to a meeting, so I can talk for a bit. How's life?"

"Fine." He hesitated. "The house is a disaster, thanks to our ever-present relatives. Dad won't say a word to them about it either. It's frustrating. I don't see how he can get so angry with you over trivial things but give a bunch of freeloaders a pass simply because they're blood."

"Don't be so hard on your father. He's going through a huge transition right now."

"I dunno why you're always saying that to me. I would think you'd love it if I hated him."

"What an ugly thing to say, Oliver Jones. Of course I don't want you to hate your father. I want you to have a good relationship with both of us." She cleared her throat. "So long as you like me the best."

Oliver snorted. "What is it with parents and bad jokes?"

"Wait until it's your turn. But in all seriousness, Ollie, your dad's side of the family believes in that whole 'it takes a village' thing. They always show up en masse, and your dad was raised to put family first."

"That's rich, considering he let ours fall apart."

"Dad didn't want to get divorced, Ollie. I did."

Oliver sucked in a breath. He'd always assumed it was a mutual decision. "You're kidding."

"Nope. He wanted to stick it out no matter how miserable we made each other. I only convinced him to give up when it became obvious that our fighting was affecting you."

"Wow, I had no idea." Oliver flopped onto his back and switched his phone to his other ear. "Kinda proves my point, though. Dad's priorities are in all the wrong places."

"Maybe. But if I can make an effort to understand him, you can too. A lot of what he does, he does for you."

That mollified Oliver in terms of his father, but not their leeching relatives. After spending the last few days with Aiden and Max, he was getting spoiled. He'd always known his family was dysfunctional, but he'd thought every family was like his.

Being with the Kingsmans, however, had thrown a sad fact into sharp relief: there were people out there who were genuinely happy. People who had relatives that not only loved each other, but liked each other too. Oliver didn't have that, might never have it. No matter how much he clung to the Kingsmans, he wasn't one of them. He was a Jones, and the Joneses were a mess.

"I guess," Oliver said, for Mom's benefit. "I'll cut Dad some slack. And the rest of them. Admittedly, it'd be easier if there were someone I got along with. All the cousins who are my age have kids, and all they ever want to talk about is daycare and prenatal vitamins."

"Yikes. Though from what I hear, you're getting plenty of companionship from outside sources." Her tone was saccharine. "Dad says you've been spending a lot of time with the Kingsmans. I assume you've reconnected with Aiden and Max?"

"Oh, yeah," Oliver said, happy for the change in subject. "It's actually kind of eerie. It's like we never stopped being friends. Granted, we have a lot of catching up to do—you should hear some of Max's outrageous stories from high school—but overall, we picked up right where we left off."

"True friends can always do that. Remember Aunt Sylvia?"

"Your best friend from high school?"

"Yeah. We only see each other every few years, but when we do, we discover we've somehow grown together instead of apart. I'm so glad to hear you're getting along with the twins. I hated moving you away from them. You cried for *days*. It was like you were heartbroken."

Oliver's face got hot. Thank God Mom couldn't see it.

But of course, she didn't need to. In true motherly fashion, she seemed to read his mind. "Now that I think about it, didn't you used to have a crush on one of them?"

Damn it.

"Mom," Oliver whined.

"Oh, come on. I'm teasing you." She paused. "Was it Max?"

"Of course not! It was Aiden."

"Ah ha! I knew it."

Oliver opened his mouth only to make a defeated, sputtering noise. "Walked right into that, didn't I?"

"Sorry, honey. If there's one thing I know about children, it's that they love to correct their parents. So, tell me about him. Is he in school? Have your old feelings returned, or are you just friends now?"

"*Mooom*," Oliver whined again. "I can't talk about this right now. I'll jinx it."

"So, there's something to jinx, huh?" She giggled. "All right, then. I won't ask about your relationship, but I will ask about him. He has to earn my seal of approval. To my recollection, he was a quiet child, though he might have seemed that way because Max was so loud."

"He definitely doesn't stand out as much as Max does, but he's unforgettable once you get to know him. He's so . . ." Oliver chewed his bottom lip. "Kind. Not only does he do nice things, but he does them before anyone can think to ask him. You know that one sandwich shop near campus that I love?"

"The one with the giant meatball sub you're always cleaning out of your shirts?"

"That's the one. The other day, I mentioned I had a craving for them. The next time I saw Aiden, he handed me a picnic basket full of their sandwiches. He'd driven into the city to get them."

Mom made an impressed noise. "That drive takes an hour, one way."

"Yeah, if traffic is light. Isn't that the sweetest thing you've ever heard?"

"Very sweet. Maybe a little self-serving."

"What do you mean?"

"If you get homesick, you might leave. Sounds like he doesn't want that to happen. I bet he'd move the whole city closer to get you to stay." Her tone was teasing.

Oliver chuckled. "Maybe, but I'm not the only one he's sweet to. You should see how he takes care of his brother. Waking him up in the morning. Bringing him coffee. Making extra food whenever he cooks because he knows Max is gonna want some as soon as he smells it. I hate to admit it, but it makes me envious."

"What do you mean?"

"Well . . . they're brothers, you know? Twins. They have a bond I'll never understand. I'm always going to be the outsider."

"I doubt either of them thinks of you that way. Also, I know I'm not supposed to jinx anything, but if you and Aiden become an item, you're going to have your own special bond. Something that will be unique to you. And remember, it's not a competition." She was silent for a beat. "You know, if you wanted to, say, bring him home next break so I can meet him, that would be nice."

"We're so not there yet." Oliver laughed. "But if we ever get to that point, I'll definitely reintroduce you. You'll love him."

"Perfect. I'm pulling up to my meeting, so I have to run." Mom hesitated again, but this time there was weight to the silence. "Ollie, before I go, will you promise me something?"

"Of course."

"Promise you'll call me if anything happens. Anything at all, day or night. I can be there in an hour."

"What could happen?"

"I don't know, but promise me anyway. Say you'll call, even if you think it's trivial or you're being a bother. You're not. Okay?"

"Okay, I promise. I love you."

"I love you too."

Oliver jabbed the End Call button with his thumb. For a long moment afterward, he stared up at his ceiling, thinking about his two parents and how different they were. Mom had always been a career-oriented city girl, whereas Dad had only ever wanted a big family and a house like the one Oliver had grown up in. No wonder they hadn't worked out. He wondered sometimes why they'd gotten married at all. Why had they had him?

He supposed it did him no good to speculate. He was here now, and he had some time to kill before he needed to get dressed for dinner. Facebook was his first stop. His handful of friends back home had been hounding him.

Adam wanted to know when he was coming back. Christine's messages started out amiable and then became increasingly peeved as he failed to respond for days on end. He replied to her first, assuring her he was still here and saying (lying) that he'd been busy with family. He truthfully said he missed her and then moved on to his notifications.

He'd been tagged in a few memes and had some new wall posts, but his friend list was short. He made quick work of proving he was still alive.

After, he dicked around on the internet for a bit. Read some articles, scrolled through the photos he'd posted on Instagram of himself with the twins, and briefly toyed with the idea of changing his profile pic to one of him and Aiden . . . But he discarded it.

Don't get ahead of yourself.

A little before dinner, he wandered out of his room and asked Dad if he wanted any help. Dad grunted in response and waved him away with a turkey baster, which Oliver took as a no. He retreated to his room, changed into nice jeans and a fresh green shirt, and reappeared right as people started arriving.

For the first half hour, the doorbell rang like church bells. Aunts, uncles, and one surviving great-grandmother who was as old as Italy itself piled into the living room, along with more cousins than Oliver could name. Literally. They all looked alike, and he'd always been bad with names.

There were hordes of children too, running from room to room, shrieking at the top of their lungs while their parents shouted fruitlessly at them to stop. The noise multiplied with each new ring of the doorbell.

And then there was wine. Oliver had never seen so much red wine in one place, outside of a vineyard. Bottle after bottle got uncorked as the living room crowd spilled over into the dining room and started claiming seats. No matter how many leaves they added to the table, they never had enough room for everyone. Someone broke out some fragrant bread, and soon they had a proper predinner party going on.

Much as Oliver complained, he had to admit, there was never a dull moment.

He snagged a seat and did his best to be invisible, but inevitably Susie, one of the cousins he actually kinda liked, spotted him. She lowered her vastly pregnant self into the wooden chair next to him and plunked a water glass full of wine onto the table.

Oliver tried not to stare, but she must have read the horror on his face.

"The doc says a glass a day is fine." She patted her swollen belly. "I usually don't, but I heard your dad made braised lamb."

Oliver wanted to point out that the doctor had surely meant one *serving* per day, but he'd learned from years of having pregnant cousins to never, ever tell someone what to do during their pregnancy. He'd once made a comment about sushi to his cousin Morgan that had gotten him an eyeful of wasabi.

"So—" Susie took a dainty sip of her wine "—how's college?"

"It's great. So much fun, and I'm learning a lot." He started to say more, but then someone pressed a glass of wine into his hands—a standard one, thankfully. He scrambled to hand it back.

Susie tsked. "Relax, will you? Have a drink with dinner like a grown-up."

Oliver hesitated for a fraction of a second before relenting. If he was the only one not drinking, he'd get comments about it all night. He could nurse one glass for the next few hours. While Susie watched, he took a sip and grimaced. Wine was so *sour*.

"You'll like it one day," she said. "I hated red wine all throughout my twenties. Then thirty hit, and suddenly I'd stab someone for a good cab."

"Oh good. Something to look forward to."

"You go to NYU, right? That's a big school. Anyone catch your eye yet? Any guys, or whatever you're into these days?"

Oliver struggled not to look as awkward as he felt. "No."

"You *are* still gay, right? Like, you haven't changed your mind or anything?"

So much for that brief respite.

He knew she wasn't being insulting on purpose—and it was kind of refreshing to have someone acknowledge his identity instead of whispering behind his back—but the question still stung.

Tongue heavy in his mouth, he worked up a response. "Nope. Still gay. I'll save you the trouble of asking: I'll still be gay tomorrow as well."

A few of the people sitting on either side of them had grown quiet. No doubt they'd heard, though whether they were eavesdropping on purpose or couldn't help but overhear remained to be seen.

Susie apparently decided now was the time to ask him all about being gay. "Have you ever actually dated a girl, though? I don't want any details or anything. I'm just not sure how you can know you don't like women if you've never been with one."

Oliver was contemplating hurling himself out the dining room window when Aunt Antonia elbowed Susie. "Don't bring that up at the dinner table. You'll give your father a heart attack."

"What? We're a modern family." Susie swatted her away. "Besides, we were bound to have a gay one eventually."

A gay one. How lovely. Oliver struggled not to roll his eyes. This was so . . . typical. He understood, on some level, that he was one of the lucky ones. His family hadn't outright rejected him when he'd come out last year. But they also hadn't welcomed him with open arms either. He was the token gay cousin, and no one was willing to discuss it much beyond that. At least, not to his face.

Honestly, in this day and age, was being gay really a whispered conversation to be had around the dinner table while the older relatives palpitated? Maybe Oliver had been living in the city for too long; this small-town nonsense seemed ridiculous to him.

The funny thing was, he was certain they'd get over it if he talked to them one-on-one. But he didn't have the energy to walk twenty people, not counting the children, through the realization that he was the same person as before. He could either get angry, or make pleasant small talk and pretend there was no elephant looming in the room.

Or you can choose secret option number three: drink another glass of wine and fake a stomach ache so you can leave.

He drained his glass, coughed, and stood up. "Excuse me for a moment. I need a refill."

There were two open bottles of wine on the table, but he breezed right past them. As soon as he vacated his seat, someone new hermit-crabbed into it, and the conversation carried on as if he'd never been there.

Right as he was about to duck into the kitchen, he spotted his father talking to Uncle Marcus by the sink. Oliver backed away and changed course like a ship avoiding an iceberg. Hell if he was going to risk another awkward conversation right now.

He snagged a bottle of wine off an end table, dumped some into his glass, and wandered off in the general direction of the living room, lost in thought.

Reconnecting with Aiden and Max had made him go from dreading this summer to wishing it would never end. But that had its own set of issues.

On one hand, he had this burgeoning romance, but on the other, it was going nowhere fast. His friendship with Max was solid, but he also had friends back home that he missed. He was getting to spend some quality time with his father, but the rest of his family came as a package deal.

I think this is one of those adulthood things. For every pro, there has to be a con. Like you can eat cake whenever you want, but you also have to pay taxes.

Or maybe the problem was with him. His family members weren't the only ones he struggled to connect with. All throughout school he'd done his best to be invisible, and college was no different. Now, he'd reunited with his oldest friends, and yet he worried about being an outsider. Why was that?

He'd always thought he'd never had a serious boyfriend because he wanted to keep things casual, but ever since he'd moved back to Irvington, he'd been thinking about relationships. Maybe it was all the moving. He didn't want to be a typical young adult and blame his parents, but sometimes he wondered if—after all those years of watching them and thinking that this was what marriage was like—something inside of him had gotten twisted up.

He eyed his wineglass. *Time to stop drinking. It's making you maudlin.*

Oliver left his wineglass in the kitchen, snagged a few bites of bread to soak up the alcohol, and mumbled his excuse. *Stomach ache. So sorry. Gotta go.* He made a beeline for his room. Nosy aunts and godparents popped up along the way like land mines, but he managed to dodge them.

When he got to his room, he shut the door behind him, trudged over to his bed, and fell face-first onto it. The next time he went shopping, he was going to buy the kind of laundry detergent his mom used. Maybe that could make this place smell like home.

Picking his head up with reluctance, he glanced at his alarm clock. The red digital letters read 8:38 p.m. It was way too early to go to bed, and yet he was exhausted. He rolled onto his back and stared at the ceiling. Striations of light streaked across it from the window. He craned his head toward it. From this angle, he could see the bottom of a fat moon, but no stars.

I miss Aiden.

They'd hung out earlier, and yet there was an ache in Oliver's chest that could only be soothed by blue eyes and brown curls. He was developing an addiction. What would happen at the end of the summer when they had to go back to school?

That was a question for another time. For now, he pulled out his phone and sent Aiden a text.

I feel like an angsty teenager.

He checked his notifications while he waited for Aiden to text back. Thankfully, for someone who wasn't demonstrably social, Aiden always replied right away.

Why's that?

Because my family totally doesn't get me. He added a wink emoji to lighten his words.

A minute passed. Then, *You all right?*

Yeah. But I'd rather be with you right now.

This was the closest they'd come to talking about their feelings. Oliver's heart pounded in his chest as he waited for a response.

He didn't have to wait long.

Me too. Whenever you're not around, I spend all my time wishing you were.

Oliver's fingers paused over the keyboard. He could tell Aiden he felt the same way . . . or he could do something about it. Maybe it was the wine, or maybe Oliver could smell opportunity on the air, but suddenly, he sat straight up in bed.

If you want to see him, go see him, he thought. *Make your own alone time. Find out how he feels. If nothing else, that'll be a weight off your shoulders.*

Was it too late to show up at Aiden's house, though? Aiden was a night owl. He probably wasn't going to sleep anytime soon, and he'd said he wanted to see Oliver.

That settled it. Talk about feeling like a teenager. Oliver was going to sneak out of his house.

He sprang to his feet and shoved his phone into his pocket, the last text unanswered. He started for his door, only to hesitate. He couldn't go out the front. There was no way someone wouldn't spot him and ask where he was going. He glanced behind himself at his window. It looked barely big enough to let him through, but barely would have to do.

The hinges screeched as he pushed them open. Thank God his family was full of loud lushes. He jumped out legs-first, compressing his shoulders inward to get his broad chest through the small opening. He landed on the grass with a *crunch* and closed the window behind him. Too late, he thought to leave a note.

Oh well. He had a phone. If Dad came looking for him, he could call.

It was a cool, clear night. The wind felt good against Oliver's feverish skin. He sneaked around the side of the house to the driveway, which was overflowing with cars.

Please let Dad's be parked on the street. He'd walk if he had to, but he was really hoping he could commit some simple grand theft auto.

Miracle of miracles, he spotted his dad's car on the street, wedged behind Uncle Charlie's pickup truck. Dad had locked his keys inside one too many times and therefore kept a spare set in a hidden magnetic case under the car.

Sneaking out *and* stealing his dad's car. It was as if he were working some latent teen rebellion out of his system. Speaking of which, he walked heel-to-toe the rest of the way to make sure those two glasses of wine hadn't gone straight to his head. He made it without so much as a wobble.

It took Oliver less than a minute to locate the key and get behind the wheel. Once there, he pulled away from the curb and made the drive to the Kingsmans'. The sight of the house alone made relief wash through him like a warm bath. Most of the lights were off, however. Had everyone turned in?

He hadn't thought about what he'd do once he got here. He supposed he couldn't very well knock on the front door at this time of night, especially if people might be getting ready for bed. It occurred to him that he should have asked Aiden if it was cool if he came over, instead of slinking up to his house like a stray cat. Maybe the wine had affected him more than he'd thought.

Fuck it. I'm not going back home now.

He knew which bedroom was Aiden's from the night they'd put Max's drunken self to bed, but finding it in the dark, from the outside, wasn't going to be easy. He parked a little ways down and pocketed the keys before tiptoeing around the side of the house.

Is this what being a rebellious teenager is all about? Sneaking everywhere?

As it turned out, he didn't have to count windows and pray like he'd planned. A bright light guided his way. Aiden was sitting at his desk with a lamp on and a book open on the polished, off-white wood. One hand held a page in preparation to turn it while the other cupped his chin. His curls were adorably messy, and his lips were quirked up. Not quite a smile, but smile adjacent. He looked peaceful. And gorgeous.

Oliver almost hated to disturb him, but seeing him made the ache in his chest grow to a burning need. He rapped on the glass with his knuckles.

Aiden jumped so hard, he fell out of his seat. Oliver had to clap both hands over his mouth to keep from laughing. Climbing to his feet again, Aiden hurried over to the window.

Oliver's laughter died in his throat when he caught sight of Aiden's sleep clothes: a tight T-shirt with *Pace Lacrosse* printed across the chest and cotton pajama bottoms that didn't conceal as much as Aiden probably thought they did.

Gulp.

Aiden unlatched the window and pushed it out. "Oliver?"

Oliver grasped at composure. "Hey."

"What are you doing here?" Aiden leaned on the window frame. He was taller than Oliver like this, his eyes bright in the moonlight. Suddenly, it was hard for Oliver to breathe.

He swallowed. "I had to get out of my house."

"Is it your dad again?"

"No. And yes." He shook his head. "Don't worry about it. I'm here because I wanted to see you. We haven't had a chance to be alone since . . ."

Even in the dim light, the blush that painted Aiden's cheeks was obvious. "Yeah, I've been dying to talk to you too, but there's always someone around."

"There's no one around now."

Silence draped itself over them, thick and loaded. Oliver had come over here specifically to get some alone time with Aiden, but now that he had it, he didn't know what to do with it.

Aiden wet his lips. Oliver followed the motion with his eyes, and suddenly, it was like they were magnetized. Oliver took a step forward at the same time Aiden leaned out the window toward him.

"Oliver." Aiden's voice was so soft, it was almost inaudible over the wind. "Do you want to come in?"

Oliver looked past him, into his bedroom. There was nowhere on earth he'd rather be. But he knew, somehow, that if he crossed that threshold, they wouldn't get any talking done. And they really needed to talk.

"I have another idea. Remember that big tree we used to climb when we were kids? The one we'd use to get onto the roof?"

"Yeah."

"Is it still there?"

Chapter 6: Aiden

Aiden was grateful for all the new upper-body strength lacrosse had given him, and for the various growth spurts he'd had over the years. When he was a kid, he'd had to stand on Max's shoulders to reach the old elm tree's first branch. Now, he reached above his head, grasped it, and hauled himself up like it was nothing. Then it was only a matter of swinging onto the branch by the roof and shimmying onto the shingles.

Once he had his footing, he turned around to offer Oliver a hand, but there was no need. Oliver made quick work of the climb. The muscles in his arms stood out as he pulled himself onto the roof with ease.

Aiden's mouth watered. He did his best not to stare, but he was still having trouble believing this was real. Had Oliver actually appeared at his window at night like a living dream? He was tempted to pinch himself, but before he could, Oliver gestured forward.

"Lead the way."

The roof had a flat spot next to the chimney. They sat down beside each other and hesitated for only a second before they both lay down, arms pillowed beneath their heads. It was exactly like when they were kids. Aiden felt like he'd stepped into a memory.

The shingles were still warm from baking under the sun all day. It heated their backs as the wind nipped at their cheeks. Irvington was far enough away from the city that brilliant swaths of stars were visible, but it was the moon that stole the show: full and silvery, peeking at them from over the treetops.

"What a beautiful night," Oliver said.

"Yeah." Aiden resisted the urge to stare at him. There was an appropriate amount of space between them, but he swore he could feel the heat radiating from Oliver's body. It made him breathless. And nostalgic for the last time they'd been on this roof. "Do you remember—"

"We were nine," Oliver said, his voice so soft it melded with the breeze. "I was spending the night. Max fell asleep the second his head hit the pillow, as per usual, but you and I were still awake. You were teaching me the names of constellations using a book your mom gave you, but I wanted to see them for myself. It was *freezing*, but we sneaked outside anyway and climbed up here. I was kinda small for my age, so you had to give me a boost."

Aiden laughed. "I can still feel your feet digging into my shoulders."

"Yeah, well, I had to pull you up after me. You were so much bigger than me, I thought we were both gonna go flying." Oliver turned his head toward him. "Do you remember what we talked about that night?"

Aiden thought back. "Bits and pieces. I remember listening to you talk." *And thinking that I could listen to your voice for hours. And being too scared to say much because of my enormous crush on you.*

"We saw a shooting star, and we were so excited I thought we were going to wake up the whole neighborhood. We got into an argument about whether or not stars could really grant wishes. We made wishes anyway, just in case. I remember thinking that if we were at my house, we never would have gotten to do this. I would have been too afraid to sneak out, in case my parents caught us and started screaming."

There was something in Oliver's tone, something sad and fragile, that made Aiden's gut clench. "Oliver . . . is everything all right at home?"

Oliver snorted. "Whatever makes you ask that?"

Aiden sidestepped that comment. "I've been thinking about it since you got back. When we were little, you never seemed to want to go home. You used to say all the time that you wanted to live with us and be our brother. I didn't think anything of it back then, but now with the things you've told me about your home life . . . I'd love to flatter myself into thinking you showed up here in the middle of the night solely to see me, but . . ."

Oliver studied his face, eyes black in the dim light. "But what?"

"You've been spending more and more time over here, like you did when we were kids. Trust me, I'm not complaining, but it makes me worry. I wonder if things aren't quite right at your house."

Oliver was silent for a long moment. Then, he turned his gaze back to the stars. "You're very perceptive, you know that? Everyone always praises you for being book smart, but you have emotional intelligence as well."

Aiden wanted to glow at the praise, but he recognized a misdirection when he saw one. There was something that needed to be said. "Oliver, if anyone at home is hurting you, we—"

"No one's hurting me." Oliver rolled onto his side, facing Aiden. "I appreciate your concern, but I promise I'm not being beaten or anything like that."

"Not all abuse is physical."

"That's true, but while my family members can be as annoying as anyone else's, they don't mean any harm. Besides, I'm a big boy. I can take care of myself."

"I know." Aiden licked his dry lips. "But I wish you'd let me help."

Oliver's eyes roamed over his face like he was memorizing it. "Let's talk about something else. I didn't come over here to whine about my problems."

"Why did you come over?"

"Because I wanted to see you." Oliver reached out and brushed one of Aiden's curls away from his brow. "Because there's something I very much want to discuss with you."

A hot flush crept up Aiden's neck. Much as he'd been dying to have this conversation, now that they were on the cusp, his insides transformed into butterflies. The light brush of Oliver's fingers against his skin didn't help.

"Right. I think I know what that is." He swallowed and steeled himself. "When you first came back, I wasn't certain we were going to get along like we did when we were kids. It seems I was right. We're getting along in a totally different way now."

"I'll say." Oliver laughed. "I don't want to be rude, but I have some questions I've been dying to ask you. Personal ones. Is that okay?"

"You can ask me anything."

"Have you ever had a boyfriend before?"

Aiden's heart spasmed at the word *boyfriend*. He had to collect himself before he could answer. "Not in the traditional sense, no. There weren't many other gay kids at the high school Max and I went to. Or at least, none that were out. Our college is a much bigger pond, obviously, but I'm not the most outgoing person."

Oliver looked like he was suppressing a grin.

"What?"

"It's interesting that you don't refer to things as yours. You don't say 'my high school' or 'my college.' It's always you *and* Max."

Aiden shrugged. "We're kind of a matched set."

"That's not how I think of you." Oliver's eyes glinted with intensity. "Not at all."

The air left Aiden's lungs. He had to draw a new breath before he could speak. "So, have you dated much?"

"Yeah, but nothing serious. I only came out last year, and there were so many new people to meet. New friends to make. And so much sex to be had."

Aiden's eyes almost popped out of his skull.

Oliver grinned. "I'm kidding, I swear. The truth is, until recently, I hadn't met anyone I was serious about."

"Until recently?"

Oliver's smile grew. "Remains to be seen. Honestly, when I first started dating, I had a run of bad luck. I didn't know what I wanted, and I ended up moving way too fast with someone I didn't care about. Things got messy, and feelings got hurt. It taught me an important lesson about communication, though." Oliver blew out a breath. "Anyway, I'm over it now. So, what was your first time like? Obviously, mine was a mess."

Aiden wasn't following. "First time doing what?"

It was Oliver's turn to go wide-eyed. "Aiden, you're not . . . Are you a virgin?"

Aiden's face must have been something to behold, because a second later, Oliver was on his back, howling with laughter.

Irritation simmered in Aiden's viscera. "It's not funny!"

Oliver was laughing too hard to respond. After a full minute, he gasped, "I'm so sorry. I'm not laughing at you, I swear. Your face was just so *priceless*." He cleared his throat and composed himself. "I promise I don't buy into the whole myth that being a virgin is funny or shameful or anything. You're not mad, are you?"

"I'm too embarrassed to be mad."

Oliver hesitated before reaching over and touching Aiden's hair again. This time, he wound a curl around his index finger. "I really am sorry. Forgive me?"

Aiden would have forgiven Oliver for burning down his house, so long as he kept playing with his hair. "Okay."

Oliver's fingers skimmed down the side of his face, featherlight. "Have you done anything, sex-wise?"

Aiden's face heated. He wondered if Oliver could feel it in the tips of his fingers. "No."

"Not even to yourself?"

"Oh. No, I've done, um, things. Like, that one thing that teenage boys are known for, and then when I started to think I might be gay—when I was maybe twelve or so—I did some research." Aiden swallowed. "Found out about that whole *other* thing you can do to yourself."

Oliver looked like he was suppressing laughter. "That's so like you, to research gay sex. Trust me, it's not like any textbook you've ever read."

"I take it you're definitely not a virgin then?"

"No." He shrugged as best he could while lying on his side. "Couldn't wait around for you forever."

Aiden's heart thudded hard against his ribs. "Huh?"

"This is embarrassing to admit, but I suppose there's no harm in telling you. I had a massive thing for you when we were younger. I dare say you were my first love."

Aiden sat straight up. He didn't care that Oliver's hand was in the way, and he smacked himself in the face with it. "You *what?*"

Oliver scrambled up as well, looking panicked. "Don't freak out. When I say *love*, I mean puppy love. I'm not saying that I—"

"Oliver, I had a crush on you too."

Oliver inhaled sharply. "You did?"

"Yeah. A big one. I was heartbroken when you moved away." *I don't think I ever got over you.*

Oliver stared at him for a long moment before he fell back onto the roof like he lacked the strength to support himself. "Oh my God. I can't believe it. Imagine if I hadn't moved away. We might have . . . We could have . . ." He made a frustrated sound.

"I know. My head's spinning with the possibilities."

"And to think, all these years I thought I was silly for pining after you."

"I did the same thing. Only my pining had an added level of angst, because I always kinda suspected you had a thing for Max."

Oliver's head snapped toward him. "What on Earth made you think that?"

"When we'd play house or marriage or whatever, you and Max were always the couple."

"Yeah. You know why?"

Aiden shook his head.

"Because Max always took charge. He'd cast himself in the leading role—usually the groom, if memory serves—and since he couldn't very well marry his own brother, guess who got to be his bride?"

"Huh, I never thought of it like that. Makes sense."

"Trust me, I would have gotten pretend-married to you if I'd been calling the shots. In fact, in my daydreams, that was how it went down."

Aiden lay back down next to Oliver, closer this time. "In mine too."

Oliver seemed to be weighing what he wanted to say next, judging by the way his eyes searched Aiden's. "I love your brother and all—he's my friend and a great guy—but if he'd turned out to be the gay one, and you were straight, you still would've been the one I liked."

Aiden's heart clenched with joy. "Why, though? We're identical, and he's so much better with people than I am. Why pick me?"

Oliver propped himself up on his elbows and looked Aiden straight in the eye. "You two aren't identical at all, in my eyes. It's true that Max is funnier and more outgoing—"

"Loving this comparison already," Aiden said.

Oliver continued as if he hadn't been interrupted. "But that's all surface, you know? It's superficial. He's smarter than he claims, but all he wants to be is the life of the party. He's not the guy who sticks around after everyone else has left to help clean up. You are. And that's one of many reasons why I can't stop thinking about you. I know it's only been a week, and we missed out on a whole decade of each other's lives, but for once, I feel like I'm right where I'm supposed to be."

It took everything Aiden had to keep breathing. He braced himself to ask the question he'd been wanting to ask ever since Oliver had shown up at his window. "So . . . what are we going to do?"

"I don't know. I guess we take it one step at a time."

"I can do that." Aiden forced himself to say the truth, no matter how embarrassing it was. "I really like you, Oliver."

Oliver shifted closer, and the air between them ignited. "I like you too. More than I should, considering we haven't so much as been on a date. You're so smart and considerate and . . . you have this steadiness to you, like the world could fall apart, and you'd shrug and start picking up the pieces. I haven't had a whole lot of stability in my life, and it makes me feel safe. *You* make me feel safe."

With Oliver so close to him, it was difficult for Aiden to think. There was so much he wanted to say. He wanted to tell Oliver how wonderful he was, how fun and charming and sweet. Instead, two warring thoughts kept flashing in his brain like a neon sign.

One, if they pursued this and it didn't work out, it could ruin everything. Aiden could lose Oliver for the second time in his life, and the thought of that paralyzed Aiden with fear. Two, he wanted to kiss Oliver. He wanted to kiss him so badly, he could barely stand it. He didn't think he'd ever, in his life, wanted anything or anyone more. Inside and out, body and soul.

There were so many things to consider. So many worries and insecurities and potential pitfalls. Aiden could waste the rest of this beautiful night analyzing every little thing that might go wrong.

But he wasn't going to do that. For once in his life, he was going to be bold.

Aiden exhaled raggedly. "Fuck it."

He grabbed Oliver's face and kissed him hard.

For a moment, neither of them moved. Aiden was so petrified, he went stiff. But then, Oliver returned his kiss with a soft, wanting sound, and everything flew out of Aiden's head. Every thought, every doubt, everything. All that mattered was the warm, sweet press of Oliver's lips against his, and his sudden, burning need for more.

Before Aiden could decide on his next move, Oliver pulled back by a hair's breadth and spoke against his mouth. "Is this your first kiss?"

"Yes." Aiden was shocked by how rough his voice sounded. "That obvious?"

"You tensed like you thought I was going to bite you." He thumbed Aiden's cheekbone. "If it's your first, I'd better make it good, huh?"

Aiden tried to say something back, but it came out garbled. His pulse was going haywire, and his body was heating up. Was this what it felt like to have real chemistry with someone?

"Relax. Don't overthink it, okay?" Oliver brushed their lips together. "Let me show you."

Aiden took a deep breath and let it out slowly, relaxing as Oliver had instructed. When Aiden's shoulders were no longer knotted up, Oliver kissed him, and this time they melted together like warm chocolate.

Aiden turned his thoughts off as best he could and focused on how it felt. Oliver's mouth was warm compared to the cool night, so firm and enticing. His body was the same, pressing against Aiden, all corded muscle and sinewy strength.

Before Aiden knew it, he was flat on his back. Oliver rolled with him, never breaking the kiss. He lay half on top of him, and all semblance of cognizance flew out of Aiden's head. Oliver's tongue swiped across his bottom lip, and Aiden made a little pleasured sound before he could stop himself.

Oliver reacted to the sound like gasoline reacted to fire. He groaned against Aiden's mouth and kissed him harder, with purpose. One hand found its way into Aiden's hair while the other slipped down his chest. Aiden was having trouble breathing, and when he broke the kiss long enough to suck in some oxygen, Oliver's lips found his neck. Aiden never would have guessed he was so sensitive there, but *wow*. Every hot, wet brush of Oliver's mouth down his throat sent sparks up his spine.

When Oliver nibbled on his neck, Aiden shivered. "Jesus."

Oliver licked the spot. "Sorry. Did that hurt?"

"No, I . . . I liked it."

Oliver did it again, and this time Aiden actually moaned. Of all the times he'd imagined what it would be like to kiss someone, he'd never thought it would feel this intense. He had to wonder if it was always like this or if it only felt this way because he was with Oliver.

Oliver kissed up the column of his throat to his jaw and found his earlobe. From there, things went from relatively innocent to downright filthy in a flash. Oliver's lips were *everywhere*. Aiden couldn't seem to touch enough of him. He ran his hands up Oliver's sides, across his broad shoulders, and down his back. Aiden could feel the heat of Oliver's body through clothing, and it seeped into his skin.

His hands found where Oliver's waist dipped in, and stroked it, pushing Oliver's shirt up to get at the skin underneath. Instinctively, Aiden grabbed Oliver by the hips and hitched him up, better aligning their bodies. Though Oliver was bigger than him, in his eagerness, Aiden moved him like he weighed nothing.

Oliver pulled back and stared at him.

Aiden blushed. "What?"

"That was *hot*." Oliver claimed his mouth again, kissing him deeply.

Aiden gave back as best he could. He was sure it was artless and sloppy, but Oliver seemed to enjoy his enthusiasm, judging by the little sounds he was making.

Now that Oliver was on top of him, it was getting harder for Aiden to ignore the fact that he was . . . well, getting harder. He'd been too preoccupied to notice it before, but with Oliver so close, his problem was only growing more persistent.

Before worry could throw him out of the moment, Oliver shifted, and Aiden felt something new and yet familiar against his thigh. For a moment, his brain fought to process the knowledge that Oliver was every bit as turned on by this as he was. Then, a fresh wave of lust sizzled through him.

Aiden must have tensed or something, because Oliver broke their kiss. Panting, he looked at Aiden from inches away, his eyes as dark as the night sky behind him. His lips were plump from kissing. There was something remarkably sexy about that.

Oliver adjusted his position, not bothering to hide the fact that he was hard. "You okay?"

Aiden nodded, too far gone for words. Even if he could speak, he didn't know what he'd say. He had the weirdest urge, however, to say Oliver's name, for the simple pleasure of hearing it.

They stared at each other, the air between them growing more charged by the second. They both seemed to understand that they were standing at a crossroads. Aiden had thought they might take a big step tonight, but he'd expected them to decide if they wanted to date or not. It hadn't occurred to him that there was something else they could decide to do, right here and now.

Aiden struggled to interpret his own feelings. This was like diving headfirst into dark, warm waters, when he'd never so much as stuck a toe in before. But his body had very clear opinions in this instance, and who better to take this step with than Oliver?

He hesitated for only a second before moving his hands—which had been splayed across the small of Oliver's back—downward to where Oliver's waist swelled up into his ass. He grabbed two handfuls, and then, with a dry swallow, he used them to pull Oliver tight to him, groin to groin.

Oliver's reaction was beautiful. He shuddered from head to toe and dropped his head until it rested on Aiden's shoulder, like he couldn't support it anymore. He made a small, desperate sound that Aiden wanted to record and listen to on repeat. He could make a whole playlist out of the noises Oliver made.

All too abruptly, however, it was over. Oliver rolled off him and sat up a good few feet away.

Aiden propped himself up on his elbows, fighting an icy tide of anxiety that was threatening to sweep through him. "Oliver?"

Oliver held up a finger. His back was turned; Aiden couldn't see his face. "Give me a second, please."

Aiden nodded, though Oliver couldn't see him, and sat up. His back hurt from the uneven surface of the roof, his shirt was probably filthy, and his erection wasn't going away anytime soon, but he felt *high*, like that one time he'd taken a hit off a joint at a party.

After a few seconds, Oliver took a deep breath and turned back toward him. "Okay, I'm better now."

"Why'd you stop? Was it something I did?"

"In a manner of speaking. I, uh, got a little too excited."

Aiden glanced away, face burning. "I don't mind."

"I know, and trust me when I say there was a part of me that didn't care either, but we're on the roof of your house. We can't . . . you know."

Aiden laughed. "'*You know*'? What are you, twelve?"

Oliver moved closer just to shove him. "I was trying not to offend your virgin ears."

"Consider me unoffended. And also kinda amazed you stopped. I don't think I would have had the willpower if you'd spent much more time kissing my neck."

Oliver shivered again. "Please don't tempt me. I had to put some distance between us for a reason."

Aiden worked up the last of his nerve to ask, "So, no sex tonight I take it?"

Oliver made a pained sound. "You could so talk me into it, but I don't think now's the time. Do you?"

Loath as Aiden was to admit it, Oliver had a point. They were going at warp speed, undoubtedly because of their history together. If what was building between them was going to be as amazing as Aiden suspected, it was worth taking the time to do it properly.

Aiden climbed to his feet and held out a hand to Oliver. "We should call it a night before one of us changes our mind. Maybe we can hang out tomorrow?"

Oliver took his hand and let Aiden haul him up. "Oh, you bet. There'll be no getting rid of me now."

Aiden made his way to the edge of the roof. A few careful maneuvers later, his feet hit the ground. He turned around to help Oliver down and ended up catching him by the arms and slowly lowering him to the grass, their faces close, like something out of a movie.

Oliver's face was half in shadow, but Aiden could still make out the brightness of his eyes and the fact that his lips were still a little swollen.

Aiden swallowed. "It's like a floodgate opened. Now that I've kissed you, I don't want to do anything else."

Oliver nodded. "You should probably let go of me, or we'll have to start this whole process all over again."

"Oh, sorry." Aiden released him and stepped away, looking down at his shoes. A second later, something warm touched his hand. Oliver laced their fingers together.

"Come on," he said. "Let's get you inside before we push our luck too far, and someone wakes up."

He led the way to Aiden's window. When they reached it, Oliver faced him. "Thanks for tonight. I needed it." He gave Aiden a chaste kiss that lingered long after he'd pulled away.

Aiden hesitated. "Do you want to spend the night?" As soon as the words were out of his mouth, he realized how they sounded. "Um, I could make up the couch for you, or you could stay with me. I don't know why, but I have the weirdest urge to sleep with you." His cheeks flamed. "I mean *actually* sleep. I want to hold you and, um, all that."

"By 'all that' do you mean cuddling? You want to cuddle?"

"Right. That." *Why am I so bad at this?* Aiden looked down at the ground and willed it to swallow him whole.

A finger brushed his chin, and he peeked up.

Oliver was smiling, bright like sunlight. "I know what you mean. I want that too. But if I spend the night, I don't trust myself to keep things PG."

Aiden nodded. "I understand, but I don't want you to go."

"Hey, I'm not leaving yet. We still need to clarify some things." His smile turned playful. "We got a little distracted up on the roof."

Aiden laughed even as a whole swarm of butterflies took flight in his stomach. "Yeah, I suppose we did. So, obviously we're attracted to each other, but we should take things slow. Do you want to go on a date maybe? See where it leads?"

"Sounds good to me. Although . . ." Oliver looked off into the shadows as if he were searching for answers in their amorphous forms.

Aiden backpedaled as fast as a professional cyclist. "Hey, listen, we don't need to decide anything right now. It's a big step, and I'm so inexperienced, and—"

Oliver shushed him gently. "Aiden, it's not that. I don't care that you've never had a boyfriend or whatever. If I have my way, that's all about to change. I was thinking . . . I don't know how to phrase it."

"Try."

"I feel like we're already dating? Like, I'm not sure how going on a date is going to be much different from what we've been doing all week. Hanging out. Going places. Having fun. I mean, what's the difference?"

"Well, for one thing, I hope Max won't be there." Aiden stepped closer. "And I'll get to do this." He kissed Oliver.

Oliver leaned into it but didn't deepen it. "I suppose that's true. I've never dated a friend before, so I'm still working through it in my head. We won't have to have any of the first-date small talk, because I already know where you're from and what you do."

"Good. I hate small talk." Aiden studied Oliver's face. "You still seem concerned. It's not like we're getting married or anything. We have plenty of time to figure things out. Just promise me that if we don't work out as a couple, we'll still be friends."

Oliver smiled. "You read my mind. That's exactly what I was worrying about. I want to stay friends, no matter what. Assuming Max doesn't kill me, of course. You know he would if I ever broke your heart."

Aiden laughed. "That's what big brothers are for, as he would say. Speaking of which, what are we going to tell him? And everyone else?"

"Right now, nothing. I'm not saying keep it a secret, but I don't think there's anything to tell yet. Besides, we don't want to get everyone excited prematurely."

"Fair enough. I suppose I'll have to be patient."

Oliver nodded. "I know how you feel. I can't help but think of the future. What's going to happen when summer ends and we go back to school?

Aiden was beyond relieved to learn Oliver had been thinking about that as well. "I've been waiting for you for ten years. I can wait a little longer. Besides, come senior year, I'll be moving to the city. We'll be a subway ride away from each other."

"I like the sound of that." Oliver cupped his face and kissed him, not deeply but with so much passion it left Aiden breathless. "Good night. I'll talk to you tomorrow."

"Night."

Aiden watched Oliver melt into the shadows. He stood outside his window and listened as a car started somewhere near the front of the house. A moment later, it was silent except for the gentle hum of the wind.

Aiden glanced up at the night sky. He had to be imagining that the stars looked brighter than they had before, but they did. Bright and twinkling with the promise of tomorrow.

Chapter 7: Max

"So . . . did something happen between you guys, or what?"

Max might have set off a cherry bomb in the middle of the game room, judging by the way Aiden and Oliver jumped.

"W-what?" Aiden stammered.

"Nothing happened." Oliver's eyes got funny-big. "I dunno what you mean."

They were downstairs, as per usual. Max was lounging on the sofa—taking up the whole thing just to be an ass—while Aiden perched on the arm and Oliver reclined in the chair next to that. It might have been a day like any other, if it weren't for the storm cloud-worthy tension crackling in the air.

Max's whole face puckered with disbelief. "Uh-huh." *Real convincing, guys.*

He didn't press the issue, but if Aiden and Oliver thought the moony looks they kept shooting each other were subtle, they were off the fucking rails. It would've been less obvious if one of the Yankees had busted into the house and started lobbing fastballs past Max's head. He had no idea what had gone down—he wasn't a mind reader, after all—but shit had clearly gotten real.

Two precious weeks of summer had passed since they'd reunited with Oliver, and the Three Musketeers had fallen into a routine: wake up, meet up, hang out, and sleep. Or at least, that was how it had been, until today.

Max studied them out of the corner of his eye while pretending to watch TV. At first, he'd thought maybe they'd had a fight. Why else would they be acting so weird around each other? But considering what he'd seen at the arcade . . .

Could this be sexual *tension? Ew.*

Max didn't want to think about his brother and his childhood friend slinking around each other like cats in heat, and not solely for the obvious reasons. He shared a face with Aiden. He now knew exactly what he looked like with a big pair of googly eyes. It wasn't flattering.

Then again, Max could be totally misreading things. What evidence did he have beyond some odd looks and awkwardness? Aiden was always awkward, and Oliver wasn't much better. But then, Max did have the much-touted twin telepathy.

He might not know much, but he knew his brother. He understood Aiden's moods, and when he was pretending to be upset versus when he actually was. Same with when he acted upbeat around friends and professors when in reality, he was downright miserable. Right now, Max's senses were telling him that love was in the air. Or, at least, lust.

As if to confirm his suspicions, Aiden and Oliver both sneaked a peek at each other at the same time, and when their eyes met, Max swore music swelled in the background.

Shit. *This had all the makings of summer loving, had me a blast. How had he not seen this coming?*

Because you never thought your geeky brother and shy friend would actually do *anything.*

Goddamn it, this could ruin their whole summer. There had to be a way to stop this train wreck before it started.

What could he do, though? Tell them to cut it out? Whack 'em with a rolled-up newspaper? Fill a spray bottle with water and squirt them whenever they looked at each other?

"Uh, Max?"

Max broke from his thoughts and glanced at Aiden. "What?"

"Are you changing channels for the fun of it, or what?"

Max had taken the remote and absently mashed the channel button in frustration. One look at the TV screen told him they were whizzing by too fast for anyone to process what was on them. So much for pretending to watch.

"Sorry, I was lost in thought." He tossed the remote to Oliver, who caught it easily. "You pick something. You're the guest."

Aiden and Oliver exchanged a look that Max did not like one bit.

"Actually," Aiden said, "we were thinking we wanted to do something today."

"Today?" Max repeated. It was already afternoon. Hadn't the ship sailed on today?

"Yes, brother dear. Today." Aiden stood up and stretched. "I know summer's supposed to be about recharging, but we can't keep lazing around."

"I like lazing around, thanks." Max didn't mean to sound so crabby, but he didn't like having his lifestyle called into question. "You guys want to play some Madden or something? We could make a mini fantasy football league."

Oliver—who came the closest to sharing Max's love of spectator sports—did him the courtesy of considering it before he shook his dark head. "If I don't get off my ass and do something, I'm going to atrophy. Last year, I fell out of my workout routine over the summer, and then when the season started again, I was way behind. I don't want to do that again."

"You fit people and your exercise," Max joked. It came out flat. "What's the plan, then? If you guys try to drag me to a gym, there will be blood."

They exchanged another look, and Max got the sense that they'd had this conversation already.

"We were thinking we might go to Hudson Park," Aiden said. "Walk around. Maybe throw a Frisbee."

The use of *we* was unmistakable. *We*, as in Aiden and Oliver. *We*, as in not Max. They'd made this plan without him.

It was bad enough Max was on the fringe of their bizarre mating ritual, but now he was left out of the decision-making process as well. Max, who had always taken charge when it came to plans and activities, was now an afterthought.

His stomach acid roiled. *Don't overreact. It's not that serious.*

"Isn't it a little hot for the park?"

"Yeah," Aiden said, "but we'll find some shade. We wanted to go this morning when it was cooler, but you slept until noon."

Am I imagining things, or did that sound a bit like an accusation?

Aiden continued. "It'll be fun. We'll bring towels so you can sit in the grass if you want. Maybe we can score a spot on the riverbank." Aiden glanced at Oliver. "You'll like that, right? Getting to hang out by the water?"

"Yeah, though I want to get some vitamin D too." He held up his arm. "I'm getting pale."

"Yeah, right." Aiden leaned over and put his arm next to Oliver's. "I guess that makes me Casper."

They giggled. Max wanted to scream.

"Well, I hope you guys have fun," he snapped.

That got their attention.

Oliver looked at Aiden, as if for guidance.

Aiden pursed his lips. "Max, what do you mean? You're coming too."

"Yeah, dude, it wouldn't be the same without you." Oliver rubbed his palms on his jeans like they were clammy. "Besides, it's a beautiful day. It'd be a shame to miss it."

Max was overcome by the pettiness building within him. "Maybe for you athletic types, but I'm the lazy twin, remember? I'd hate to make you bring blankets just so I'll have somewhere to sit around and do nothing. You'd be better off without me."

Max himself was shocked by how bitter he sounded. Where the fuck had that outburst come from? How long had he been stewing on that particular insecurity, and why was it bubbling up now?

He was about to apologize and try to smooth things over, when Aiden and Oliver exchanged another infuriating look. Max shut his mouth with a smack of lips.

"If you want to stay in, we can stay in." Aiden's tone wasn't patronizing, per se, but it was a little too fake-soothing. As if Max were a toddler, and Aiden was the long-suffering parent. "We don't want to exclude you."

There was that *we* again. Max was struck by the oddest urge to reclaim his territory. He jumped to his feet. "On second thought, I could go for some fresh air. Let me change clothes, and we can leave. Oliver, do you want to borrow some shorts or something?"

Oliver's relieved expression punched Max in the gut. "That would be great, yeah."

"I guess jeans are gonna be too hot, huh?" Aiden frowned down at his own denim-clad legs. "I'll change too, and we can meet in the living room."

Aiden went off to his room while Max led Oliver to his. As soon as he walked in, he wished he'd thought to tidy up. It looked like a suitcase full of dirty laundry had exploded inside, but whatever. Oliver had seen worse.

It wasn't until Max closed the door behind them that renewed unease crept over him. Perplexed, he tried to shake it off as he sifted through his bureau for two pairs of clean shorts.

"Can I have the green ones?" Oliver asked.

Max scoffed but tossed them to him. "Trying to bring out the color of your eyes?"

He'd meant it as a joke, but there was a noticeable flush in Oliver's face as he stripped off his jeans and pulled the shorts on.

At the first flash of bare skin, Max suddenly realized why he felt uneasy. Before, he would have thought nothing of changing in front of Oliver. Hell, they'd taken baths together when they were little, and Mom had the embarrassing photos to prove it. But now . . .

This isn't because he's gay, is it? Because if so, you're gonna have to kick your own ass.

Max did a quick self-analysis and determined that wasn't the issue. So what was?

"Dude." Oliver interrupted his thoughts. "I'm comfortable with my body and all, but could you not stare?"

"Right! Sorry." Max turned back to the drawer, blushing so hard he must have looked like Aiden. Well, more so than usual.

He selected a pair of black shorts and started to undress, but his hands hesitated on the fly of his jeans. Did this sudden weirdness have something to do with Aiden? Or the changes between him and Oliver, or—

It was like a damn light bulb went off above Max's head. Aiden was in better shape than him, hands down, but they were still twins. Undressing in front of Oliver was kinda like giving him a peek at what Aiden looked like naked. Would Oliver see it that way?

Max glanced over his shoulder. Oliver had taken a seat on his bed while he waited. He wasn't ogling Max, but he also wasn't facing the other way either.

"You change your mind or something?" Oliver asked when he noticed Max looking at him.

"Uh, no." *Stop being weird. It's Oliver. You watched him eat a crayon once.*

Max stripped down, but he was tense the whole time. His mind whirred with errant thoughts. If he hadn't volunteered to let Oliver borrow his clothes, would Aiden have? Would Oliver be in Aiden's room right now? Undressing?

The unfamiliar emotions that had been churning in Max's stomach finally boiled over. What *was* this? Was he jealous or something? What did he have to be jealous of?

"Hey, are you okay?" Oliver stood up and moved to his side.

Max waved him off. "I'm fine." He finished dressing, ran a hand through his curls, and took a deep breath. "Ollie, can I ask you something?"

Oliver's face sobered. "Sure." Aiden probably thought Max was too oblivious to pick up on what was happening, but judging by the caginess of Oliver's expression, he was expecting a blow.

Max opened his mouth, but as soon as he did, it occurred to him that he wasn't sure what to ask. *Are you dating my brother? Are you guys serious or fucking around? Is this any of my business whatsoever?*

He closed his mouth.

"Max?" Oliver looked him over, as if checking for signs of trauma. "You were gonna ask me something?"

"Um, yeah." Max flipped through a mental rolodex of possible questions before settling on a genuine curiosity of his. "How can you always tell me and Aiden apart?"

Oliver blinked. "What do you mean?"

"You've never mixed us up. Not once in the past two weeks. Our own mother gets us confused every now and then."

"Really?"

"Well, it's rare, and it usually involves seeing us out of our element. Like, if she looks at Aiden from behind, or if I'm reading a book. Anyway, I'm curious as to how you can tell which of us is which."

Oliver rubbed his chin. "Well . . . it's hard to put into words. It's sort of a vibe, but not in, like, a New Age kind of way. Aiden has this calmness that radiates off him, whereas you're more energetic. It's odd to say, but when I look at Aiden, I get the same feeling I get when I look out over the water. I feel . . . peaceful." He ran a hand through his hair. "I'm babbling, sorry. I hope that answers your question."

Max stared at him, heart jackhammering in his chest.

"Max?" Oliver waved a hand in front of his eyes. "Do you need medical attention? You keep spacing out."

"I never thought . . ." Max wiped his brow. "It never *occurred* to me that . . ."

"What?"

Max didn't know how to finish that sentence. A moment ago, he'd thought he was so perceptive. He'd thought Aiden and Oliver were the dense ones for thinking he wouldn't notice what was going on. But he'd had no idea.

They were in *love*. Or, at least, Oliver was in love with Aiden. After that little speech, there was no question. And why wouldn't Aiden love him back? They got along great, they'd been friends forever, and they'd already met each other's family. Plus, they had everything in common. Upbringing. Goals. Hobbies. They had all the ingredients for an epic romance lined up and ready to go.

And fuck, Max hadn't seen it coming. He'd suspected, but just because he'd spotted the light didn't mean he was prepared for the train currently smacking into him.

The silence had stretched on for way too long. Max gave himself a mental shake. "Sorry, forget I said anything. I'm having an off day. Let's go meet Aiden. He's probably wondering where we are."

Oliver nudged him in the side, grinning. "Hopefully he doesn't think any funny business was going on."

Yeah, right. You're in love with my brother. Like you'd come anywhere near me.

Max led the way to the living room, trying to pretend he wasn't caught up in his own head. Sure enough, Aiden was standing by the front door with a bitter look on his face, the same one he got when Max made him late for class.

At the sight of Oliver, however, he grinned. "Took you long enough."

"Sorry, I was coordinating my ensemble." Oliver walked right up to Aiden like he intended to kiss him, but at the last second, he stopped short. They both looked at Max like they'd forgotten he was there.

Aiden cleared his throat. "Are we ready to go?"

There was a flicker of a moment in which Max considered faking a cramp to get out of this whole thing. He'd been perfectly happy watching TV, and if he was going to be a third wheel, he'd rather stay home. Besides, if they really were in love and didn't know it, having some alone time might do them some good. They might figure this whole thing out, and then . . .

And then what? Where would that leave Max?

His chest tightened with yet more emotions he couldn't quite interpret. Maybe that cramp idea wasn't so far from the truth.

"Yeah," he found himself saying. "Let's go."

Aiden drove, as per usual, and Oliver called shotgun, which meant Max was relegated to the back seat. Oliver chattered on about some class he'd taken last year while Aiden balanced driving with staring at him. If they died in a fiery crash, at least Max could comfort himself with the knowledge that it was *totally* worth it.

For the life of him, Max couldn't figure out why this whole thing bothered him so much. He tried to dissect his reactions as they reached their destination and snagged a parking spot beneath a tree. The park, which was aptly named Scenic Hudson Park, was every bit as pretty as Max remembered. Crisp green grass stretched up to the rocky bank of a river that wound off toward the horizon. Park benches and shady trees dotted the idyllic scene. The sun was dripping down the cloudless sky in preparation of what would undoubtedly be a gorgeous sunset.

It was hot, but not as oppressively so as Max had anticipated. He spotted a handful of people jogging and some children playing on one of the baseball fields, but otherwise it was quiet.

Oliver stretched his hands up until his spine cracked. "Oh, yeah. This is exactly what I needed. I'm like a lizard. I get my energy from the sun."

Aiden nudged him. "Or a flower."

"No, trust me. Lizard."

They laughed, and Max found himself laughing along with them. Some of his paranoia ebbed away as they trotted toward the riverbank. Maybe things weren't changing after all. They were all still friends. They were still hanging out, still laughing and joking. Maybe he'd gotten all worked up over nothing.

"Hey, Max," Oliver asked as they scoped out a shady spot. "Whatever happened with that girl? The one from the arcade?"

"Danielle?" Max shrugged. "I called her, but she didn't pick up. Probably because she didn't recognize the number. I'll try her again soon."

"Did you leave a voice mail?"

"Hell no. I'm old-school. I'm not wooing a girl over a machine. Besides, I've seen too many sitcoms where people fuck up their messages, and then everything cascades from there. If I'm going to make a fool of myself, I want to do it in real time."

Aiden chuckled. "That's my brother."

They spent the next hour doing nothing in particular, and it was wonderful. They found an abandoned soccer ball and kicked it around until they got bored of that, and then Aiden and Oliver raced each other to the riverbank. Aiden won by a sliver, Oliver demanded a recount, and Max was called in to act as referee. He ruled in Aiden's favor—of course—which sparked a lively debate about nepotism that had Max laughing until he couldn't breathe.

Afterward, they lay in the grass and talked and talked, like they used to when they were kids. If they could live anywhere in the world, where would they go? What did they want to be when they grew up? Aiden recounted the tale of the Christmas when they were eight.

Oliver's dad had given him a toy police kit with a real fingerprint duster. They'd spent the whole afternoon dusting his house and fingerprinting each other. They'd been fascinated to discover that Max and Aiden had different prints. The ink hadn't come off their hands for days. All three of them had different stories about how they'd finally gotten it off.

As the sun moved doggedly across the sky, they started talking about leaving.

"I don't want to go home just yet, though," Oliver said. "We still have hours before dinner."

"We could see a movie." Max was lying in the grass with his hands folded beneath his head. When they started to go numb, he held them in front of his eyes, admiring the latticework of marks the grass had left in his skin. "All this sun has made me want to go chill in the dark for a couple of hours."

"I'm down for that." Oliver was sitting at the base of a nearby tree with his back to the bark. Aiden was also sitting beneath the tree, but he'd settled the exact right amount of distance away. Not so far that it looked weird but not so close that anyone would think they were sitting *together*. As someone who knew how analytical his brother could be, Max wanted to laugh.

"What should we see?" Aiden asked. "There's that one film about the service animals used in the Vietnam War that's supposed to be fascinating."

"Veto," Max said. "I don't want to see anything I have to think about. How about *Fist of Impact*?"

Aiden crinkled his nose. "That action movie with all the explosions? Um, no. There's a difference between not thinking and being induced into a coma."

"Then again." Oliver looked over at Aiden. "We could sit in the back and make fun of it the whole time."

Aiden pursed his lips. "I dunno. I swore off hate-watching movies after the fifth Pirates of the Caribbean film. The joke was on me, that time. What about that one kids movie? The one with the balloon factory?"

"Dude!" Oliver clapped his hands together. "I've seen it, and let me tell you, it's *awesome*. I'm not ashamed to admit I teared up at the end."

"Wanna see it again?"

"Hell yeah! Sounds perfect." Oliver jumped to his feet, pulled Aiden up, and was about to offer his hand to Max when he paused. "Max? Is something wrong?"

Max had grown increasingly tense as he'd listened to Aiden and Oliver. "So, that's it? We're not going to discuss this any further?"

Oliver's hand fell limply to his side. "You don't want to see the balloon movie?"

"Oh sure, now you ask me. After you two have already decided that's what we're seeing." As frustrated as Max was, he had to ask himself if he was really as opposed to seeing this movie as he was acting.

100

No . . . but it's the principle of the thing.

Oliver and Aiden exchanged another look, and bile rose up in the back of Max's throat.

"Well, I hate to say this, but it's two against one," Aiden said.

That was the wrong argument. Max's temper sparked up like a flare. "What, there's no such thing as compromise in this new democracy of ours? If you'll recall, Oliver was also okay with seeing my movie. *Fist of Impact* has two votes, which makes it a tie."

"But I was going to see it to make fun of it." Oliver shuffled his feet. "If it comes down to it, I'd much rather see the kids movie again. It had a great soundtrack."

Max's ire was rising by the second. "We're twenty. We're too old for that sort of thing."

Now, Max knew for a fact he didn't believe that. He still watched cartoons while wearing his Batman pajamas. But irritation was bubbling up in him like a geyser about to explode, and he couldn't seem to keep a lid on it.

"I guess . . . we could split up?" Aiden sounded unsure. "You can see your movie, and we can see ours?"

The last of Max's self-control snapped, and irritation bloomed into white-hot anger inside him. "You're *ditching* me?"

Aiden's eyes widened. "I didn't say that. I—"

"That's exactly what you said. I don't want to see your movie, so you're gonna go without me instead of trying to compromise."

"Not for nothing," Oliver said, "but the kids movie *was* the compromise. You didn't want to watch Aiden's movie, and he didn't want to watch yours, so we picked a third option."

"A third option that I don't want to see. I can't believe you guys are gonna make me watch that crap."

"We're not making you do anything," Aiden said. "Don't blame us for this. You're the one who's throwing a temper tantrum because you didn't get your way. You're such a child sometimes."

The second the words were out of his mouth, a hush fell over them.

Max stared at his brother without really seeing him. Despite the heat, he felt cold. A mixture of humiliation and betrayal washed through him.

Max *was* being ridiculous. He knew he was. But hell if he was going to admit it to Aiden, the world's biggest know-it-all.

Oliver hesitated. "Max . . . is something else bothering you?"

That was a spectacular question.

Max had always been the leader. He'd always taken charge and made the plans, because if he didn't, Aiden would never do anything social. But now Aiden and Oliver were making their own plans, and Max was left to either tag along or get left behind. He swore he could almost feel the power dynamic shifting around them.

"I guess this is how things are going to be now," he said to no one in particular. "You two vote together, and I always lose."

"Oh, please." Aiden rolled his eyes. "This is so dramatic."

Max opened his mouth to say something nasty—he didn't know what, but it was going to *hurt*—when Oliver stepped between them.

"Guys"—he held up his hands—"you both need a time-out. This is exactly like when we were kids. Max, you would explode over something small that you'd probably get over in five minutes if left alone. But then Aiden would slowly build up to being angry, and right as you were ready to calm down, he'd get you going again. I've seen you guys fight for hours this way, and that's not how I want to spend the rest of my day."

Max worried his bottom lip. Oliver was right. No one knew how to irritate him better than his twin. There was a part of him that was willing to admit Aiden had a point: he was causing a big stink over nothing. He wasn't even sure *why*.

He was contemplating offering up an apology when Oliver turned to Aiden and whispered something under his breath. Max couldn't make out most of what Oliver said, but he caught his name loud and clear.

Wow, way to talk about me like I'm not here, Ollie.

That would have been reason enough for Max to get irritated all over again, but then Aiden whispered back, "Stop making excuses for him. If he's going to be like this, he can go home."

"Well, fuck you too, brother dear." Max climbed to his feet, heart pounding. "Going home sounds great to me. You two can do whatever the hell you want with your night. Drop me off, or if that's too much trouble, I'll walk."

"It's five miles," Aiden said.

It didn't escape Max's notice that he didn't try to talk him out of leaving. "I know it is, genius. Believe it or not, I can count."

"Max, stop it." Oliver looked back and forth between them. "Aiden, you're no better. You guys are fighting over nothing."

A stray thought flitted into Max's mind as if planted there: *That's rich, considering this all started when you showed up.*

Holy shit. Where had that come from?

Max would have to examine it later. He'd finally thought of the nasty thing he wanted to say. He shot Aiden a saccharine smile. "You know, if you wanted some alone time with your new boyfriend, you could have asked."

Aiden paled. "Oliver's not . . . We're not . . ."

"Bull*shit*. You can't lie to me, twin. I'd recognize your clumsy attempts at flirting anywhere. Guess you don't know everything after all."

He whirled around before either of them could reply and marched back to the car. He stood with his arms crossed and stared pointedly at the ground until he heard shuffling feet approach, followed by the *click* of the door unlocking. Max threw himself into the back seat without another word.

The first half of the drive was library-silent. As they neared their house, however, Oliver tried to talk Max into coming with them. Aiden didn't speak, and Oliver never once offered to see the movie Max wanted to see.

Not that Max would have agreed to go even if they'd both caved at this point. In truth, he was too embarrassed when he thought back on how he'd acted. He wasn't totally at fault, sure, but he'd started the whole thing, and for what? He needed to figure out what the hell was chewing his ass before he wrecked his two closest relationships.

When they pulled up into the driveway, he wordlessly exited the car. He trudged up to the house without looking back. Part of him hoped his brother would come chasing after him—like when they fought when they were little—but after a tense few seconds, he heard their shared car back out of the driveway and speed away.

Which was remarkable, really, considering the car had just lost its third wheel.

Max stabbed his key into the front door and opened it with such force, the wood creaked.

"Boys?" called Dad's voice from the kitchen. "Is that you? Your mother and I are were just thinking about starting dinner."

Max forced himself to sound neutral. "It's me, Dad. Aiden and Oliver went to see a movie."

Mom's head popped into the hallway. "Without you? That seems kind of rude."

"Yeah, no sh—" He stopped himself in the nick. "I'm not feeling well. I'm gonna go lie down."

Mom eyed him, as if she sensed something was up, but all she asked was, "Want some water? Juice? Healing mom kisses?"

"Later. Love you."

"Love you too."

Max trundled to his room, feeling more exhausted with every step. He reached his door and was about to push it open, but on impulse, he turned down the hall and went into Aiden's room instead. It was much neater than Max's—he'd actually taken the time to put his clothes into drawers. The desktop lamp had been left on, illuminating Aiden's bookshelf and the corkboard that hung above his workspace.

School papers, tickets, and photos had been tacked onto it. The last time Max had looked at it, the photos had all been of them. Prom. Their graduation. Moving into their first apartment. There were other people here and there, but the central theme was clear: the Kingsman twins.

Now, however, there was an open shoebox of old photos on the desk, and from it, Aiden had made some new additions. Max didn't have to look twice to recognize who was in the new-old photos. Oliver.

Fucking figures.

A school photo of him had taken the place of the picture of Max and Aiden in their caps and gowns. Same went for the one of Max and Aiden standing by their car on their sixteenth birthday. And there was another one of all three of them in the backyard, but Max's face was hidden beneath the corner of an old essay.

Max scoffed. The metaphor was so blatant, even he could have written a thesis on it. He was being replaced. By a guy they hadn't talked to in a decade. Max grumbled under his breath. Oliver was great and all, but Aiden was his *brother*. Where was the loyalty? Where was the literal bros before figurative bros?

And all because they have the hots for each other. Fuck this.

Maybe if Max talked to Aiden, he could get him to realize what a mistake he was making. After all, at the end of the summer, Oliver was going to go back to the city. He wasn't going to be there for Aiden like Max was, like Max had always been. Aiden couldn't see it because he was caught up in the romance. As his older brother, it was Max's responsibility to force him to be reasonable.

Before the thought had fully solidified, Max shook his head to himself. "Am I really gonna turn on Oliver like this? Am I gonna be that shitty friend? All because I'm ..."

He sucked in a breath, and his mental voice finished his sentence for him. *Jealous.*

Shit. He'd been told more than once that he was immature, but he'd always thought he was supposed to be at this age. He couldn't even drink legally, after all. If people were going to expect him to have all the answers, they were going to be disappointed.

But he didn't want to be immature about this. No matter how much he wanted to blame Oliver and let his temper take over, he wasn't going to let that happen. For once in his life, he was going to think this through like a goddamn adult.

He wandered over to Aiden's bed and flung himself onto it. Might as well start at the top of the list. Why was he so jealous of Aiden and Oliver's budding romance?

Well, it took attention away from Max. That much was a given. But it had to run deeper than that.

They were hiding the relationship from him. He shook his head. On some level, it stung that Aiden wasn't sharing this part of his life with him, but Aiden was also *oblivious*. He couldn't share something that he hadn't fully explored for himself.

Max thought harder. He was being third-wheeled. That would upset anyone. But Oliver and Aiden had gone out of their way to invite him to things, though it had certainly backfired. They obviously weren't *trying* to exclude him. Then again, judging by what had gone down at the park, he felt excluded regardless. He filed that away as a possibility.

What else was there? He wasn't the leader anymore. After a lifetime of big-brothering, he didn't like being relegated to a minor role.

All of these were perfectly good reasons for him to be jealous, but he was starting to think he wasn't asking himself the right questions.

Maybe it's not about why you're jealous, but rather who you're jealous of.

The obvious answer was Aiden. He was calling the shots now, and he'd gotten Oliver on his side. Max felt like he was being dog-piled by his own brother and friend.

But then, Oliver was *only* a friend. Maybe Max was jealous because Oliver was taking Aiden away from him. His baby brother. The one who turned to Max when he was upset. Max's confidant. His best friend. Aiden could now turn to Oliver for support instead of Max. Maybe that was part of it. Aiden was more interested in someone else now.

What if it's both of those things?

Something like a gameshow bell went off in Max's head. *We have a winner.*

He didn't want Oliver to take Aiden's attention away from him. At the same time, he hated that Aiden had someone else who was important to him. Max had lots of friends, but he'd always given Aiden priority, especially since Aiden didn't have many friends of his own. And now, Aiden had glommed onto Oliver, abandoning Max in favor of a newer, shinier relationship.

Jesus, Aiden was right. I am dramatic.

Max needed to remind himself that they'd had one fight, and Aiden and Oliver weren't dating yet. Max was acting like he'd been abandoned by his one and only precious sibling, when in reality, they all needed to figure some things out.

Namely, Max needed to accept the fact that if things didn't work out between Oliver and Aiden, that wasn't the end of this conundrum. There would be other boyfriends.

Even if it wasn't until years from now, someone was going to come along and steal Aiden's heart. They'd have their own, special bond that

Max could never be a part of. And the same went for Max. He'd never had a steady girlfriend before, but he was bound to someday, and when that happened, the Kingsman twins would split up into couples.

That was surprisingly hard to swallow. They were twins. They were a pair. They weren't meant to be broken up.

Max was beginning to understand why he'd gotten so angry. He was losing a part of his identity. Big brother. Twin. The hero who swooped in and saved Aiden from bullies and loneliness. Only, in the end, Aiden had moved on without him.

"What a fucking mess," he grumbled to both himself and the ceiling. He remembered how silent Aiden had been in the car ride. After years of falling in line, it seemed little brother was ready to stir some dissent in the ranks.

Max needed to defuse this before it blew up in his face as dramatically as he'd blown up earlier. Talking seemed like the easiest fix to him.

"The next time I see Aiden," he whispered to himself, "I'll explain everything. He'll listen to me. I'm his big brother, after all."

Chapter 8: Oliver

There Oliver was, on his first technical date with Aiden, and he couldn't begin to enjoy it.

He should have been ecstatic. He should have been making jokes about good-night kisses and enjoying the nuclear blush that surely would have swept over Aiden's face. But, instead, all he could think about was Max.

The fight had left Oliver a jittery mass of nerves. He'd lived through his fair share of Kingsman squabbles, but he'd never heard Aiden and Max be that nasty to each other. And then after, when Aiden had let Max leave without trying to fix things . . . That was a coldness he'd never seen Aiden display before.

A small, foreboding voice in the back of Oliver's mind whispered to him all throughout the movie, warning him that this was a precursor. The first rumble of thunder before the oncoming storm.

They ended up seeing the war film Aiden had proposed in the first place, and it felt like a betrayal. Like, now that they'd gotten rid of Max, they were free to do what they *really* wanted. Oliver knew that wasn't what had gone down, but his gut seemed to have other ideas.

He spent the whole movie tense and distracted. When Aiden had slipped his hand on top of Oliver's, Oliver couldn't bring himself to lace their fingers together. Max's words kept bubbling up into his thoughts: *"You two vote together, and I always lose."* In his head, a mantra had started to repeat like an echo off the cold walls of a cave.

They're fighting the same way my parents do; only this time, I know it's because of me.

His head was in a fog as they walked out of the theater.

Aiden looked at him askance. "You okay?"

"Yeah." It was the most blatant lie Oliver had ever told. He kept his eyes trained forward so Aiden wouldn't see through him as easily as a pane of glass.

Something warm brushed his wrist. Aiden's fingers. "I had a really good time." He hesitated. "I hope you did too."

Oliver wanted to take his hand. He wanted to stroll through the parking lot full of movie-goers with his date by his side and act like any other couple. He wanted to offer to walk Aiden to his car, despite the fact that they'd driven here together, and kiss him against the door. Aiden would taste like salt and butter from the popcorn they'd shared, and it would be the perfect end to what should have been a phenomenal first date.

"Yeah," Oliver said again. "I think we need to talk about some things, though."

Aiden winced. "Should I be worried?"

"Honestly, I'm the one who's worried. Let's go home and we'll talk." He didn't want to worry about tense, emotional driving on top of everything else.

They went straight to the car and got in. No kiss. Nothing.

Once they were on the road, Aiden started talking about the movie. He must've been bursting to ask Oliver what was up, but he refrained. It was a considerate gesture, and one that Oliver appreciated.

Oliver must've participated well enough, but in truth, he didn't hear a word. In his head, he was rehearsing what he was going to say to Aiden when they stopped. It wasn't a conversation he was looking forward to having, but the more he replayed the day's events, the more convinced he became that it needed to happen.

For everyone's sake.

A small eternity later, Aiden pulled into Oliver's driveway. There was room, for once. It seemed there'd been no family dinner. Oliver was actually a bit sad he'd missed an opportunity to share a meal with just his dad. He'd have to make it up to him later.

"Oliver."

He glanced over to the driver's seat.

Aiden was watching him. "I can tell you're trying to delay having this conversation, but if you do, I might explode."

"Sorry. I wasn't trying to act all mysterious. I needed some time to think of what I wanted to say."

"Is this about Max? Forget what he said before. I won't let him—"

"Stop." Oliver held up a hand. "Seriously, you need to cut your brother some slack. Can't you see how hurt he is by all this?"

Aiden's eyebrows shot up. "Why would he be hurt? He's the one who picked a fight with us earlier."

"Yeah, because he sensed that something was going on between us, and then we teamed up against him. He obviously feels left out."

"So, what, he gets a free pass to act like a complete brat?"

"No. This is an explanation, not an excuse. He shouldn't have blown up like that, but honestly, you shouldn't have been so dismissive."

Aiden had an honest-to-God pout on his face. "I guess."

Oliver studied him. "What's with you? You're usually good at reading people and understanding their emotions. Why are you refusing to see your brother's side of this? Both of you are being immature, and I'm not going to get dragged into the middle of it."

Aiden let out a breath. "I'm sorry you feel like you're in the middle. I admit I wasn't the most sensitive with Max, and I shouldn't have forced you to be a tiebreaker between us. But I had to, Oliver. You don't know my brother."

"Don't I? I know I wasn't there for all of your formative years, but for the past couple of weeks, it's been us three against the world. I think I understand you both pretty well, and I have the advantage of knowing you differently from how you know each other."

Aiden nodded. "That's true, but like you said, you missed a lot. A lot of fights, and frustrations, and most infuriatingly, the fact that Max *always* gets what he wants. Like when we were at the arcade. Did we want to talk to those girls? No, but Max did, so guess what we ended up doing. Now that I have you to back me up, I couldn't miss an opportunity to veto him. For once, I got *my* way."

Oliver took a steadying breath. It seemed he was dealing with two hurt brothers, not one. And to think, he'd always assumed Aiden was happy to follow Max's lead. Maybe that'd been the case at one point, but it was obvious now that something had changed. What did that mean for all three of them?

I feel like I'm about to see what happens when an unstoppable force meets an unmovable object.

Good thing family conflict was Oliver's specialty. "There's something I need to say, and I want you to let me say it in full before you comment."

Aiden studied him with guarded eyes. "All right. I think I can manage that."

Oliver pivoted in his seat to face Aiden. "You know how I have family issues that I don't like to talk about?"

"Yeah?" Aiden tensed. "Did something new happen?"

"In a manner of speaking. I . . ." He rolled words around in his mouth, as if he could taste which ones were right. "I already feel like I cause problems in my own family, okay? I can't be a problem in yours too."

Aiden gasped. "Oliver, you're not—"

"Please let me finish. Please?"

Aiden fell silent. He looked so devastated, Oliver had to direct his next words at the sunroof.

"I don't know if I ever told you this, but I was happy when my parents got divorced. In fact, I was *thrilled*. I didn't go through any of the stages of grief some kids experience. I wasn't angry. I didn't blame myself. Hell, I didn't mind having to travel back and forth across the country. They were miserable together, and I knew that. Sometimes, I wondered why they got married in the first place.

"After they split up, I thought things would quiet down, and in some ways, they did, but new problems cropped up too. Holidays became nightmares. Mom and Dad would be forced to see each other, and they'd start fighting again as if they'd never stopped. As I got older, I kept thinking to myself, 'Why do they do this to themselves? Why don't they agree to never see each other ever again?' And then one day, I guess I was finally old enough, because I understood: it was because of me."

Aiden looked like he was itching to say something, but he remained quiet.

Oliver continued. "I'm what's forcing them together. As long as I'm alive, they're stuck with each other. And I hate it. If they'd gotten divorced before Mom got pregnant, they'd never have to see each other." He paused. "Before you freak out, I don't mean that in a I-wish-I-was-never-born kind of way. I'm stating a fact."

Breath escaped from Aiden as if he were a tire with a leak. "Thank God, because I was *dying* to ask."

Oliver's lips twitched. "You know why my dad moved back to Irvington?"

"To be with his family?"

"Sort of. It's because I turned eighteen two years ago. I wasn't legally obligated to spend breaks in California with him anymore. I have anyway, but I think he understood that when I graduate and get a job, that's not going to be possible anymore. He came here to be close to me, but he didn't move to the city, because that would be too close to Mom."

Aiden blew out a breath. "That's rough. Why do they hate each other so much?"

"I don't think they hate each other. I think they made a fundamental mistake."

"What's that?"

"They were never friends. They loved each other, but they didn't like each other. After a while, the infatuation wore off, and they were left with all the other stuff. Mom's ambition. Dad's need for a quiet life. All the things they *didn't* have in common."

Aiden's brow furrowed. "But if they're divorced now, why are they still fighting?"

"I don't know for sure, but if I had to guess, I'd say they rubbed each other raw. When you fight with someone long enough, it's like it primes you to fight with them again. Your nerve endings get exposed, and the tiniest thing can set you off. I once watched my parents go from zero to sixty over a frozen pizza."

"That sounds awful." Aiden reached over, slow enough that Oliver could stop him if he wanted, and touched his hand. "I'm sorry you have to deal with that. Your parents should care enough to knock it off when you're around. You know that's on them and not you, right?"

"I guess." He squeezed Aiden's hand. "Anyway, the point is, I've had my fair share of familial tension. Your house was always my haven, the place I went when I needed to get away. I can't watch things between you and Max escalate."

"What makes you think they're going to escalate? We had one fight."

"You're right. They might not. But this all started when we got closer, so I can only imagine it's going to get worse as our relationship deepens. I can't handle the idea of causing tension between you and your brother. It hits way, *way* too close to home. In fact . . ."

Oliver exhaled. *It makes me think you'd be better off if I left again.*

"What?" Aiden's eyes searched his. "What is it?"

"Nothing. I think having all this free time over the summer is making everyone a bit melodramatic. The point is, I want to be Max's friend, and I want to be with you. But not if it's going to cause problems."

Aiden was quiet for a long moment. "May I have official permission to speak?"

Oliver nodded.

Aiden grabbed Oliver and crushed him to his chest. He hugged him so hard, the air left Oliver's lungs. At first, Oliver was too surprised to react. Then he hugged back with equal ferocity. He hadn't realized how much he'd needed that.

After a second, Aiden pulled back. He held Oliver at arm's length and fixed him with a fierce look. "Oliver, I need you to understand that this isn't your fault. The problems Max and I have run deep, and they've been festering for a long time."

"You're just saying that to make me feel better."

"I'm not, I swear." Aiden let his head fall back against the headrest. "I'll admit you were the catalyst that got me to recognize them, but you're not the source. This has been going on all our lives, but I think I realized it when we left for college. Max . . . stifles me. When we go to parties, he doesn't so much as let me introduce myself. I'm 'my brother, Aiden' before I can open my mouth. All my friends are his friends, minus the guys on my lacrosse team. We *live* together, for Christ's sake. We have our whole lives."

Oliver nodded. "I've wondered before if you guys might be a little dependent on each other, but I didn't want to make assumptions."

"Exactly. And you've seen for yourself how he answers for me and makes me out like I can't function without him. I want to be my own person—not Max's twin—and I think Max can't handle that. The fight we had earlier was a long time coming."

There was so much new information to process, Oliver's head was spinning. "Part of what you're saying is fair, but you're also not giving your brother a lot of credit, which brings me to my final point." He took a breath. "I need you to talk to Max. ASAP. Be as open and honest with him as you were with me a second ago, and find a way to fix this. All three of us need to come out of this as friends, or we're going to have a problem."

Aiden muttered something along the lines of, "I don't see why you'd *want* to be friends with that immature, controlling—" But Oliver silenced him with a glare.

"Talk. To. Your. Brother, Aiden Kingsman. You'll be a lot happier once you do, and I'm not going to be able to relax until the air is clear."

Aiden reached over and brushed his fingers through Oliver's hair. "That's all the reason I need. I might not get the chance until tomorrow, though. Is that okay?"

Oliver leaned into the touch. "Take all the time you need. But make things right."

"Maybe this isn't the right time for jokes, but—" Aiden grinned "—I feel like such an adult. We're having a mature, honest conversation about our feelings. We're nailing this whole communication thing."

Oliver laughed. "I suppose we are."

"For the record, I appreciate that you didn't do this solely for us. You did it for Max too, and I love that about you. I'm angry with him right now, but he's still my brother, and you reminded me of that."

Oliver's lips quirked up. "You love that about me?"

Aiden blanched. "I didn't mean . . . Well, I mean, I *meant* it, but I didn't—"

Oliver giggled, and Aiden made a series of inarticulate squawking noises.

"That's so *mean*, Oliver. I didn't think you had a mean bone in your body."

Oliver shrugged. "In my defense, you walked right into that."

They sat for another moment, breathing quietly together. Oliver took Aiden's hand and brushed his thumb over it, trying to work up the nerve to kiss him. To his surprise, Aiden beat him to it. He leaned over in his seat, and Oliver met him halfway. It wasn't a deep kiss, or a long one, but the potency of it left Oliver dizzy.

When Aiden broke away, he was panting slightly. "Good night, Oliver."

"Good night," Oliver replied as he tangled his free hand in Aiden's curls and pulled him in again.

It was several minutes before Oliver actually got out of the car. Aiden didn't drive away until Oliver had unlocked the front door, waved goodbye, and disappeared inside.

Oliver leaned against the closed door and let out a long breath. Stressed as he was about the whole situation, he felt better now that they'd talked about it. They could nip this in the bud. He was sure of it.

Pushing off the door like a springboard, he made his way through the darkened house. He found his dad sitting in the living room in his old recliner, reading a book by the light of a lamp.

He looked up when Oliver entered the room. "Hey, kiddo. You're home kinda late."

"I went to see a movie. We're not having another family dinner, are we?"

"No, it's going to be quiet tonight." Dad seemed to sense his exhaustion, because he offered up a way out of the conversation. "Going to your room?"

"Yeah. See you at breakfast. Love you."

"You too."

Despite the early hour, Oliver went directly to bed. He slept so hard, it seemed to him that all he did was close his eyes, and suddenly his alarm was blaring. He turned it off and stretched until his joints popped. The sound of talking and banging around reached him from the kitchen, which meant some of his family had already arrived. He moved through his morning routine slowly, relishing the last few moments of peace he had left.

When he could delay no longer, he emerged from his room and found his uncles making breakfast while his father sat at the table and read the newspaper aloud. Oliver was preparing himself for yet another drunken brunch, when he looked around the kitchen.

There wasn't a beer in sight. Uncle Marcus was roaring with laughter while Uncle Charlie tried and failed to flip a single, hopelessly burned pancake. Dad was egging them on. It seemed . . . normal.

Uncle Marcus spotted him and wiped a tear from his eyes. "Morning, Oliver."

"Morning." Oliver wandered over to the coffeepot and poured himself a cup. "Need help making breakfast?"

"I'll say." Uncle Charlie dropped the skillet onto the stove and wiped his brow with his sleeve. "Clearly, I can't be trusted with this. You any good with a spatula?"

"I like to think so."

"Then by all means." Uncle Charlie dumped the burned pancake in the trash and waved at the bowl of batter. "We'll repay you with the spinach omelets I'd planned to make next."

Oliver took over, making a dozen sand-dollar-sized golden-brown pancakes. His uncles ate them as fast as he could get them out of the pan, raving as if they were juicy steaks. When the batter ran out, they commandeered the frying pan to make the aforementioned omelets. All the while, Dad sipped coffee and watched them with a rare smile on his face.

Afterward, the uncles helped clean up before they declared they had to be at work. Oliver saw them to the door and waved while they drove off. All in all, it was the most pleasant family encounter he'd had since he'd arrived back in Irvington. Had something changed?

He mulled it over as he wandered back into the kitchen. Dad had gotten up and was pouring himself another cup of coffee.

He glanced over when Oliver walked in. "Much better, right?"

Oliver stopped halfway through lifting his own mug to his lips. "What do you mean?"

"Your uncles. They were much better behaved, right?"

"Um, yeah. I suppose they were. But why—"

"I know all young people think their parents are out of touch, but—" Dad shrugged "—I like to think I'm a little more observant than that."

Oliver swallowed. "Huh?"

"I noticed what you were doing. Missing dinners with the family. Spending all your time over at the Kingsmans' house. Excusing yourself to your room. It was like when your mother and I were going through the divorce. You needed to escape a lot back then too."

Oliver started to say something, but Dad cut him off. "You're not in trouble. I am. I should have done something sooner, but I guess I wanted to act like everything was fine. I had a talk with your uncles last night while you were out."

"What'd you say?" Oliver could only imagine the fuel this could give to their family gossip mill.

"I told them there'd be no more late-night poker games over here. No day drinking on their days off. And I told them to stop acting like tough guys around you. I gave them an ultimatum: get over the fact that Oliver is gay, or you won't be allowed over here anymore."

Oliver's chest tightened with emotion. "How'd they take that?"

"There was a lot of macho posturing at first, but . . . kiddo, you know they love you, right? It took them all of five minutes to cave."

"Wow, Dad, I . . ." Oliver wasn't sure how to express the relief he felt. "Thanks for sticking up for me."

"Well, you know." Dad shifted his weight from foot to foot. "I want you to want to spend time here. I don't get to see you all year, so when you run off every chance you get . . . it hurts."

Cold fingers grabbed Oliver's lungs and squeezed. "I'm sorry."

"It's okay. I understand, I swear. I'd want to be off spending time with my friends too." He cleared his throat. "But things are going to be different now, all right? We're having dinner with the family tonight. You can see for yourself. And be ready to listen to your cousin Susie talk about her pregnancy, because if I have to one more time, I'm going to be halfway to a gynecology degree."

Oliver laughed. "I'll be at dinner. I don't have anything planned anyway." He paused, wondering how far he could push his luck. "Things between me and the twins are kinda weird at the moment."

"Oh?" Dad hesitated, as if he were bracing himself. "Wanna talk about it?"

Oliver had never talked about boys with his father before. This might be scarring for them both. But then, Dad had made it through a whole talk about feelings without flinching. Maybe Oliver should give him a chance.

"I should warn you, I'm having boy troubles." He sucked in a breath. "Feel free to run screaming."

Dad grimaced but didn't back down. "Well, I've had my fair share of dating disasters, and I'm not even talking about your mother. I might be able to help."

Oliver relaxed. "That'd be great."

They moved into the living room. Dad claimed his chair while Oliver took a spot on the couch. Once there, he paused, uncertain of how to begin this conversation.

Dad spared him the trouble. He cradled his coffee mug in his hands, staring at it instead of Oliver. "Your boy troubles and your twin troubles wouldn't happen to be linked, would they?"

"You caught me. I kinda have a thing for one of them, and it's caused some issues."

Dad looked at him sidelong. "It's not Max, is it?"

"No."

"Thank God. Nothing against the kid, and lord knows I haven't seen him in years, but I remember the mouth he had on him. Always talked at top volume too."

Oliver laughed. "That hasn't changed much, though add in near-constant swearing. Anyway, no worries. I'm interested in Aiden."

"What's the problem? Does he not like you back? Is he straight?" Dad's expression grew fierce. "If those boys are giving you shit for being gay, I'll go down there right now, and—"

"No, no." Oliver waved him off. "Mind your blood pressure. Aiden is gay too, and he likes me back."

"Huh. Well, if you have to date someone, you could do a lot worse. He was always a smart kid, and his parents are decent folk."

"I thought you weren't fond of Kim and Roger."

It was Dad's turn to wave him off. "I only said that to rile your mom up. Although, I do think they're a little too perfect. Kind of *Stepford Wives*, if you ask. But that's probably the jealousy talking."

"You're jealous of the Kingsmans?"

Dad eyed him over the lip of his coffee mug. "Aren't you?"

Touché.

Oliver was tempted to delve into that a bit more, but he didn't want to get sidetracked. "Aiden and I aren't a couple quite yet, FYI.

I'd like to be, but things have been weird between him and his brother. I don't know what to do about it."

"Why are things weird?"

"Apparently, the twins have some issues, and then when Max picked a fight yesterday, everything sort of boiled over. At first, I thought Max was acting out because he felt excluded, but now I think he might be jealous of me and Aiden."

"Wait, jealous as in, he wants to date you? His twin brother's boyfriend? Sounds like a soap opera."

"No, Max is straight, as far as I know. It's more like he's jealous of me for stealing his brother away." He shook his head. "It's complicated, as you can tell. I told Aiden to talk to Max and work it out. Hopefully he will, sooner rather than later."

"Can I give you some fatherly advice?"

Oliver leaned forward. "Please. I need it."

"The people you love most on this planet—the people you're closest to—are the ones who can hurt you the most. More than any random stranger on the street. They know where all your soft spots are, and in moments of anger, people can be vicious. It's a sad fact—" he looked away, as if lost in thought "—but it's true."

Oliver swallowed. *Is he thinking about Mom right now?*

Dad seemed to come back to himself. "If Max and Aiden are out of sorts, they need to fix it now, before it has a chance to fester. Two brothers . . . and twins no less . . . I can imagine what a knockdown, drag-out fight between them would look like, and it's not pretty."

"I don't want that to happen, but what can I do?"

"If it were me, I wouldn't go near that ticking time bomb until some progress has been made. If you're right and Max is jealous of you, then hanging around him is only going to rub salt in the wound. Aiden will be much more motivated to talk things out if you're not around to distract him."

Oliver scratched his cheek. "You want me to give Aiden an ultimatum? Tell him I'm not coming over until things are cool between him and Max?"

"I wouldn't do anything that drastic. People don't like ultimatums. I would give them some space. Maybe let a few calls go to voice mail.

They're smart boys; it won't take them long to figure out why you're being distant, and then I'm sure everything will work itself out."

Oliver's mouth turned down in a thoughtful way. "Hm. That's solid advice. Thanks, Dad."

"You're welcome, though you don't have to sound so surprised. Keep in mind, I'm getting something out of this too. With you ignoring the twins, I might actually get to see you." He winked. "Well, this was much less scarring than I thought it would be. I survived my first boy talk. How'd I do?"

Oliver chuckled. "You did great, Dad. Perfect score."

"Glad to hear it. Fun as this has been, I gotta get down to the office. I've come in late a few too many times under the pretense of 'settling in.' If I do it again, Mrs. Perring will skin me."

Dad exited in the direction of the master bedroom, leaving Oliver alone to mull over his advice. It seemed simple enough: make himself scarce while the twins dealt with their issues. But then, he hadn't gone a day without talking to them since they'd reconnected. His fingers were already itching to pull out his phone and text Aiden good morning.

He'd have to be strong. This was for their own good, and his too.

As if cued by his thoughts, his phone vibrated in his pocket. It was Aiden, wishing him a good morning. Oliver put it away without responding and busied himself washing the breakfast dishes. By the time he waved goodbye to Dad from the front door, he had another text.

What are your plans for the day?

It felt rude to ignore Aiden like this. Oliver's resolve was already wavering when another text popped up. This one, however, was in the group chat with both brothers, which hadn't been touched since the fight.

It was from Max. *I'm going to lunch with a friend who got into town yesterday. You guys are welcome to join. She's picking me up at one.*

Oliver studied the message. That sounded civil enough. Was there a chance he and Aiden had already made up? Oliver had expected them to need at least a day to cool off, talk, probably fight some more, and then hug it out.

He was considering breaking his vow of silence—if only to ask for an update—when Aiden replied in the group chat.

No thanks. Have fun with your friend.

So much for that.

Not a minute later, Aiden texted Oliver privately.

With Max out of the house, we'll have the place to ourselves.

Oliver's resolve made worrisome creaking noises beneath the weight of that temptation. *Don't give in. Aiden is blowing Max off to spend time with you. Isn't that the root of this whole problem?*

Oliver put his phone on vibrate and stuck it in a kitchen cabinet. Out of sight, out of mind. He felt strangely naked without it, and without the Kingsmans, for that matter. The past two weeks of his life had revolved around them. What had he done before?

There was one thing he definitely needed to do. Go for a jog. He hadn't had a proper workout in far too long.

He changed into his athletic wear and went for a long, vigorous run. The exercise made his unused muscles scream and cleared his mind of other distractions, leaving him plenty of room to dwell on his current predicament.

When he got home, he showered, changed into normal clothes, and attempted to watch TV. That lasted for all of ten minutes before he came across a romantic comedy and decided TV was dangerous. He'd brought some books with him, but he only made it a few pages into one of them before a love-angle between a girl and two brothers made his head spin.

What else was there to do? If he had his phone, he could waste some time on Instagram or check his email. Maybe his school sent him something important...

No. He was going to be strong.

He made himself some lunch, cleaned up the living room, and then took another crack at the books he'd brought. He managed to distract himself for another hour or so, but by the time afternoon had set in, he was crawling out of his skin.

It's been hours. Surely there's been some sort of progress.

Oliver retrieved his phone. He had three more texts from Aiden and a missed call. He texted him back faster than he ever had in his life: *Have you talked to your brother yet?*

Just hitting Send was a huge relief. He hadn't realized how used he'd gotten to having the twins in his life. At the end of the summer, when it was time to go home, what was he going to do?

Aiden texted back before Oliver could stumble down that rabbit hole. *No, I'm sorry. I was exhausted last night, so I went straight to bed. Max slept until noon, as per usual, and then he went to lunch with his friend. I barely saw him. Come over? The house is empty, and I miss you.*

Oliver's willpower was stretched so thin, it was translucent. All summer, he'd been vying for alone time with Aiden, and now that he had it, he couldn't take advantage of it. If Max came home and found them together—hanging out without him yet again—it would exacerbate everything.

Oliver put his phone back in the kitchen cabinet. "Being a good person is the *worst*."

He marched into his room and threw himself facedown on his bed. This was going to be the longest day of his life.

It'll be worth it, though. When this is all over, and there's no more drama or hurt feelings, it'll be so worth it.

Oliver read the same page of a book twelve times before he wandered into the kitchen for some water. He was halfway through filling a glass when he heard a faint but persistent vibrating sound. It was coming from a familiar cabinet.

Oliver stared at it, eyes widening. "Is it calling out to me?" He opened the cabinet, and sure enough, his phone was buzzing like an agitated beehive. One glance at the screen told him what he'd already suspected: Aiden was blowing up his phone.

Would temptations never cease? The call brought up the photo Oliver had assigned to Aiden's contact info: a selfie they'd taken at the arcade. They were standing cheek to cheek with big, carefree smiles plastered on their faces.

Seeing it again made Oliver miss Aiden so much, it hurt like a bone-deep ache. He slammed the cabinet shut with unnecessary force and plodded back to his room, intent on hurling himself onto his bed again. He'd just walked through the door when something rapped against his window. He peered at it, curious, and nearly jumped out of his skin.

Aiden was standing outside, fist raised to knock on the glass.

Oliver blinked owlishly at him. Was he hallucinating? Had he somehow conjured Aiden here through the power of his thoughts?

Aiden knocked again, dismissing the hallucination theory. He was real all right.

The sound jolted Oliver into action. He ran over and threw his window open. "Aiden?"

"Oliver, thank God. Are you all right?"

Oliver was too bewildered to answer. "What are you doing here?"

"You weren't picking up, so I came over." Aiden's phone was still in hand. "I knocked, and then when you didn't come to the door, I panicked. I'm so glad you're all right. I was starting to think something had happened to you. You've never not answered me before."

Oliver must not have heard Aiden knock. He looked him over. Aiden's eyes were wild, and he was flushed, like he'd been running. He really must've panicked.

"How did you know which window is mine?"

"I didn't. I looked in them all."

"Jesus." Oliver stepped back. "Come in."

Aiden hooked a leg over the ledge and followed it with his head and torso until he was standing in Oliver's bedroom. He looked around at the blue-and-white-striped walls and the open suitcase on the floor. "I have to admit, this isn't what I expected."

"I didn't get a say in the decorating. I promise my room back in the city has more personality."

"I believe you."

They stood together in awkward silence. As happy as Oliver was to see him, now that the initial shock had worn off, he realized this ruined his whole avoid-the-Kingsmans plan.

"Why are you here exactly?" he asked. "Not that I'm not happy to see you. But coming over here because I didn't respond to you for half a day seems a little extreme."

"Yeah, I agree. We're in serious trouble."

Oliver looked him over. "Are we? Why?"

"Because not seeing you all morning and afternoon was *hard*. So much harder than I thought it would be." Aiden stepped closer, eyes bright and so, so blue. "Was it hard for you too?"

Oliver couldn't lie when Aiden looked at him like that. "It was. I hated every minute of it. Isn't that weird? We were apart for ten years with no problem, but now . . ."

"It's because things are different now." Aiden reached up and lightly skimmed his fingers along Oliver's jaw. "Now that you're back in my life, I don't ever want to be apart from you again."

His words tugged Oliver closer. He took a step forward, despite the lack of space between them already, and the air crackled. "Aiden, what are we going to do? When summer ends, that's it. Who knows when we'll get to see each other again."

Aiden glanced down. "I know. I've been trying not to think about it."

"Me too. But we can't keep pretending we're in some happy summer bubble that's never going to burst." He sucked in a breath that felt like little shards of glass. "Right now, we're on the precipice of something. If we go any further, we could end up getting really hurt. If we date, it'd be long-distance for at least a year while we're in school. There will be times when we won't get to see each other for weeks."

"I know," Aiden said again, his voice soft and pained. "There are so many complications, so many things that could go wrong. It's frightening, but . . . doesn't it feel right to you?"

Oliver swallowed. "What do you mean by 'it'?"

"This." Aiden slid his hand into Oliver's hair, and the feel of Aiden's fingers dragging against his scalp made Oliver weak. "What if nothing goes wrong? What if all this happened for a reason, and we're right where we're supposed to be? Isn't it worth the risk?"

Oliver knew he should pump the brakes. He had real concerns and issues that needed to be addressed. But Aiden was looking at him with such pure longing, such real and intense need. It was impossible not to get totally sucked in. Was dating your best friend always this complicated?

If there was one thing Oliver knew for certain, it was that he didn't want to hurt Aiden. He'd leave now if it meant sparing him the heartache.

Aiden was watching him, probably waiting for an answer to his questions. Oliver couldn't bring himself to say no—it was too much of a lie—so he said the next best thing. "We shouldn't. We're rushing into this. If we were able to wait for ten years, we should be able to wait until we've figured things out."

"We should be able to, yeah. But can we?" Aiden tilted his head, and a few of his curls spilled over his brow. "If that's what you want, I'll do it. I'll do anything you say. But the USS Take Things Slowly sailed the second you walked back into my life. If we broke things off now, we'd still get hurt. We're already in too deep, and I think we both know it. What are you really afraid of?"

I'm scared of how badly I want this. How badly I want you. And the power that gives you to completely devastate me. But at the same time, there's no one I'd sooner trust with my heart.

Oliver exhaled hard and pressed his face into Aiden's warm touch. "How can you be so sure about this?"

"There are some things I just know. I know your eyes look green, but they have a ring of brown right around the irises. I know you're scared of lightning but not thunder, and that you hate mushrooms. And I know, with complete and utter certainty, that if things don't work out between us, we'll still be friends. Like we've always been. You know that too, right?"

Oliver answered without hesitation. "Yes."

Aiden closed the last of the distance between them. "Then, for as long as we can, I want to be with you. I want to spend as much time with you as possible, to have as much of you as I can take."

Oliver shuddered, closing his eyes, and was not at all surprised when Aiden's lips brushed against his. He chased the sensation, tilting his head up until he got the perfect, firm contact he'd been craving since the moment Aiden had climbed through his window.

The kiss grew heated within seconds, with Oliver grabbing a handful of Aiden's soft shirt, and Aiden moaning against his mouth. Oliver couldn't seem to get close enough to him, even as he pressed Aiden back against his desk.

The furniture hit the wall with a loud thump, dislodging several books, but neither of them seemed to care. Aiden's hands found their way into his hair again, and when Aiden's fingernails raked down the nape of his neck, Oliver saw stars.

"Aiden," he moaned as arousal flooded into him. "I—"

Aiden nodded, mouth open and breaths coming in pants. "Me too."

Instinctively, Oliver shifted until he could slip one of his thighs between Aiden's legs. The moment he did, he realized how hard he was, from so little contact. And, more importantly, Aiden was too.

Aiden seemed to notice it the same second Oliver did, because he broke the kiss and pulled away enough to look Oliver in the eye. Something unspoken passed between them, and suddenly, Oliver's whole body was hot. He claimed Aiden's lips again, this time with intent.

It occurred to him, as if through a fog, that for once there was nothing stopping them from having sex. Besides their stolen rooftop kiss, they'd gotten so few chances to be physical with each other. But right now, they were in an empty house, and the ache in Oliver was growing with every frantic surge of Aiden's mouth against his.

Oliver leaned back, and Aiden whined like he couldn't handle the three inches of space between them. He stopped, however, when Oliver reached down, grabbed his own shirt, and yanked it over his head. He tossed it to the side and turned back to Aiden, searching his face for a reaction.

Aiden's mouth was hanging open, possibly because he was breathing hard, possibly from awe. His kiss-reddened lips were a splash of beautiful color on his fair face.

Oliver waited for a response with bated breath. Aiden's eyes roved down his chest. Oliver was confident in his body—he worked hard to be—but he'd never felt so acutely vulnerable. Yet safe at the same time. If Aiden didn't want this, Oliver still knew the feelings between them were real.

As it happened, Oliver had no reason to worry about rejection. When Aiden looked up from his scenic trip down Oliver's body, his beautiful eyes had been completely overtaken by his pupils. He looked hungry in a way Oliver had never seen before. It was hopelessly hot, knowing he'd taken this shy, cerebral man and turned him into a carnal thing.

Aiden's voice was rough. "Is your dad home?"

The air between them sizzled with obscene intent.

Oliver almost couldn't draw the breath to answer. "He's at work."

"Perfect."

With that, Aiden kissed him with such passion, such raw need, Oliver thought it might consume him.

And he wanted it to.

Chapter 9: Aiden

Aiden was going into sex the way some people went into Olive Garden: with absolutely no expectations. He knew more or less what to do, and where everything went, of course, but beyond that, he was at a loss. His sexual experience was limited to masturbating and what he'd gleaned from movies, and he highly doubted the latter had given him a realistic outlook.

Relax. Don't overthink it.

That was a surprisingly easy order to obey. He'd assumed he would be nervous, but the moment he kissed Oliver, all his thoughts had quieted. It was like someone had hit a mute button in his brain. For once, he was simply feeling, allowing himself to get swept up in the new sensations, and it was intoxicating. Exhilarating. Maybe a little frightening.

When Oliver had slipped a thigh between his legs, need had resonated in his bones. It was unlike anything he'd ever experienced before. The emotion had hints of the crush he'd had on Oliver, but it was deeper, and bigger somehow. He couldn't put a name to it, but it was clearly Oliver-specific, and it was spreading like wildfire. Aiden felt a thrum deep within him, a hunger so acute it burned. It left room in his head for only one undeniable truth.

He wanted Oliver, and he wanted him *now*. In a way he'd never wanted anyone else.

Oliver seemed to feel the same way. He had Aiden pinned against his desk and was kissing him with single-minded enthusiasm. Aiden tried to give back as good as he got, but it seemed Oliver was happy to take the lead. His hands were everywhere at once, and his lips never ceased their sweet, firm slide against Aiden's.

Aiden couldn't stop himself from making little, helpless noises. When Oliver answered with a deep moan that made his lips tingle, kissing suddenly wasn't enough anymore. He wanted Oliver's pants to join his shirt on the floor, he wanted out of his own clothes, and as much as he liked being pinned, he wanted to get a lot more horizontal.

He broke their kiss long enough to stammer, "B-bed?"

Oliver didn't bother answering. He took Aiden by the shoulders—still kissing the cognizance out of him—and spun him around before giving him a gentle but decisive push. The backs of Aiden's legs hit the mattress and he fell onto it.

He blinked up at Oliver. "That was . . . Wow."

"Just you wait."

Oliver didn't hesitate to crawl after him. He straddled Aiden, one leg on either side of his, and brought their faces close. Aiden naturally lay back as Oliver moved, and soon they were chest to chest, looking at each other from scant inches away.

The intensity of it made Aiden dizzy. Now that he had the object of his desire on top of him, astride his hips, he couldn't breathe. Or think. Or do anything but stare, really.

Everything about Oliver felt incredible. His hands. His lips. The light kisses he was now feathering all over Aiden's face. He was warm and solid and heavy in the best way. Feeling his weight on top of Aiden was a special kind of turn-on.

Delirious with lust, Aiden panted, "You always end up on top of me."

Oliver's lips turned up into a smile against his skin. "Problem?" He rolled their hips together.

Aiden gasped and arched up. "Nope. No problem."

Oliver laughed. "You're wearing far too much clothing." He sat up—groin to groin with Aiden—and reached for Aiden's shirt. Aiden helped him pull it off and toss it aside. Self-consciousness flared up in him as Oliver's eyes tracked down his chest.

Oliver wet his lips. "Better than I'd imagined."

Aiden hesitated for a second before he touched the tattoo on Oliver's stomach, fingers tracing over the shape of the waves and then around the circle that enclosed them. He could feel Oliver trembling beneath the light touch, and it made him giddy. "When you showed this to me in the game room, I thought I was going to faint."

"I might faint right now if you keep touching me like that." Oliver fumbled for Aiden's jeans and started to undo them.

Aiden seized up without meaning to.

Oliver immediately pulled his hands away. "Sorry. Too fast?"

"No, it's fine. I'm . . . I dunno, is it possible to be *too* ready? Everything feels so intense, and yet not enough at the same time."

"I know what you mean." Oliver leaned down and nuzzled Aiden's neck, his mouth finding its way up to Aiden's ear. "We don't have to do this, you know."

"No, I want to. Believe me"—he squirmed—"I want to."

"How about I go first, then?" Oliver pushed himself into a kneeling position and reached for his own jeans. He had them open and pushed down in a blink, and Aiden almost wished he'd drawn it out. Almost.

It took some shimmying, but Oliver got his pants off and onto the floor, leaving him in nothing but black boxers. Tight ones.

Aiden swallowed. He'd known Oliver was hard, of course—he'd felt that much for himself—but seeing the outline of his cock through the fabric of his underwear made it so much more real. He'd done that. Oliver was turned on because of *him*.

The thought made fresh arousal flood into him. Aiden was turned on to the point of pain, and he hadn't seen Oliver fully naked yet. Once he did—once they took this final step—it would be like the last barrier between them had been torn down. They'd know each other inside and out. Aiden wanted that. Maybe more than he wanted sex. He wanted to touch Oliver, feel him, and learn his body the way he'd learned Oliver's mind.

Oliver didn't move, as if he were giving Aiden time to digest. He didn't seem in any way self-conscious, which emboldened Aiden to go for his underwear. Oliver shivered when Aiden's fingers brushed his stomach, and he rose up on his haunches. The message was clear: whenever Aiden was ready, he could pull Oliver's boxers off.

And Aiden was more than ready.

His fingers shook as he slid the fabric down Oliver's hips, revealing first skin, then black hair, and then Oliver's cock. Oliver shivered again as Aiden's eyes roved over him, as if he could feel Aiden's gaze like a physical touch. Aiden hadn't spent a lot of time imagining Oliver's cock, and yet it was somehow precisely what he'd expected. Darker than his tan skin, reddened at the head. Average-sized, but thick in a way that made Aiden's mouth water.

Without thinking, Aiden curled his fingers around it. Oliver gasped, and his eyelashes fluttered, but his body stayed in place. His cock fit in Aiden's hand like it was meant to. It felt incredible: hot, heavy, and so, so hard.

Aiden gave him a slow stroke from head to base. Oliver gasped and pushed his hips forward, as if trying to get more of the touch. Aiden obliged him and pumped him three times in rapid succession. The sound that poured from Oliver was like sex and music rolled together. It made Aiden's own cock twitch with envy.

"That's good," Oliver breathed. One of his palms found its way to Aiden's chest and splayed over it, like he needed it for balance. "A little tighter."

Aiden did as he was told, and this time when he stroked Oliver, a bead of liquid appeared at the head of Oliver's dick. Aiden smeared it with his thumb without thinking, and Oliver jolted like he'd been shocked, eyes clenched shut.

"Shit." His stomach muscles flexed. "That shouldn't feel as good as it does."

"Why do you think it does?"

Oliver opened his eyes. "Because you're doing it."

Aiden licked his dry lips. "I'm ready to be naked now."

Oliver scrambled off his lap, removing his boxers from around his thighs as he went. Aiden fumbled with his jeans, unzipping them and pushing them down in one clumsy movement. He hadn't thought to take off his shoes earlier. Some kicking was required before he could get everything off and on the floor where it belonged.

He'd known he was turned on, but he hadn't realized how much until he saw his cock sticking straight up from his body. He expected to feel self-conscious when he was finally naked, but the way Oliver's eyes dragged down him—catching on his groin before darting all over like they couldn't decide where to land—made him dizzy.

Oliver climbed back on top of him, and the feel of being skin to skin was *heaven*. So much more intense and intimate in a way Aiden couldn't have imagined. Oliver lined their hips up, and the silky-hot feel of his erection made Aiden's vision blur.

It only got more potent when Oliver reached between them and gripped them both in a long-fingered hand. Aiden hissed and canted his hips up, desperate for it. Oliver gave it to him, stroking them together. There was no lubrication to speak of, and the friction was almost too sharp, but Aiden was going to burst out of his skin if he didn't get more.

"We gotta talk about a couple of things." Oliver mouthed the skin below his ear, breath warm and ragged.

Aiden had to mentally drag himself out of the haze of lust that had descended on his brain. "Like what? How much I love your hands right now?"

Oliver chuckled, his breath tickling Aiden. "I meant safe sex and who's gonna do what."

"Oh, right." Aiden sucked in a breath. "I'll think better without you touching me."

"Sorry." Oliver removed his hand but kept their bodies close. "I don't have lube or condoms. I didn't think I'd need them over the summer, considering I'm here to spend time with my family."

Aiden bit his lip. "I have a condom."

Oliver's eyebrows shot up to his hairline. "You do?"

"Yeah, it's in my wallet."

"If it's been in there for a while, we can't use it."

"It's been there for three hours."

Oliver's expression was something to behold.

Aiden was grateful his blood was busy elsewhere, or it all would have rushed into his face. "Sorry if this was presumptuous of me, but when I thought we were going to have the house to ourselves this morning, I wanted to be prepared. So, I went to the store. I didn't think to get lube, though. Virgin problems."

Oliver let out something that sounded suspiciously like a laugh and covered his mouth with a hand. Aiden was wondering if he should be offended when Oliver seized his chin and kissed him with feeling. Aiden made a surprised sound but didn't pull away.

When Oliver released him, he was grinning. "You're so thoughtful. Do you know that? I don't think I've ever met anyone who thinks ahead like you do."

"I'm glad you're pleased."

"Oh, I'm *thrilled*. Without it, there'd be a limit to what we can do." Oliver kissed him again before sliding off the bed. "Is your wallet in your pants?"

"Back pocket."

Aiden was treated to a glorious view of Oliver bending over to dig in Aiden's jeans: ass round and muscular, and through the space between his thighs, his balls were barely visible. When Oliver had his prize, he flipped the billfold open and unerringly dug the condom out of the place where Aiden had hidden it.

Guess I'm not as subtle as I thought.

He came back to the bed, set it within reach, and busied himself kissing Aiden into a boneless pile of limbs.

"What about lube?" Aiden panted against his mouth.

"We'll make do." Oliver skimmed his lips down Aiden's neck. "The condom was the important part." He bit down on Aiden's collarbone, and Aiden's breath hitched. *Holy shit.* Why did that feel so good? "There's one other thing we have to talk about. I—"

"I want you to fuck me," Aiden blurted out.

Oliver jerked his head back to look at him. "What?"

The blush finally won out and spread over Aiden's face like a conquering army. "That's what you were gonna ask, right? I thought about it, and that's what I want. If, um, you want it too."

Oliver's green eyes *blazed*. "I've never wanted anything, or anyone, more."

He grasped Aiden's hip and thrust against him. The motion was shallow, barely enough to rub their cocks together, but it made Aiden's body burn. He grabbed Oliver's shoulders and closed his eyes, sinking into the sensation. Oliver shifted on top of him, and he heard a rustle. Then Oliver pulled away.

Aiden looked up, ready to protest the loss of contact, just in time to watch Oliver roll the condom down his length. Desire, sharp and heady, pulsed between his legs. This was really happening. He was really going to have sex with one of his oldest friends.

He's a lot more than that to you now.

Oliver held the base of his cock with one hand and stroked Aiden's thigh with the other. "You've fingered yourself before, right?"

Aiden swallowed. "A couple of times, yeah."

"So, you know how it's supposed to feel? What feels good and what doesn't?"

He nodded.

"Okay." Oliver nudged Aiden's legs apart and spit on his hand. "Tell me if I hurt you, or if anything feels wrong. Try to stay relaxed."

Aiden let his head fall back against the pillows and willed himself to go pliant. He must have done a decent job, because Oliver had one slick finger in him before he could exhale. It felt all right, up until Oliver added a second finger. That was when the stretching started to get uncomfortable.

He must have tensed, because Oliver paused. "You okay?"

"Yeah." Aiden squirmed. "Feels kinda weird, though."

"Like, call-an-ambulance weird or still-getting-used-to-it weird?"

"The second one."

"I think I can help with that." With his free hand, Oliver grasped Aiden's flagging erection and gave it a slow but firm pump. Aiden startled and spread his legs more on instinct. Oliver spat on his hand again and opened Aiden with his fingers in time to the strokes. Before long, the pain faded, and all Aiden felt was pleasure. His cock was leaking pre-come; between that and the spit, everything was slick and hot.

"I'm ready." His hips were arching off the mattress of their own accord, trying to get more of Oliver's fingers.

Oliver swore. "Good, because watching you writhe like that was making me itch." He positioned himself between Aiden's legs and pressed the head of his cock against Aiden's hole. "You sure?"

"Oliver." Aiden took Oliver's face in both of his hands and looked him dead in the eye. "Fuck me."

"Jesus." Oliver shivered, and his hips stuttered forward, seemingly on instinct. The head of his cock popped into Aiden. "Tell me how it feels."

Aiden wasn't sure yet. Oliver's cock was a lot bigger than his fingers, and Aiden was aware of every inch of it. Of all the times he'd fingered himself, nothing had prepared him for what it was like to have a dick enter his body. There was discomfort, sure, but mostly he was *full*. When Oliver sunk all the way in and gave a little thrust, like he wanted to go deeper, Aiden thought he might overflow.

Oliver kissed the side of his face. "You all right?"

Aiden wriggled beneath him. "Yeah, I think so."

"Fuck." Oliver's eyes shut. "Stay still. You're clenching around me."

Despite what Oliver had said, Aiden hooked a leg around Oliver's waist, trying to find an angle that worked for him. "You can move now."

"Give it a minute. If I move too soon, it'll hurt."

It already hurts.

Aiden slid a hand into Oliver's hair and kissed him, tasting salt and sweat. "Oliver, it's okay. I want more."

Oliver exhaled hard, breath tickling Aiden's skin. Oliver started moving, slower than Aiden wanted, but he felt it throughout his whole body. It wasn't *good*, expressly, but there was so much stimulation, Aiden could drown in it. The sound of Oliver's moans, his warmth, and the weight of him all rolled around on the edge of Aiden's awareness.

Before long, the discomfort faded, leaving a purer sensation in its wake. Aiden had never been this close to someone before, physically and emotionally. He didn't want to wax poetic about how connected they were, or how intimate sex was, but as he started to move in time with Oliver, they hit a rhythm that seemed as natural as breathing.

Just then, Oliver changed angles and did some sort of grinding motion. Aiden cried out.

Oliver froze. "You okay?"

"Yeah, that felt . . . good." He squirmed, trying to find the right spot. "Can you do that again?"

Oliver flicked sweaty hair away from his eyes. "I'm not sure what I did."

"Wait, let me see if I can . . ." Aiden rolled his hips, angling for where he thought Oliver had been, and pleasure bloomed within him. "Fuck, right there."

"Like this?" Oliver thrust hard into him.

Aiden threw his head back and moaned. He would have been embarrassed by how loud he was being if he weren't so preoccupied. "Feels so good. More."

Oliver started fucking him in earnest, and it was all Aiden could do to hold on for dear life. He lost all sense of volume, or what he was saying, in the honesty of his reactions. He couldn't believe they'd waited so long to do this.

If he were being realistic, it was only this good because of the feelings between them. No one's first time went this smoothly. Aiden wasn't sure if it was their history or something deeper, but it soothed an ache inside of him that he hadn't realized was throbbing. It was like the years they'd spent apart melted away. Aiden knew Oliver—trusted him, wanted him—and now he had him in every sense.

Aiden had no clue what he was doing, but his body seemed to. It moved in whatever way felt good, and in time, he learned to let it. Mostly he matched Oliver's thrusts, as if he could somehow draw Oliver deeper into him. He couldn't seem to get enough.

Oliver gave a particularly hard thrust that wrung a low, deep moan out of Aiden. Then his rhythm faltered. "Aiden, I'm getting close." He sounded wrecked, like it was all he could do to form words. His pace altered to shallow rocks, and his face found its way into the sweaty crook of Aiden's neck. "I can slow down if you're not there."

"No, I'm there." Aiden angled his hips up into Oliver's movements and let his head fall back. "I just— I need . . . I'm not sure what."

"I know what." Oliver changed positions so he was kneeling between Aiden's legs. With one hand, he gripped Aiden's hip and used it as leverage to slide devastatingly into him. With the other, he grasped Aiden's cock. His strokes were sloppy and rhythm-free, but they got the job done.

The dual sensations hit Aiden like a revelation. Pleasure crackled up his spine and then pooled between his legs. "Oh God, Oliver."

"Feel good?" Oliver panted.

"Yeah. How close are you? Because I feel like I could—" Oliver hit his prostate dead-on, and Aiden tensed, right on the edge of orgasm. "Fuck, I'm there." He'd go off if Oliver so much as blew on him.

"I'm right behind you. Go ahead and come." He sped up both his hand and his thrusts.

Aiden only had time to shout a garbled version of Oliver's name before he came unraveled, tensing from head to toe as pleasure rolled through him. Oliver's thrusts stuttered, and then he shoved hard into him before stilling. If he made any noise when he came, Aiden was too far gone to hear it.

When the final wave crested and broke within him, Aiden's bones liquefied. He seemed to fall against the bed, though his body had never left it. He pulled Oliver's hand from his cock when oversensitivity set in, but otherwise, all he could do was breathe.

Oliver collapsed on top of him, somewhat crushing him, but his weight was strangely comforting. Aiden didn't even consider asking him to move. He freed a hand and ran his fingers down Oliver's sweaty back, feeling the bumps of his spine.

For several minutes, all they did was breathe together in the loud silence of Oliver's room. Eventually, Oliver pushed himself up, found Aiden's mouth, and smeared their lips together, as if he was too tired to put any skill into it. "That was amazing."

Aiden focused his bleary eyes on him. "Yeah. Not at all what I expected."

"In a good way?"

He nodded. "I didn't think . . . I mean, I thought it was all hype, you know? What they say sex is like in movies and songs. I didn't think it was going to be so intense." He chewed on his bottom lip. "Is it . . . always like that?"

Oliver's voice was so soft, Aiden almost couldn't hear him. "No, it's not. That was different for me too."

Aiden's heart thumped in his chest like it was trying to break out. "Well, I guess you've spoiled me, then."

"Good. You deserve it." Oliver pushed himself up with a groan and pulled out of Aiden. Aiden tried to hide his wince, but Oliver must have seen it. "Sorry. I shouldn't have been so rough."

"No, it's okay. I liked every part of that. Well, once I got used to it."

Oliver disposed of the condom in a small bedside trash can and then climbed back into bed, snuggling up next to Aiden. "How do you feel now?"

"Good. And I know it's cliché, but satisfied too." He yawned. "And tired."

"Take a nap."

"It's the middle of the afternoon."

"So? We can cuddle. That's the best part, in my opinion." Oliver buried his face in Aiden's damp curls like that was the end of the conversation.

Aiden laughed. He craned his head to look at the clock on Oliver's nightstand. "Your dad works a nine-to-five, right? Won't he be home in like an hour?"

Oliver jolted upright. "Okay, now I'm awake."

Aiden's laughter shook his whole body. "Imagine if he came home and found us asleep together."

"I'd rather not. I don't want to give myself palpitations." Oliver wiped his sweaty brow. "Jesus, and he would find us too. He expects me at dinner tonight. If I didn't show up, I'm sure he'd peek in on me." He shook his head. "Yeah, I'm not going to think about it. I've exerted myself enough for one day."

"That you have." Aiden reached out for him. Oliver allowed himself to be guided back down and into Aiden's arms. They lay together, limbs tangled, fingers running through hair and over skin, for a small infinity.

Unfortunately, time didn't care what they wanted, and it continued to tick forward until Aiden could no longer ignore how much he needed to get going. "If I leave right now, your father probably won't catch me as I'm backing down the driveway."

Oliver groaned. "You're the worst alarm clock ever." He rolled off the bed and started hunting around for his clothes.

Aiden watched him. Much as he needed to get dressed, he couldn't tear his eyes away. Oliver's hair was matted, and he was coated in sweat, but he was more beautiful than Aiden had ever seen him.

"I'd invite you to shower before getting dressed, but I don't think I could resist joining you." Oliver pulled on his jeans, jumping a little to get the tight fabric over his thighs. "How are you feeling, by the way?"

The question prompted Aiden to get up and start gathering his own clothes. "Sore, honestly. But good. A little weak-kneed." Right on cue, he almost fell over stepping into his pants.

Oliver reached out and steadied him. "That's normal. If anything starts to hurt, though, let me know."

Aiden smiled. "I'm not fragile. Stop fussing."

"Sorry. I—" He looked down. "I wanted so badly for it to be good for you. It was your first time, and our first time, and . . ."

Aiden stepped into his space and cupped his chin. "It was. It wouldn't have been as good with anyone else, with anyone I felt less for."

Oliver sucked in a breath that trembled like leaves on a branch and kissed him again. It very nearly turned into another heated make-out session, but Oliver pushed him away. "I really can't get enough of you, can I? It's going to have to wait for later, though."

"All right, fine. I'm leaving. Kicked out of bed by my own boyfriend." Aiden froze halfway through pulling his shirt back on. "Um . . . I . . ."

Oliver didn't miss a beat. "I'm not kicking you out." A grin spread across his face like daybreak. "I just don't want the first time my boyfriend meets my family to be impromptu." He twirled one of Aiden's curls around a finger. "When they meet you, I want it to be under the right circumstances, so they'll be as enamored with you as I am."

Aiden had to blink to keep his eyes from misting over. "I want that too. And hey, you've already met my family, so that's out of the way."

Oliver nodded, but his expression was sober. "Don't think I've forgotten about your brother, by the way. When you get home, talk to Max."

"But I'm so tired," he whined. "I want to take a nap."

Oliver silenced him with a pointed look.

Aiden sighed. "Okay. I suppose it's for the best."

"I know it is." Oliver pulled him in for a brief but firm kiss. "Have everything?"

Aiden checked his pockets for his wallet, phone, and keys before surveying the floor one more time for any wayward clothing. "I think so. And if not, it's not like I'll never see you again."

"Oh, I think you'll be seeing a lot of me over the next few days, both literally and figuratively. Now, off you go."

Oliver shooed him out the window while Aiden laughed. When he was standing safely on grass, Oliver leaned on the sill, looking like something out of a fairy tale. "Drive safe."

"I will." Aiden took one step toward the front of the house before he turned back. "Oliver?"

"Yeah?"

The words weighed on Aiden's tongue. He wasn't sure what he wanted to say, but he could almost feel it. Some emotion was expanding in his chest, trying to get out. Something like . . . love? Was that what this was? Would it be the most cliché thing ever to tell Oliver he loved him right after they had sex?

He drew a breath, still not sure what he wanted to say. "Oliver, I . . ."

"I know." Oliver smiled, and it was the sweetest thing Aiden had ever seen. "I feel it too. I'll miss you."

"You too."

It wasn't until he was in his car and backing down the driveway that he dissolved into giggles. He had to take several deep breaths before he could compose himself.

So, that was sex, huh?

It was . . . weird, to be perfectly honest. Chock-full of embarrassing noises and fluids. But it was wonderful too.

He wasn't so trite as to think that having sex had changed him in any sort of fundamental way. But his feelings for Oliver had become clearer, as if they'd been written in pencil before and were now outlined in ink.

In all the times he'd imagined the future—his career and house and partner—he'd never been able to picture his husband's face. Now, all he saw was Oliver. His bright smile. His expressive eyes. His warmth.

Aiden shook himself back to the present before he drove off the road. A minute later, he pulled up to his house and cut the engine. For a moment, he sat there, stewing in unrestrained glee, before he got out of the car and trotted up to the house.

When he walked in, he half expected to find his parents waiting for him. In his head, they somehow knew he'd lost his virginity and had prepared a lecture. But he was greeted by silence.

That made sense. It was still early. They weren't home from work yet. That gave him some time to perfect his poker face.

It also gave him a chance to talk to Max without them in the house. If things got ugly, he'd rather they didn't interfere.

I bet Max is in the game room, as per usual.

He shuffled through the house into the living room. Sure enough, he heard the sound of the TV blaring from the basement. Max was down there all right.

If Aiden wanted to, he could walk right past and go to his room. Take a nap. Talk to Max later when he was refreshed and not suffused with leftover hormones.

His exhaustion begged him to do precisely that, but he'd promised Oliver. When he thought about how much distress this feud with Max was causing him, Aiden's heart clenched.

I'm so whipped. And I kinda like it.

With a final deep breath, Aiden steeled himself and made his way down the stairs into the game room.

Chapter 10: Max

Max was parked in front of the TV—an Xbox controller in one hand and a fresh bag of chips in the other—when his little brother deigned to waltz down the stairs.

"Well, look who it is," Max said without taking his eyes off the virtual football players on the screen. "Finally decided to come home, huh?"

He hadn't intended to sound so hostile when he saw Aiden next, but after being stuck at home alone with no car, he'd had plenty of time to stew.

Aiden didn't even have the decency to look guilty. "I was gone for a couple of hours. Not exactly newsworthy." He stopped at the foot of the stairs and stood there like he hadn't decided if he was going to stay or not.

"Well, thanks for taking the car without asking. I loved being stranded here with no idea where you went."

"You weren't stranded. God forbid you walk somewhere."

"Right, because walking for miles during a New York heat wave sounds like a great idea. Maybe after that, I can invade Russia in the winter."

"Fine!" Aiden snapped. "Sorry I took the car for a whole afternoon. I didn't realize I'd be depriving you. Maybe we can get a celebrity to sponsor a charity for you, since you have *so* many problems."

Max stared at him, incredulous. "Seriously, bro? Why are you being such a dick?"

Aiden looked down at his shoes. "Sorry. It's been a long day."

"Aiden . . ." Max paused his game and tossed the controller aside. "Look, I don't want to fight anymore. In fact, I planned to apologize when I saw you next, but then you disappeared, and you didn't answer any of my texts. Did you not get them?"

"Oh, whoops." Aiden dug his phone out of his pocket and checked it. "Yeah, I got them. Sorry. I didn't have my phone on me."

"Since when? You *always* reply. I've joked before that it's because you have to have the last word. Were you ignoring me?"

"No, I swear. I was busy."

Max huffed. "I want to talk this out, but I can't do it alone. Are you going to work with me here or not?"

Aiden's face softened. "I think I can manage that."

"Cool. Grab a seat." Max waited for Aiden to fall into one of the chairs. "I'd ask where you've been all day, but I think I can guess."

Aiden hesitated. "I was with Oliver."

"Yeah, no shit. You guys hung out without me. Again."

"Well . . . yeah."

"You didn't think to invite me? I invited both of you to lunch."

For some reason, Aiden's whole face turned red, as if he'd been dunked in paint. "We weren't trying to exclude you. It wasn't planned. You were at lunch anyway."

"Yeah, but I texted you guys as soon as I got back. Neither of you thought to call me?" He eyed Aiden. "Where were you guys, anyway?"

"What does it matter?" Aiden's tone was getting defensive again. "We weren't here, and apparently that's a crime now."

Max's temper flared like a roman candle. "If you're going to feed me bullshit and cop an attitude, then we don't need to talk after all." Not that Max was being especially well-mannered, but he was the injured party here. He was entitled.

"I don't want to be interrogated." Aiden still wasn't looking him in the eye. "I'm exhausted. I was planning to take a nap before Mom and Dad get home, but instead, I came down here to talk to you. And this is the thanks I get? Sarcastic comments and accusations? I don't have the energy for this."

Max frowned. "Why are you so tired? Did you and Oliver go rock climbing or something?"

Aiden froze, and even in profile, the embarrassment on his face was so palpable, Max swore he felt it as much as saw it. For a moment, his brain struggled to comprehend what it meant. Then, the implication slapped him across the face.

"Oh." Max gaped at him. "*Oh.* I— Wow, okay. Didn't see that coming."

"See what?" Aiden looked cagey. "I didn't say anything."

"Bro, come on. Twin telepathy. You and Oliver . . . um." He swallowed. "You know what? I don't think I can say it."

"Please don't." Aiden covered his ears. "I'll die."

Max shifted his weight in his seat as his annoyance melted into awkwardness. Jesus. His little brother, deflowered by the boy next door. He wasn't sure why it hadn't occurred to him that two young, virile men in love might do the do. Maybe because he hadn't wanted to think about it. His brain had conveniently skipped over that possibility, but now it was staring him in the face.

His stomach lurched. For a brief moment, he thought it was because he was bothered by the idea of his brother having sex. With their mutual friend, no less, who now knew what Max had going on downstairs. But all of that was superficial. What upset him the most was the fact that Aiden hadn't come to him first.

"Well, Aiden." Max hesitated, not sure where to begin. "I want you to know that I love and support you, of course. But, um, I have to admit I'm a little hurt."

"Hurt?" Aiden's head jerked up. "Why would you be hurt? I'd think you'd be surprised, if anything."

"I am surprised, but it kinda pales in comparison to the fact that you didn't talk to me about this. When I thought I was going to lose my virginity, you were the first person I came to. Not my friends, not our parents. You. You didn't do the same, and . . . Well, it sucks."

The remorse on Aiden's face intensified. "I didn't plan this, Max. It just sort of happened. I didn't mean to—"

"Exclude me. Again. Yeah, I'm sensing a theme here." Max tried to push down all the negative emotions that were bubbling up in him, but they kept rising: sadness, anger, resentment, and a whole, heaping dose of rejection. Max pushed through it, though. No matter how upset he was, it was time to be the big brother. "Well, I'm here now if you want to talk about it."

"Actually, I want to go to bed." Aiden stood up like he meant to leave. "I need some time to process."

Anger won out. "Wait, seriously? After dropping a bomb like that, you're gonna walk out on me?"

Aiden rubbed one of his temples. He looked like he was fighting back a fresh bout of irritation. "What 'bomb,' Max? I'm twenty years old. I had sex with a boy I'm dating. It's not a big deal. It's . . . a decision that Oliver and I made together. I get that we're brothers and all, but you can't be involved in *everything* I do. What happened was between Oliver and me."

Max swallowed around the sudden lump in his throat. "Okay. I get that. We were supposed to talk about other things, though. I was going to apologize for being a jerk earlier."

"Apology accepted."

Max waited for him to add more. The silence stretched on until it was so thin, it snapped. "I thought maybe you'd like to apologize too. For ditching me."

"I'm sorry we ditched you. I don't think either of us intended to do that, and I know Oliver was really upset about it." He paused. "You might have to get used to it, though. Now that Oliver and I are dating, we're going to want to spend time together as a couple. Things aren't going to be like they were at the beginning of the summer."

The emotions inside of Max bubbled over, black as tar. "So, that's it, huh? You get a boyfriend, and suddenly you don't have time for me anymore?"

"Honestly, Max, this is for the best. We could stand to spend the summer apart. There are some aspects of our relationship that are unhealthy, and I think deep down you know that. In particular, I need some space to figure out who I am when I'm not being your twin brother. I've never gotten to do that before, and it's long overdue."

Max recognized, on some level, that what Aiden had said was insightful and poignant, but his brain had already plunged into full-blown panic mode. Alarms blaring. Red lights flashing. Sirens wailing in the distance. In their entire lives, they'd only been apart in the brief moment between their births. Ridiculous as it was, Max had assumed they'd never be separated again. What would he do without his brother by his side?

As fear washed through him—cold as deep, dark water—Max did what he always did when he was afraid: he got angry. "What the fuck, Aiden? You think you're Oprah now? You can keep your armchair psychology to yourself, because I'm not buying it."

Aiden frowned. "It doesn't matter if you buy it or not. It's the way things are going to be from now on."

"I can't believe you. I've been there for you through *everything*. High school. Puberty. When you came out. And now, you'd rather spend all your time with him?"

"I don't know what to tell you." Aiden shrugged. "It's not a you-versus-him thing. We're all going to have to learn to live together."

"You know, for someone who's so smart, you sure can't see what's right in front of you."

"What's that supposed to mean?"

"You say you need space to figure out who you are, but you're going to fill that space with Oliver. Instead of being 'Aiden, Max's twin,' you're going to be 'Aiden, Oliver's boyfriend.'"

It was a baseless accusation, but it sounded good, and Max would have said anything to make Aiden doubt his decision.

It seemed to have the opposite effect, though. Aiden's eyes hardened, and the look he leveled at Max was pure ice. "I'm sorry, Max. I've made up my mind. Maybe . . ." He seemed to steel himself. "Maybe I don't need you as much as you need me."

It would have been kinder if Aiden had punched him. Max wanted to tell Aiden off, but one look at his brother's face, and he couldn't do it. Beneath the nonchalant façade Aiden was putting on, Max could see gears turning in his head. What Max had said had gotten to him. It was a small consolation, but it kept Max from losing hope entirely.

"I'm going to bed." Aiden made for the stairs.

Max called after him. "I hope you're happy."

Aiden paused with his hand on the stair railing. "I can't tell if that's sincere or sarcastic."

"Neither can I."

Aiden left. Max stared at the door long after Aiden had closed it behind him. All of a sudden, he understood what Aiden had meant about being exhausted. He attempted to get back into his game, but he barely made it fifteen minutes before he threw the controller down and went upstairs. He had no idea what he intended to do once he got there, but he couldn't sit still any longer.

He poked his head into the hallway that led to their rooms. Aiden's bedroom door was closed, and there was no light visible beneath it. It seemed he really had gone straight to bed.

At least he hasn't graduated to lying to me. Yet.

Max let his thoughts wander as he debated his next move. He'd wanted to apologize to Aiden, and he'd accomplished that, but that was about the only good thing to come out of their talk. Max understood, more or less, why he was angry, but Aiden had never been this irascible with him. Where had his mild-mannered brother gone?

Maybe you don't know Aiden as well as you think you do.

That was a troubling idea.

Max ended up going to his room and flopping onto the bed, though he'd only woken up a few hours ago. He pulled his phone out, and a persistent flashing light told him he had notifications. Probably Facebook messages, texts, and shit. His friends from back in Westchester had been blowing him up the past few days. He'd been ignoring them in favor of spending time with Aiden and Oliver.

And why wouldn't he? They were here and his easiest source of companionship, besides Jessica, the friend he'd had lunch with.

Looks like I bet all my money on the wrong horse.

He sighed. Why was he so bitter about all this? So his brother had gotten a boyfriend, and now he was more interested in him than he was in Max. Big deal. It sucked, but it was no Shakespearean tragedy. There had to be something more going on.

The last thing that Aiden had said to him stuck out in his head. *"Maybe I don't need you as much as you need me."*

At the time, Max had dismissed it as a jab said out of anger, but now he wondered if there wasn't some truth to it. It was true that Aiden relied on him for social energy and support, but Max needed Aiden for attention, affection, and to feel like he was the best at something:

being a big brother. Had he spent all these years playing up how much he did for Aiden because he needed to be needed?

It was possible. He and Aiden were such different people, after all. If they weren't brothers, would they be friends?

"Damn," he whispered to his ceiling, "I'm *deep*."

Normally, he'd laugh at his own joke, but right now, he didn't have it in him. All this thinking was wearing him out.

He was contemplating taking a nap of his own when he heard the front door open, followed by the sound of his parents' voices.

"Well, fuck." He rolled out of bed. "Can't we cancel the rest of today?"

Mom and Dad had brought home taco ingredients. Max hung out with them in the kitchen while they cooked, and tried to distract himself. Aiden didn't appear until dinner was ready and Mom had called him twice.

They ate in relative silence. It was unusual for the Kingsman household, but not so much so that Mom and Dad got suspicious. Several times, Max tried to catch Aiden's eye, but not once did Aiden glance his way.

When dinner was over, Aiden disappeared back into his room, and that was the last Max saw of him. He spent a few hours playing video games, but after he died a series of bloody and avoidable deaths, he admitted his heart wasn't in it. He went to sleep, praying that things would be clearer in the morning.

He couldn't remember exactly what he dreamed, but it involved Aiden, and Max was anxious the whole time. He was pretty sure they were yelling at each other over some sort of fictitious problem. Max had borrowed Aiden's hover scooter without asking or something.

What bothered him most about the dream was that it never got interrupted. In the past, when they'd argued, Aiden couldn't sleep until things were right between them. It'd started when they were kids, and hadn't changed over the years. Aiden would sneak into Max's room after a fight and tug on his foot until he woke up. They'd sit cross-legged on his bed and talk it out.

But Aiden never came. Max had never been so sorry to sleep through the night.

Around eight in the morning, he woke up to find himself sticking to the sheets with sweat. He considered shaking off his bad dream and going back to sleep, but for once, he didn't want to spend half the day in his room. If he was going to be ignored, he intended to be present and accounted for.

Rolling out of bed, he ducked into the bathroom, took care of everything he needed to do in there, and got dressed. When he walked out into the living room, Mom and Dad were awake but it seemed Aiden wasn't.

"Morning, Aiden," Mom said without looking up from her newspaper. She was seated at the breakfast table while Dad fussed in the kitchen.

"It's Max, actually."

Dad stopped halfway through scooping bacon out of a pan to glance at him. "Oh, hey. You're up early."

"Sorry, Max." Mom's brown eyes crinkled at the corners. "I'm so used to Aiden being the first up."

"It's okay. Is there coffee?"

Dad gestured at the pot with a spatula. Max poured himself a cup and then doctored it with enough milk and sugar to make it arguably not coffee anymore. Precisely how he liked it.

He sat down at the table next to Mom and sipped it while fucking around on his phone. He was halfway through a tell-all message to Jessica when Aiden's door opened, and out strolled the man himself.

Aiden made it three steps into the living room before he stopped short. "Max, you're up early."

Max didn't look up from his phone. "So I've heard."

"How'd you sleep, honey?" Mom asked.

Max couldn't resist the opportunity to cut in. He glanced up. "Oh, I bet he slept great. He was all tuckered out from yesterday."

A line appeared between Mom's eyebrows. "What happened yesterday?"

Aiden didn't glare daggers at Max so much as swords, dipped in poison, that were also somehow on fire. "Nothing. I didn't sleep well. Isn't that right, Max?"

"Sure." Max's smile was beatific. "Why not?"

Mom looked between them. "Boys, I've been a lawyer for thirty years and a mom for twenty. I know when something's up. What's going on?"

"Nothing, really." Max turned his smile on her. "I'm teasing my brother."

She looked unconvinced, but a glance at her watch sent her scrambling to put her dishes in the sink. "I have to run. Be good today, boys. Say hi to Oliver for me."

Funny how she assumes we're going to see him.

Mom kissed Dad goodbye and dashed for the front door. Dad turned back to the stove and called to them. "Want some breakfast?"

"I'd love some." Aiden took a seat at the table across from Max. "I'm starving."

"Sex will do that," Max muttered.

"What was that?" Dad asked.

"I said 'Eggs will do, Dad.'" He grinned. "If we have any."

"Coming right up."

Dad busied himself frying eggs while Aiden glared murderously at Max and Max pretended not to notice. After a while, Aiden pulled out his own phone and started texting. Max tried to peek at the screen, but Aiden held it away from him. Max would have bet money that he was texting Oliver.

"Here you go." Dad appeared with a plate of eggs, bacon, and toast for both of them. He produced a pair of forks from the pocket of his apron. "I have to head into work as well. I trust you boys can fend for yourselves until I get home."

"We'll be fine, Dad," Aiden said.

"Merff," Max said while shoveling eggs into his mouth.

Aiden's lip curled up.

Dad laughed. "All right. See you boys for dinner."

No sooner had the front door shut behind him that Aiden pounced.

"*What* is the *matter* with you?"

Max didn't look up from his phone. "I don't know what you're talking about."

"Don't pull that shit with me."

Max was so startled to hear his brother curse—something Aiden usually saved for special occasions, like their birthday and Christmas morning—he looked up. Aiden's eyes had narrowed. Aiden's face was different than Max's in anger. Max tended to get red and veiny, whereas Aiden got pinched and pale, like a crumpled piece of paper.

Judging by the creases around Aiden's mouth and forehead, he was plenty angry now. "What were you thinking, saying those things to Mom and Dad? Did you think it would be *funny* to tell them I'm not a virgin anymore? Before I've had a chance to tell them Oliver and I are together? Or was that some kind of sick revenge because I blew you off?"

Max pressed his lips together. What he'd done was wrong, but hell if he was going to admit it. "Oh, I'm sorry. I didn't know you were keeping it a secret. Maybe if you'd *talked* to me, I would have known."

That shut Aiden up. Max grinned triumphantly.

Aiden stood up from the table. "I'm gonna invite Oliver over. When he gets here, I want you to play nice. It's not his fault you're—" he stopped and corrected himself "—we're having some issues."

"Fine by me. I can play nice. Oliver is *my* friend, after all."

Aiden glowered but didn't speak as he stalked off toward the basement. Great. Now Max couldn't go down there like he'd planned. Aiden had probably done that on purpose.

"Whatever." He finished downing his breakfast and dropped his plate and mug off in the sink. He started to go back to his room, but at the last second, he took a detour for the second time that week and walked into Aiden's room instead. It was messier than it had been last time, and there were more photos tacked up on the corkboard.

Max plucked one off the board at random. Aiden had the curtains drawn, so it was a shade too dark for details, but Max recognized the scene: their joint eighth birthday party. The photo featured two rows of kids sitting at a long table at some sort of pizza place. Aiden and Max shared spots at the head of the table while a host of small faces leaned forward so the camera could see them around their neighbors.

Of course, Oliver was there, sitting right next to them, sporting the terrible bowl cut his mom had given him that year. He was looking at the camera, eyes and smile sparkling. In fact, everyone in the picture was looking at the camera, except for Aiden and Max.

Aiden was looking at Oliver. Max was looking at Aiden. It was so damn fitting, Max wanted to cry or rip up the photo. He couldn't decide.

Was this how things had always been, and he'd been too self-involved to see it? In all the years he'd taken the lead, was he secretly chasing after Aiden?

This raised all sorts of uncomfortable questions Max didn't want to deal with. Who was he if he wasn't Aiden's big brother? What role did he fulfill? What was their relationship going to be like now that so much had changed?

He had no idea how long he stood there, staring at the photograph while stray thoughts wreaked havoc in his mind, but he was startled back to the present when he heard a knock at the window.

He dropped the photograph. For a second, he thought he was hearing things, but then the knock sounded again.

"What the fuck?" He pulled the curtains aside and blinked in the sudden light.

It was Oliver. He waved at Max and gestured at the window like he wanted to be let in. Max threw it open without thinking.

"Hey, I see you got my text." Oliver climbed over the sill. Once he was in, he shut the window again and drew the curtain back, dimming the light. "I thought this would be more fun than the front door. It's like our thing, you know?"

Max was too confused to form words. *The fuck is he on about?*

What happened next in no way helped him regain the ability to think.

Before Max could react, Oliver swooped in and kissed him. With enthusiasm.

Max stiffened like a corpse. It all happened so fast, he didn't know what to do. But there was one thing he *definitely* didn't do. No matter how angry he was with Aiden, no matter how much he resented Oliver . . .

He did *not* kiss Oliver back.

It took Oliver all of three seconds to realize his mistake. He wrenched his mouth away, eyes wide with horror. "M-Max?"

"'Fraid so," Max said, still stunned. His eyes actually hurt, they were open so wide. "Nice to see you too, buddy." He didn't know where the humor came from, but it was all he could do not to giggle like a nervous child.

Of all the thoughts that flitted into his head, the most troubling was how comfortable he was with the idea that he'd kissed another dude. He wouldn't say he'd liked it, per se, but he suspected that was because it was Oliver.

Now's not the time for a sexual-identity crisis, said a voice in his head. *There are more pressing matters at hand.*

He touched his fingers to his lips. "So . . . that happened."

Oliver stumbled back a step and covered his mouth. "Max, I am *so* sorry. I—"

There came the sound of footsteps in the hall. "Oliver? Is that you? I got your text."

Aiden entered the room a second later. Max and Oliver didn't have time to do more than look up in terror.

Maybe it was the fear on Oliver's face. Maybe it was the fact that Max was touching his lips. Maybe it was how they'd jumped away from each other, guilt hanging so heavy in the air it seemed to blot out the light.

Whatever it was, Max could tell right away that Aiden knew exactly what had happened.

"Aiden," Oliver said, his voice pitched too high. "Hey. I just got here."

Poor Oliver, Max thought. *He doesn't know it's too late. This is where twin telepathy comes in handy.*

He was completely unsurprised when Aiden rounded on him, eyes sharp as knives, and snarled, "Get the fuck away from my boyfriend."

Though that didn't make it hurt one bit less.

Chapter 11: Oliver

Congratulations, Oliver thought. *This is the worst you've ever fucked up.*

He'd realized his mistake almost right away and yet was powerless to correct it. The damage was done. He'd kissed Max, and now he was watching the Kingsman twins square off against each other like they were in a bad spaghetti Western.

How? *How* had Oliver made such a mistake? He was an expert in telling the brothers apart. Except, he supposed, when Max was in Aiden's room for no reason. And when Oliver had texted Aiden and asked to meet there. Plus, it was dark, and Max hadn't spoken. If only he'd said something. If he'd said so much as a word, Oliver would have realized.

There was no point in dwelling on it. It was over. It wasn't just that Oliver had made a mistake. He'd made the worst mistake he could have possibly made at the precise worst moment. Bards could write poetry about how epically he'd fucked up. He'd launched a bottle rocket into a gunpowder keg. When Aiden had invited him over this morning, Oliver had specifically asked if he'd fixed things with Max. Aiden had said yes.

Well, so much for that.

In his panic, Oliver said possibly the most cliché thing ever. "Aiden, this isn't what it looks like."

Aiden, who had been glaring at Max, jerked his head toward Oliver. "So, my twin brother didn't kiss you?"

Fear rippled through him, as if Aiden had thrown a stone into the pit of Oliver's stomach. He stared at his feet. "I kissed him. But it was an accident. You have to believe me."

"I do."

Oliver whipped his head up. "What?"

"Of course I believe you, Oliver." Aiden frowned, like he was offended Oliver had to ask. "I know you'd never do that to me. You probably got us mixed up, right? It was bound to happen. You were a little *too* good at telling us apart."

Relief thundered through Oliver. "Yes! That's exactly what happened. Oh my God, I'm so relieved. Does this mean you're not angry?"

"I'm not angry with *you*." Aiden rounded on Max again. "You, on the other hand. I don't believe for a second that you didn't have some hand in this. What were you doing in my room, anyway?"

"Nothing!" Max appeared as startled as Oliver felt. "I was looking at your photos."

"Uh-huh. For no reason at all, you were in here at the exact time I was meeting Oliver, and you just happened to kiss him. Is that what I'm supposed to believe?"

"Aiden, calm down," Oliver tried.

But Max jumped in. "Dude, what the fuck? What are you accusing me of? You think I *wanted* to kiss Oliver?"

"I don't know what to think. It's a little convenient, though. We had a huge fight about Oliver, and the next thing I know, you do the one thing that could drive a wedge between us. Well, sorry, brother dear, but it's not going to work. I trust Oliver."

Max's face turned red, but not like Aiden's did when he blushed. Rage radiated from him like heat. "You trust him, but you don't trust me? Wow, your opinion of me sure has changed since Oliver got back into town. Look me in the eye right now and tell me that you honestly believe I'd do that to my own little brother."

Aiden fell silent, but his accusatory expression was now tinged with doubt. "The way you referred to me is a perfect example of our problem. You always think of me in terms of you. Your little brother. And for the last time, Max, you're *five minutes* older. Not five years."

Oliver's gaze darted between them as he scrambled to think of something to say to diffuse the situation. "Aiden, Max didn't do anything. He didn't kiss me back. That was part of what made me realize he wasn't you."

Aiden's resolve flickered on his face. "He didn't?"

"Not at all. Besides, he's straight. He wouldn't kiss another guy to piss you off."

Max's expression was pinched with discomfort. "Right. Straight."

It distantly occurred to Oliver that while Max hadn't kissed him back, he also hadn't pushed him away.

Aiden interrupted that thought before it could fully form. "None of this makes things okay."

Oliver took a tentative step toward him. "I think we should all calm down and talk about this. It was an accident. There's no reason for anyone to fight."

"There are plenty of reasons." Aiden glared at his brother. "Hey, Max, why don't you tell Oliver about the stunt you pulled at breakfast? You know, when you kept dropping hints to our parents that he and I had sex."

Oliver gasped. "Max, you didn't."

Max grimaced. "I was fucking around. I wasn't going to actually tell them."

"Dude, joke or not, that's fucked up." Oliver shook his head. "I have a whole relationship with your parents too. We should be allowed to tell them we're together in our own time."

"Well, don't leave it up to Aiden." Max crossed his arms over his chest. "If you do, he'll never tell them. He didn't come out until I spent weeks assuring him everything would be fine. Not that he's ever thanked me for all the times I've supported him."

"You are so *arrogant*." Aiden's voice rose. "I can't believe you're taking credit for me coming out. Did it ever occur to you that you never give me a chance to do things on my own? You answer for both of us before I've heard the question. I don't bother introducing myself when we meet new people, because I know you will before I can open my mouth. I would be fine if you weren't around. Sometimes, I wish you *weren't*."

By the time Aiden had finished, he was breathing heavily. He seemed surprised at himself, like he hadn't known what he was going to say until he'd said it.

There was a pregnant pause. Then Max deflated. "You wish I wasn't around?"

Oliver took a breath and held it, praying that Aiden wasn't about to say something he'd regret.

Thankfully, Aiden looked down at his socked feet. "I didn't mean that."

"Didn't you? You said before that you need space. Have I been stifling you this whole time? There has to be a reason you're so mad at me." Max seemed to have blown through his share of anger and was now coming down. "I admit I haven't been a perfect big brother—"

"Five minutes, Max," Aiden grumbled.

"Will you let me finish?"

Aiden pressed his lips together, appearing none too pleased about it.

"I've been thinking a lot these past days, and I get why you think our relationship is unhealthy. I even get that I was holding you back or whatever. Stifling you. But you know what? At least I'm willing to admit it. You still haven't apologized for the way you've treated me since Oliver arrived."

"That's not true. I said I was sorry."

"Yeah, sorry for ditching me. That's not the only thing you've done."

Aiden shifted his weight from one foot to the other and didn't speak.

Max continued. "You need space. Fine. I can live with that. But you're trying to cut me out entirely, and that's not good for either of us. We're *brothers*, Aiden. Forever. I thought I knew you better than anyone else on the planet, but this new person you've become in the past few weeks—the one who accuses me of kissing his boyfriend on purpose—I don't know that guy. And I don't particularly like him."

Aiden's uncertainty was plain on his face. "You can't turn this back on me. You're the one who fucked up."

"Yeah, I did. I was jealous and petty and small. I admit it."

"Admitting it doesn't make it okay. This is so typical of you. It's like when we were kids and you'd break a toy sooner than let me have it."

"Whoa." Oliver held up a hand. "I've been trying to stay out of this as much as possible, but I have a big fucking problem with being compared to a toy."

Aiden blanched. "Oh shit. Oliver, I didn't mean that. I was—"

"What? Being a jerk to your brother?" He shook his head. "I swear, I always talk about how different you two are, but you're more alike than you think. My dad told me something the other day, and I wasn't sure how true it was, but now I think it's spot on: the people who love you the most can also hurt you the most. Both of you need to say you're sorry and remember that you're family."

"Yeah, *we're* family," Max groused. "And you've always tried to encroach on that."

"Yeah, because my family's a mess. Ever since we were kids, I've wished I had half of what you and Aiden have. Parents who respect each other. A beautiful, welcoming house. A sibling, and not just any sibling: a *twin*. Warmth and stability and love. Do you two realize how *lucky* you are?"

Aiden hung his head, guilt plain on his face.

Good. Maybe something got through to him.

Max, on the other hand, rolled his eyes. "I don't feel very lucky right now. My brother thinks I'm the reason he has no personality. Be sure not to invite me to the wedding. Aiden will accuse me of trying to deliver his vows for him."

Aiden's anger returned, quick as a flash flood. "Get over yourself, Max."

They started talking at the same time, voices rising until they were yelling over each other.

Oliver had seen them fight before, but this was something else. Max was usually the first to get angry, but also the first to cool off. Aiden took longer, but when he got going, he was like an avalanche. There was no stopping him until he stopped himself.

Fuck this. I can't.

Over the years, Oliver had prevented many a fight. He'd kept Aiden's fuse from running out, or he'd gotten Max to cool off fast and apologize. But he wasn't going to do that this time. He'd reached his personal quota of listening to people scream at each other. He was starting to get the short-of-breath, rib-squeezing feeling he got when his parents argued. It was compounded by the knowledge that this was partially his fault.

All of this had begun when he'd run into them in that grocery store. On some level, he understood that this fight would have happened eventually anyway. Max and Aiden had clear issues. This was one stick of dynamite that was destined to go off. But that didn't mean he felt any better about being the one who'd brought the matches.

He needed some air. He stumbled for the door. Aiden and Max were too busy yelling at each other to notice. At first.

Oliver got all the way out into the hall before he heard Aiden, or maybe Max—he couldn't tell anymore—say, "Oliver? Where are you going?"

By then, he was in the living room and had no intention of stopping. There was the brief sound of footsteps, as if someone were chasing after him, but then the shouting started again.

In his haste to leave the house, he slammed right into something. Or someone, as it turned out.

"Oliver." Kim Kingsman blinked at him with doe-like brown eyes. "Are you all right?"

"I'm fine," he lied. "I was on my way out."

"Why don't you stay for lunch? I brought sandwiches." She held up her arm, which had a plastic bag hanging from her elbow. It smelled heavenly, like fresh bread and cheese. "I was going to surprise the boys."

He hesitated, and in that second of quiet, the shouting reached them like a creeping mist.

Kim frowned, peering around Oliver in the direction of the noise. "Are they fighting? I knew something was up. They've been like dogs marking the same stump for days now."

"I'm so sorry. I really have to go." Oliver tried to edge past her.

She touched his shoulder. "Oliver, look at me."

Though he was an adult now, he was still hardwired to obey. "Yes?"

"Are you okay? You seem like you're upset about something."

Understatement of the century. How could he explain everything that had happened since he'd walked back into this house? The answer was simple: he couldn't.

"It's nothing." He began to pull gently out of her grip. "I need to go home. My family's waiting for me."

She looked unconvinced, but she dropped her hand. "Okay. But Oliver, you know you're always welcome here, right? We're your family too."

Oliver almost burst into tears. He nodded and turned away. "I know, Kim. I'll see you later."

As he made his way to the front door, he had the strangest feeling that he was lying to her.

Outside, the bright sunlight and the gentle wind calmed him somewhat. He took what felt like his first breath in fifteen minutes. As his head cleared, he realized he had a problem: his dad had dropped him off here on his way to work. He'd expected Aiden to give him a ride home when they were finished hanging out. He was stuck here.

Fuck that. I'll walk if I have to.

Dad's house was six miles away, and the afternoon heat had settled in, thick as a blanket. This was going to be brutal, but it was better than staying here.

He made it halfway down the driveway before he heard the front door open behind him. Part of him wanted to keep walking, but with a sigh, he glanced over his shoulder. Aiden was running toward him, looking frantic. He waited for Aiden, growing tenser with every step.

"Hey, are you leaving?" Aiden was flushed, and the sight of him all cute and disheveled almost shook Oliver's resolve. "Don't go."

"I have to, Aiden. I can't listen to you and your brother fight. It strikes every nerve I have."

Aiden flinched. "I'm sorry. I forgot fighting makes you anxious. But you know it's not directed at you, right? I'm not angry at you, and neither is Max, no matter what he says."

"I know, but somehow that doesn't make me feel any better." He started down the driveway again.

Aiden caught his arm. "At least let me drive you home. Please? We can talk in the car."

Sweat trickled down Oliver's back. "Okay."

They got in, and as they backed out onto the street, Oliver stole a peek at Aiden. His eyes swept over familiar features—messy curls, beautiful eyes, a long neck—and lingered on an unfamiliar one: the furrow between his eyebrows that said he was troubled. Oliver would have given anything, *anything*, to smooth away all the worry on his face.

God, I think I love him.

In that moment, Oliver knew exactly what he needed to say. "Aiden, I can't see you anymore."

Aiden slammed on the brakes. "What?"

The seat belt cut into Oliver's chest like a dull blade. He had to suck in a new breath before he could speak. "Please don't do that."

"Sorry." The car started moving again. "I panicked. What did you say?"

This was going to take all the strength Oliver had. "You heard me, Aiden. Until you and Max have worked out your problems—and I mean *really* worked them out—we can't see each other. I hate to give you an ultimatum like this, but I can't think of any other way to get you and Max to stop this before you do some real damage to your relationship."

"Oliver, you're being ridiculous."

Oliver's temper spiked. "Don't you call me ridiculous, Aiden Kingsman. I'm not. You're being unjustifiably stubborn. I used to think you were like stone: steady and unshakable. I still think that, and I still love that about you, but now I think it's half the problem. You can't see all the ways you contributed to this. Or the ways I did."

"You don't mean that." Aiden was staring forward like he couldn't risk looking at him. His voice was shaky and broken. "Please don't tell me you regret yesterday. Because I couldn't stand it."

Oliver's heart cracked like glass in his chest. "Of course I don't regret it. I want to be with you, Aiden. But I can't do that while things are the way they are."

Aiden looked like Oliver had set him adrift at sea. It was heart-wrenching. "Are you breaking up with me?"

"No, I'm not. I care about you. I want to be with you so much it hurts." *I love you.* "But someone has to be the grown-up here. If you and Max don't clean out your wounds, they'll fester. Trust me, I've watched it happen."

"Why can't you be around while we do that?"

"Did you not see what happened in there? For whatever reason, I'm like gasoline on the fire when it comes to you two. Your brother said himself he's jealous of me, and you've been acting like a different person ever since we got together."

They pulled into Oliver's driveway.

Aiden put the car in park and swiveled in his seat to face him. "I haven't changed, Oliver. I'm still me. I swear it."

"Aiden." Oliver fixed him with a hard look. "Did you lie to me this morning? When you said you and Max made up?"

Aiden's throat moved, suggesting that he'd swallowed. "What do you mean?"

"When you invited me over, I specifically asked if you and Max had made up. You said yes. But one little mishap later, and you were at each other's throats. I heard the things you two said to each other. Those weren't the words of two brothers who'd sorted out their differences. Did you, or did you not, *lie* to me?"

Aiden's face gave Oliver an answer long before he spoke: it was heavy with shame and remorse. "It's wasn't a total lie, but it wasn't the truth either. Max and I did talk last night, and we both apologized, but I knew things weren't totally right. I didn't think it was that big of a deal." Aiden put a hand over Oliver's. "Please don't go."

Oliver stared at him for a long moment, his heart shattering in his chest. Finally, he moved his hand away from Aiden's and put it on the door handle. "Aiden?"

"Yes?"

"If you ever lie to me again, I *will* break up with you."

At that, Aiden's eyes dropped to his lap like a curtain.

Oliver opened the door and got out. He walked up to his house without looking back. As soon as he got in, though, he peeked out the window by the door. Aiden's car was still in the driveway. Oliver knew him well enough at this point to know he was composing himself before he attempted to drive. A solid minute passed before the car finally backed out and disappeared down the street.

The tears Oliver had been holding back sprang up in his eyes. He blinked them away. He'd done the right thing. He knew he had. So, why did it feel so horrible?

Because it's not enough. This is part one of what you need to do.

There were a handful of things that Oliver knew for certain. One, Aiden was the most stubborn ass Oliver had ever met, and he meant that with love. Aiden wasn't going to get over the idea that this was all Max's fault overnight. Two, preserving Aiden's relationship with Max was more important than anything. More important than Oliver's feelings. More important than his burgeoning relationship with Aiden.

And three, Oliver wasn't strong enough to stay away from them. Not indefinitely. He loved both brothers too much, in so many ways. If Aiden came to him tomorrow and said everything had been magically fixed, Oliver would eat it up. Next thing he knew, he'd be back over at their house, and the whole ugly cycle would start again.

Which was why he had no choice but to remove himself from the equation. Aiden had thought it was okay to lie to him once. Oliver needed to make sure he never did that again.

Oliver would go back to the city. He'd move away, like he had when they were kids. Without him around, the brothers would be right back where they'd started: with only each other. Oliver couldn't think of a better way to get them to deal with their issues than sticking them in time-out together.

It was a huge risk, and there were all sorts of complications. Dad was going to be furious, and there was no guarantee Aiden and Max would fix things quickly, if ever. They might not reconcile until the end of summer, just in time to say goodbye again as they headed off to their separate schools. Or worse, absence might make the heart forget. Oliver remembered well when he'd moved away the first time, and the letters had gradually stopped coming.

But whatever happened, it would be worth it. Oliver was positive he was doing the right thing. For himself, the man he loved, and his good friend.

His house was empty. He staggered through it to his room, shut the door behind him, and fell into bed. He allowed himself a moment to lie there before he rolled over and dug his phone out of his pocket.

Mom was at the top of his recent-calls list. He tapped on her name and pressed the phone hard to his ear as it rang. She was at work. It'd probably go to voice mail. But he prayed with everything he had that she'd answer.

"Oliver?"

"Mom," Oliver said, sniffling. "I'm so glad you picked up."

"Honey, are you okay? You sound terrible. Is it your father?"

"No, Mom, it's me." He sucked in a breath that seemed to rattle his bones. "Remember when you said you'd come get me if I needed you to? Well, I need you."

Chapter 12:
Aiden

As Aiden drove away, a thought rang in the back of his head like distant church bells: *never, ever lie to Oliver Jones.* Seeing Oliver's normally playful green eyes glint with anger had scared a gray hair onto Aiden's head.

Aiden hadn't meant to lie to him. When he'd told Oliver that morning that everything was fine, he'd known it wasn't the whole truth, but it hadn't seemed like a big deal. He'd wanted to see him so badly. It was embarrassing to admit, but he'd just lost his virginity to the guy. He'd needed confirmation that this wasn't all in his head. The closeness he'd felt with Oliver, the intensity of their sex . . . he still had trouble believing it.

Was this what falling in love felt like?

It didn't excuse what he'd done, but how could he have known things with Max would escalate the way they had?

For that matter, how could he have known Oliver would accidentally kiss Max? Aiden understood why it'd happened, and he wasn't angry exactly. More like . . . uncomfortable. His brother and his boyfriend had kissed.

Oh God, what if Max is a better kisser than I am?

Aiden shoved that thought violently away and focused instead on a more troubling realization. Oliver, who had always been able to tell them apart, had gotten them mixed up. Looking back, Aiden wondered if that wasn't the real reason he'd gotten so angry at Max.

All his life, he'd been a part of a matched set. The Kingsman twins. Never really his own person, but rather half of this separate identity. Then Oliver had come along, and he'd made it so clear, so obvious, that Aiden wasn't simply Max's brother. He was a whole person in and of himself, and that'd made Aiden want so badly to figure out who that person was.

It wasn't Oliver's fault he'd gotten them mixed up, but it'd poked a sizable hole in Aiden's new inflated sense of self. Oliver wasn't infallible, and Aiden wasn't as different from Max as he'd thought. There was a very real chance this had led Aiden to overreact the tiniest bit.

If he was smart, he'd apologize to Max for accusing him of kissing Oliver on purpose, among other things. He wasn't certain he could do that, though. Not right now, at least. He was still furious with Max for all the petulant stunts he'd pulled, and now Oliver wasn't speaking to them to boot. Besides, Aiden couldn't offer up an apology and expect that to be the end of it. He had to fix things for real, or Oliver would make good on his threat.

"If you ever lie to me again . . ."

Aiden shuddered as he pulled into his driveway and parked. He couldn't risk losing Oliver. He'd have to work through his issues with Max ASAP, no matter how ugly or painful things got.

When he walked into the house, the sound of voices led him to the dining room, where Mom and Max were sitting with a bag of sandwiches open in front of them. Max was wolfing down what looked like half a cow on bread, in a manner that reminded Aiden of Animal Planet. Mom was watching him with a look of mild concern.

She smiled when she spotted Aiden. "Hey, honey. Want a sandwich?"

Aiden hesitated. He was starving, but after what had happened at breakfast, he didn't want to risk sitting at the same table as Max.

Max glanced up, eyed him, and then went back to his sandwich as if Aiden weren't there. Aiden took that as a silent promise of ceasefire and fell into a chair, reaching for a turkey club.

Mom nibbled on her own sandwich, looking nonchalant. "So, what were you two fighting about before?"

Aiden flinched. He did *not* want to have this conversation right now. He saw Max draw a breath as if to answer for them. *Nope, not this time.*

He blurted out, "Nothing. It was a little sibling squabble."

Max shot him a sidelong look but didn't contradict him.

Mom pursed her lips. "Sure sounded like a full-blown fight to me. I could hear you yelling from the living room."

"Honestly, it wasn't a big deal." Aiden took a bite and pretended to fiddle with the wax paper, hoping Mom would move on.

He had no such luck.

"Oliver left in a hurry." She set her food down. "He looked upset. In fact, I've been to sentencings that were less dour. Any idea what that was about?"

Aiden kept his expression neutral, but across the table Max wilted like old lettuce.

Mom's eyes snapped over to him. "Max, is there something you'd like to say?"

Aiden glared at him. He'd always thought Max's "twin telepathy" was a joke, but that didn't stop him from broadcasting, *Play it cool, play it cool, play it cool.*

Max opened and closed his mouth several times. "It's all Aiden's fault."

Goddamn it.

Aiden bristled. "How is this *my* fault?"

"If you hadn't thrown such a giant tantrum, Oliver wouldn't have left."

"I threw a tantrum? Me? You're the one who—"

"Boys."

That one word, said with all the gut-wrenching force of a frustrated mother, stopped them both in their tracks.

Mom massaged one of her temples. "I don't know what's going on between you two, and frankly, I don't care. I have my suspicions, but since you seem determined to act like children instead of young men, I'll cut to the chase. Do you two remember having sleepovers with Oliver when you were children?"

"Of course," Aiden said.

Max frowned. "What's that got to do with anything?"

"Remember how he was the only one of your friends who was allowed to stay over on a school night?"

Aiden thought back. "Actually, yeah. Why was that?"

"Because your father and I knew he was having a hard time at home. We made a point of welcoming him here. He was such a sensitive boy, and a good influence on you two. We were *thrilled* when you all started hanging out again."

Max rolled a shoulder. "Not for nothing, Mom, but what's your point?"

"My point is"—her tone became sharp and cold, like a winter storm—"if I find out you two chased that young man off with your petty arguing, there will be hell to pay. Especially if you're fighting over him like he's one of your video games."

We're fighting over Oliver all right. But not the way you think.

Aiden peeked across the table, only to catch Max watching him. He was still frowning, but his eyes had a watery look that made Aiden's chest clench.

I should say something. But Mom's here, and I don't think I have the words. Maybe Oliver's right. I am stubborn.

Aiden finished his sandwich in two bites and stood up. "I'm going to my room."

Neither Mom nor Max attempted to stop him. After a brief detour to the kitchen to throw his sandwich paper away and grab some water, he locked himself in his room.

For two whole hours, he managed to keep himself busy. He checked his school email, sent some of his old notes to a former classmate in need, and caught up on some much-neglected reading. Before long, though, he started to get antsy.

It went without saying that he missed Oliver, and although he was angry at Max, he was used to having him around. Normally, by this point in the day, Max would have cajoled him into a game of pool, or a movie marathon. Aiden had to admit, much as he'd complained that Max was stifling him, he had no idea how to be alone.

I thought my main motivation for patching things up with Max would be getting Oliver back. It didn't occur to me I'd genuinely miss him.

He gave up on pretending to read and wandered out of his room. Mom had gone back to the office, but at some point, Dad had gotten home and was busying himself in the kitchen. That wasn't all that unusual these days. Since Dad's practice had hired more on-call dentists, he was able to get home earlier.

When Aiden entered, Dad looked up from the produce he was unpacking. "Hey, buddy. What's going on with you?"

Aiden frowned. "What makes you think there's something going on?"

"That sour face of yours, for one thing, and also the fact that I'm in an open and honest relationship with your mother."

"Perfect." Aiden wrinkled his nose. "Mom told you."

"More or less. She told me what she suspects. Want to talk about it?"

"No. I appreciate the offer, but it would take a lot of explaining."

Aiden expected his father to press the issue, but instead he shrugged. "All right. Then you can help me chop vegetables for dinner. I'm making chicken tortilla soup."

Aiden pursed his lips. "In summer? We'll die."

Dad pulled several large tomatoes out of one of the grocery bags and tossed them to him. "You live in an air-conditioned house in an affluent region of a developed nation. You're not going to die from eating soup. Especially not soup that was made by your father, a remarkable and talented chef. Now get chopping. Those tomatoes need to stew for twenty minutes."

Aiden did as he was told, and after a while he fell into a rhythm. The sound of his knife hitting the wooden cutting board, along with sizzling onions and Dad's off-key humming, made his mind wander. And by wander, he meant make a beeline for his debacle with Max and Oliver. How had so much happened in a few weeks? He'd rediscovered an old flame, become estranged from his brother, and maybe fallen in love.

And to think, none of this might have happened if Oliver hadn't spotted Max at the store. But then, considering what a loser Max made me sound like in the beginning, it's a wonder Oliver—

"Ouch!" Aiden had nicked the tip of his finger with the knife.

Dad materialized by his side. "Run it under water." He took Aiden by the wrist and guided him gently over to the sink.

The lukewarm spray of the water didn't hurt, but Aiden grimaced at the sight of the runny blood swirling down the drain. "It's not deep, but I think I need a bandage."

"I'll get you one. Keep your finger under the water." Dad disappeared only to reappear a moment later with a small first aid kit. "Let me see."

Aiden turned off the water and held his finger up.

Dad took a cursory look before applying the bandage. "You'll live. Though it was a near thing." He winked.

Aiden tried to smile, but his facial muscles wouldn't cooperate. He went back to chopping vegetables, more carefully this time.

"You seem distracted." Dad's tone was casual, but Aiden caught him watching Aiden out of the corner of his eye. "Penny for your thoughts?"

He's not going to let this go until I talk about it. Damn emotionally supportive parents.

Aiden did his best to summarize the issue without revealing too much. "Things have been weird lately. Max and I are fighting, and Oliver isn't speaking to me."

Dad nodded knowingly, confirming that Mom had already told him as much. "What are you fighting about?"

"Lots of things. I think Max and I realized some things about ourselves this summer, and they weren't all good things."

"That's part of growing up, kiddo. You didn't think you and Max were going to stay the same forever, did you?"

"No . . . but also yes. I guess I never put much thought into it. Things have been one way for so long now."

Dad set a large pot on the stove and poured chicken stock into it. "You know what we old people call that?"

Aiden shook his head.

"Growing pains. And believe me when I say the pain part is accurate. These are the years in which you're expected to make all kinds of big decisions. Ones that will affect the rest of your life. And yet you don't have enough life experience to know for sure what you should do. Seems kinda unfair, doesn't it?"

"Well, when you put it like that." Aiden scraped the chopped tomatoes into the pot as his dad instructed. "Can I ask you something?"

"Shoot."

"When you and Mom were dating, how did you know you loved her?"

Dad dropped his knife and looked at him. "Why do you ask?"

"No reason." Aiden fought not to blush.

"I see. Well, I suspected I loved her long before I worked up the nerve to tell her. I think we'd only been dating for a few weeks. I felt like I was floating whenever I was around her. She could make my heart skip with a look. I wanted to spend every spare minute I had with her."

Aiden's mind whirred. That was exactly how he felt about Oliver. He hadn't thought he could fall in love so fast, but if Dad had fallen for Mom that quickly . . .

"Of course, that was more infatuation than love," Dad added. "It wasn't until later that I realized the difference."

"What happened?"

"Nothing." Dad smiled. "Literally. My heart stopped skipping. I stopped floating whenever she was around. The infatuation wore off, but what was left was better. Trust. Understanding. Genuine affection that was based on something more solid than attraction: friendship."

Oliver and I were friends before we were lovers. Does that mean we'll have what Mom and Dad have some day? Only if I fix things with Max, I suppose.

Dad put a hand on his shoulder, interrupting his thoughts. "Aiden, do you think you're in love with someone? Perhaps someone who has recently come back into our lives? Someone dear to the whole family?"

Aiden's face grew hot enough to boil the soup on the stove. "Um. Well . . ."

Dad laughed. "Damn. I owe your mom twenty bucks. Not that I'm not thrilled. Oliver's a wonderful young man."

"Don't pay up yet. Every time Oliver and I take a step forward, something goes wrong."

Dad turned back to the stove and dumped more ingredients into the pot. "I'm guessing your fight with Max is related. You know those growing pains I mentioned earlier?"

"Yeah?"

"Your brother is going through them too. And even though you're twins, you're experiencing them in completely different ways. Try to keep that in mind, and don't be so hard on Max. On that note, don't be so hard on yourself either. Legally, you're adults, and I know young people think they know everything, but for the record, no one expects you to have all the answers. Okay?"

"Okay." Aiden sniffled. "Thanks, Dad."

"No problem." He gave the now-full pot a stir with a wooden spoon. "I don't need any more help in here if you want to go do something else. Maybe go down to the game room?" His tone was pointed. Max must be down there.

Aiden got the hint. "Yeah, I think I'll do that." He trudged reluctantly away. Dad had made some good points, but that didn't mean Aiden was looking forward to talking to Max. If this time went anything like the last few times . . .

He made his way down the stairs and found Max in his usual spot on the sofa. Max glanced at him briefly before directing his attention back at the TV without a word. Silence was a marked improvement over yelling, at least.

Feeling strangely like he was at a job interview, Aiden sat on the opposite end of the couch. Max had a bag of chips open next to him and some baseball game playing on the TV. Aiden had always found that interesting about them: one of them watched sports but had no interest in playing while the other was the opposite. He considered making some sort of joke to break the ice, but nothing was forthcoming.

Instead, he asked, "Who's playing?"

Max shot him a sidelong look. "You don't know anything about baseball."

"Well . . . maybe I'd like to learn."

Max was silent for a beat. "It's Team Rocket versus the Vampire Slayers."

Aiden furrowed his brow. "Those aren't real teams, are they?"

"Nope." He grinned.

Aiden couldn't help but smile back. "Very funny. You know, Team Rocket almost sounds like it could be a real thing."

Max made a strange face, but Aiden wasn't sure why. They fell into silence that was caught somewhere between uncomfortable and familiar. It reminded Aiden of all the times they'd argued in the past over much smaller issues. They'd mastered the art of ignoring each other while sitting in the same room.

That gave Aiden a thought. "You know we've lived together for twenty years, right?"

Max stopped midway through shoveling chips into his mouth. "Huh?"

"Most siblings don't spend that much time under the same roof. They move out when they're eighteen, and if there's an age gap, they spend even less time together. But us? We had bunk beds as kids, spent our teen years in the same house, and then when it was time to go to college, we rented an apartment together. We've never lived apart from each other except for that one year in the dorms, and even then we saw each other every day."

"What's your point?"

Aiden shrugged. "I dunno. I've been thinking about how easily you and I blew up at each other. Everything was fine one minute, and then it wasn't. Why was that?"

"You know my theory." Max sniffed. "Oliver."

"Be real, Max. Oliver couldn't have done all this. I think there are a lot of nuances to our issues, but one I've been ignoring is the fact that I'm going to a different school in a year."

"What's that got to do with anything?"

"Well . . . to be honest, I'm scared to leave you. It's been you and me since day one. When we left for college, I knew that if I made zero friends, I'd still have you. Soon, I'm going off on my own, and I won't have that safety net anymore."

"I thought that was what you wanted." Max's tone was bitter as black coffee. "I've been holding you back, remember? This is your chance to go off and be someone else. Someone besides my twin."

Aiden's chest clenched. "I know what I said, and I stand behind it, but . . . that doesn't mean I'm not going to miss you every single day. Aren't you a little scared of being on your own too?"

"No." Max paused. "I'm a *lot* scared. I've been avoiding thinking about it. If I pretend it's not going to happen, then maybe it'll go away."

Aiden laughed. "Same. That's the point I'm trying to make. I think as next year looms closer, you and I have been dealing with this on some level, but in different ways. You've been clinging to me, and I've been pushing you away. We're both trying to make it hurt less when the inevitable happens and we have to learn how to live separate lives."

Max fell silent, eyes bright in a way that made Aiden wonder if he'd teared up a little. After a minute, he shoved the bag of chips within Aiden's reach. "Way to get all sappy, dude. I blame all those foreign films you've been watching. They've made you *broody*."

Aiden figured that was as close to an olive branch as he was going to get right now. He ate some chips as a sign of goodwill, and they spent the rest of the evening in civil silence. They even managed to get through dinner without snarking at each other, though that might have had something to do with the hawk-like way their parents monitored their every exchange.

All in all, when Aiden went to bed that night, he felt as though progress had been made. He was optimistic that with a few more mature conversations, they could get this sorted out. And then Oliver would come back. The thought made Aiden wriggle with delight beneath his covers.

It sucks that we're losing these days together. We have so few left before the end of the summer. But if it'll make everyone happy and stop all this fighting . . .

Oliver had said not to call him until everything was fixed. Aiden wanted to respect that, but if he didn't give updates, how would Oliver know his feelings were being taken seriously? What if Aiden sent him a quick text?

He grabbed his phone off the nightstand and composed a message. *Hey, I know you said not to contact you, but I want to share the good news. Max and I did some talking after you left. We haven't worked through all our issues yet, but it went well. I think this whole thing will blow over soon. Which is good, because I miss you so much.*

He read it over to check his spelling and then hit Send. For half an hour, he pretended to care about his Facebook feed while he waited for a response. When none was forthcoming, and when exhaustion threatened mutiny, he went to sleep.

His alarm woke him at 8 a.m., same as always. He turned it off and immediately reached for his phone, cracking one eye open enough to see his notifications.

His heart almost stopped. He had a new text.

Please be from Oliver. Please be from Oliver.

Sure enough, it was. His heart sprouted wings and floated up into his throat. A second later, however, it came crashing down as he read the message. It contained the four words most feared by anyone who was in a relationship.

We need to talk.

"Uh-oh," Aiden said to his empty room. He texted back.

Sure. Want to meet up, or should I call you?

He stared at his screen for several minutes, tapping it so it would stay lit, but Oliver didn't reply. Eventually, Aiden rolled out of bed and got dressed just to have something to keep him from bursting out of his skin.

The second he heard a vibration, he dove for his phone so hard, his headboard smacked against the wall.

I want to do this in person, but I'm afraid I won't be able to. I don't know if I can handle a phone conversation either.

All the air left Aiden's lungs at once. Worst-case scenarios blared into his skull. He typed with trembling fingers.

Did you change your mind about breaking up with me?

The response was immediate, thank God.

No, not at all. I'm so sorry if I'm scaring you. There's something I have to do that I don't want to do, and it's hard.

Aiden was halfway through composing a response when another text popped up.

I'm going back to the city with my mom. She's picking me up in an hour and taking me home. I know summer's not over, but honestly, I think if I stay here, I'll be doing more harm than good. Max still resents me, and I don't want to be the carrot on the stick that encourages you to fix things with him. You should want to fix them because he's your brother. So, I'm leaving.

Aiden read the message three times in rapid succession before it sank in. Oliver couldn't leave right as things were looking up. On reflex, he hit the Call button.

The phone rang once before going to voice mail. He tried again, and the same thing happened. Oliver was rejecting his calls.

Aiden texted back. *Oliver, don't go. Max and I are doing so much better, and yesterday I realized I wanted to fix things because I genuinely missed him.*

Oliver replied right away. *How do I know you're not just saying that?*

Don't you trust me?

There was no response. In Aiden's head, he imagined Oliver turning to him and saying, *You've lied to me before.*

Shit. He tried a different approach. *Can't you give it a week? I'm sure everything will be fine by then.*

A minute passed. Then, *That's exactly the problem. In your head, you're already calculating how to do this quickly, not well. You and Max have serious, deep-rooted issues that can't be fixed with a wave of a magic wand. Deal with your shit, and deal with it knowing that when it's finished, I'm not some prize that'll be waiting for you. You need to prioritize your family over the guy you're dating.*

I am prioritizing Max, Aiden replied. *But you're so much more to me than the guy I'm dating.*

Aiden considered saying more, telling Oliver that he thought he was falling for him, but he couldn't. Desperate as he was to keep Oliver around, he wasn't going to sully the first time he said those words by doing it over text, during a fight. Besides, Oliver would think he was trying to manipulate him. He couldn't bear it if he confessed his feelings, and Oliver thought it was a cheap ploy.

His phone vibrated with another message, only this time it seemed more like a portent of doom.

I'm sorry. I wish I were strong enough to stay away, but I'm not. This isn't the end, though. When all is said and done, I'll be here, whether it's next summer or another ten years from now. I'm turning my phone off now. Goodbye, Aiden.

Despite Oliver's words, that sure felt like an ending. This couldn't be it. It couldn't.

Aiden climbed to his feet and wobbled unsteadily, his vision clouding over with tears. He had to fix this somehow. But what could he do?

He could drive to Oliver's house and beg him to reconsider.

No, that would make things worse. Oliver would be furious and even more convinced that leaving was the right thing to do.

He could let Oliver go, for now. In a week or so, when everything was better, he could call and ask him to come back. But Oliver couldn't keep uprooting his life and moving back and forth between the city and the suburbs. His parents would get fed up with that in no time, especially his dad.

If only it were simply physical distance threatening to keep them apart. Aiden could live with that. But there was emotional distance too. If Oliver wasn't speaking to him, how could they keep this budding relationship alive? When classes started again, and they both got caught up with school and friends, it'd be sure to wither and die.

Aiden couldn't afford to play a long game here. He needed to do something now, or he'd risk losing Oliver forever. A glance at the clock told him he had forty minutes left until Oliver's mom came to pick him up. He needed to think of something *fast*.

His body was urging him to act, to drive over to Oliver's house and scoop him into his arms, but he'd already nixed that idea.

A puzzle piece slotted into place in his head. *Maybe I can't go to Oliver. But there's someone who can.*

Aiden was up and out the door so fast, he didn't remember moving. He skidded to a halt in front of Max's door and opened it with such force, the hinges groaned in protest.

Max—who was sprawled across his bed—startled at the noise, blinked at Aiden, then squeaked like a mouse. He pulled his sheets up over his bare chest. "Dude, can't you knock?"

"Oh, calm down. I see you naked every time I take a shower." Aiden tossed his phone at him. "Read this."

"Is this some self-help article about overbearing siblings? Because it's too damn early for—"

"Just read the fucking text log, Max."

That woke Max up. He took the phone and tapped on it, blinking at the light from the screen. He scrolled up to the start of the conversation and read, eyes growing wider by the second. "Oh wow. He's leaving. Gotta say, I didn't see that coming."

"You have to stop him."

Max almost dropped the phone. "Me? Why me?"

"Because he won't listen to me, but he will to you."

"I don't want to stop him. He can go back to the city if he damn well pleases."

Aiden huffed. "You don't mean that. No matter how angry you are at me, Oliver is your friend. If he leaves, we might never see him again. Look me in the eye and tell me that's what you want."

Max's gaze immediately dropped back down to the phone screen. He seemed to be rereading the texts. "Do you really think he'll go, though? Seems a little extreme to derail his summer plans just to teach us a lesson."

"No, if Oliver says he's going, he's going. I've never known him to make empty threats, and he has this whole self-sacrificing streak. Normally, I find it endearing. I promise he's packing his suitcase right now. We have to act fast. There's time for you to get over there and convince him to stay."

"Didn't he say he's not coming back until we've fixed things? I dunno if you've noticed, Aiden, but shit isn't fixed between us. I don't see any reason why I should go over there and embarrass myself."

His words hit Aiden like a blow, and strangely, it felt like they dislodged something. Something that had been clogging up his chest. Words came bursting out of him before he could stop them.

"Max, I'm in love with Oliver."

Max blinked. "You're what?"

"I love him. I love him so much, it hurts. If he leaves, I don't know what I'll do. It could be forever this time. Please say you'll help. Not only for me, but for all three of us. It can't end this way."

Max wiped his mouth with the back of his hand. "I've suspected for a while now that you two are in love, but I wasn't expecting you to admit it so soon. Or to me. Once upon a time, I would have thought I'd be the first person you'd tell, but since that hasn't been the case in the past . . ." His tone was defensive, but his face was nothing but pain.

Aiden couldn't understand how he'd missed it before. Oliver had told him several times that Max was hurt, but he must've been refusing to see it. It was obvious to him now. All those things Max had said, all the times he'd lashed out . . . They suddenly made sense.

For being the alleged "smart twin," Aiden had been remarkably unobservant.

"I'm sorry." Aiden sat on the edge of Max's bed. "I mean it. I shouldn't have shut you out like I did. If I'd told you about Oliver and me from the start . . . but instead I kept things from you and pushed you away. Then I acted all shocked when you felt left out. Some brother I am, huh?"

Max eyed him. His expression was a mixture of suspicion and hope. "You mean that?"

"I do. I was so convinced this was all your fault, but I have an equal share of the blame. I'm willing to accept that."

"How do I know you're not saying all of this because you want my help?"

"Oliver said something similar. I guess I have a lot to prove before I regain your trust." Aiden tried for a joke. "We both know how stubborn I can be. I admitted I was wrong. Doesn't that show how serious I am?"

Max snorted and then looked angry with himself, like he hadn't meant to. "Do you still think I've been holding you back all these years?"

"Yes and no. I think you never missed an opportunity to take the lead, but I also think if I'd really wanted to strike out on my own, I would have done it sooner. It comes back to that whole safety-net thing. Blaming you was easier than examining my own actions. Or inactions, I suppose."

"I guess that's fair." Max appeared to consider his words before saying, "Honestly, I could have done more to encourage you. I treated you like my kid brother when we both know that's a joke. I guess I didn't want you to figure out what you ended up knowing anyway: you don't need me."

"I do need you, though, Max. I never should have said I don't. I love knowing there's someone who's always in my corner no matter what. I need your humor. I need your support. And I need you to get me to put on real clothes and leave the house every now and then, because otherwise I'll become one of those weird recluses with twelve pet reptiles who writes articles about how millennials are killing the sock industry."

Max laughed. "That's sweet of you to say. I suppose me and you have some work to do when it comes to setting boundaries, but if you're game, I'm game. Though I gotta admit, this seems a little convenient."

"'Convenient'? We fought for three straight days and sent Oliver running for the hills."

". . . You raise an excellent point. All right. I'll try to convince Oliver to stay. I gotta admit, it's a lot more fun having him around."

Aiden took his phone back and checked it. "We have twenty minutes left until his mom comes to get him. That's enough time to drive to Oliver's house."

"Not for nothing, but why does it have to be me again? You're his boyfriend."

"It's *because* I'm his boyfriend that I can't go. If I show up, he'll think I'm saying what he wants to hear. But if you go, he'll know you and I are on the road to recovery, and more importantly, he'll know that you don't actually blame him for all of this."

Max flinched. "Fuck. I guess I should apologize for that while I'm at it."

"You're a good person, Max." Aiden stood up and offered him his hand. "Let's get you on the road before it's too late."

Max eyed his hand. "I would take that, but I'm not wearing any underwear."

"Oh. Right. Maybe put some clothes on first, and then you can go."

"I think that'd be best."

Chapter 13: Max

Max rolled out of bed, shook himself awake like a dog, and threw on whatever items of clothing were closest. According to Aiden, Oliver was leaving with his mom for the city at 9 a.m. sharp. If Max broke every traffic law in the state of New York, he'd barely make it to his house in time.

He'd do it, though. He'd do whatever it took to get there. That was what big brothers were for, and there were things he needed to say to Oliver. Apologies he needed to make.

When he opened his bedroom door, Aiden was waiting for him outside. Impatience radiated from him in waves.

"Finally!" He grabbed Max's shoulder and steered him toward the front door. "Go, go, go!"

Mom and Dad were busy in the kitchen, as per usual. They glanced over as Aiden drove Max by like a plow.

"Where are you boys off to?" Dad asked.

"Nowhere," Aiden said without slowing down. "Max has somewhere he needs to be."

Max focused on not falling on his face. If he did, he suspected Aiden might pick him up and carry him bridal-style to the car.

When they got outside, Aiden pressed the keys into his hand. "Do you have any idea what you're going to say?"

"None whatsoever, and we don't have time to come up with a plan. I'm gonna have to wing it. Good thing that's my specialty." He unlocked the car, started to get in, but then turned back long enough to pull Aiden into a fierce hug. "I'll stop him, okay? I won't let you down."

"You won't," Aiden whispered, squeezing him back. "No matter what happens, you won't."

Max didn't want to let go, but he imagined he could hear a clock ticking in his head. He got into the car and sped off toward Oliver's. It felt like he was moving through Jell-O. Every red light made him grind his teeth, and the way he rolled through stop signs suggested he was actually in California.

After a gut-wrenching eternity, he pulled onto the correct street and raced up to Oliver's dad's house. He parked on the street and was about to jump out when he noticed something that pushed all the air from his lungs.

There were no cars in the driveway. Oliver's mom should have been here by now. Was he too late?

Please don't let him be gone already. Aiden will be crushed.

He stared at the dingy house, wondering what he should do. Before he could decide on anything, however, a black car appeared on the street. As he watched, it pulled into Oliver's driveway, and a woman with dark hair exactly like Oliver's got out. It'd been a hot minute, but Max recognized her from the handful of times she'd picked Oliver up when they were kids. That was his mom all right.

Max didn't know how the hell he'd beaten her there, but he wasn't about to start questioning miracles. As he watched, she stood next to her car, looking at the house like she was debating going in. After a moment, she pulled a phone out of her pocket and held it to her ear. She had a brief conversation with whoever answered and then hit a button on her keys, popping the trunk. The front door to the house opened a second later, and Oliver appeared, hauling a suitcase.

Seeing him jolted Max into action. He hopped out of the car and jogged over to them.

Oliver's mom spotted him first. "Don't even think about it, Aiden. Oliver said you might try to stop him, but we're leaving whether you like it or not."

"I'm not—"

"It's okay, Mom." Oliver eyed him warily. "It's not Aiden. It's Max." He tossed his suitcase into the trunk and shut it. When he turned back around, he was frowning. "What are you doing here?"

"Uh, well." *So much for winging it.* "I came to convince you to stay."

Oliver's mom bristled. "Absolutely not. He's coming home with me."

"She's right. I'm leaving. It's for the best." Oliver glanced at Max. "Though I gotta admit, I'm surprised to see you. I would think you'd be helping me pack."

Max looked down at his shoes. "Listen, I owe you an apology. I didn't mean to act like I don't want you around. You're my bro, and it wasn't fair of me to blame you for my issues. I hope you can forgive me." He peeked up.

Oliver gave him several once-overs, and with each pass, his expression grew more uncertain. "That's . . . shockingly mature of you, Max. Of course I forgive you. I know you didn't mean what you said. But that doesn't change anything. I still have to leave so you and Aiden can sort things out."

"That's why I'm here, though. We have sorted things out. Aiden and I are cool again."

Oliver shook his head. "You're only saying that because you want me to stay."

"Buddy, I love you and all, but if you think I'd drag my ass out of bed at this hour for you, then you've underestimated my laziness."

"Okay, so Aiden talked you into it."

"Exactly. If I were still angry at him, would I be doing him any favors? Would I risk getting my throat ripped out by your mom?"

He glanced at her, and she nodded as if to say *Damn straight.*

Oliver's frown deepened. "I guess not . . . but there's no way you guys fixed everything already. I stand by what I said. As long as things aren't right between you two, I can't be here. It'll be better if I leave."

"Oliver, seriously, I appreciate your willingness to martyr yourself in the name of brotherly love, but this isn't necessary. Aiden and I—"

"We don't have to listen to this," his mom butted in. "Oliver, tell your friend we're leaving. We have a long drive ahead of us, and I took time off work to come get you."

"Right, sorry." Oliver started toward the passenger side of the car, but then he stopped. When he looked at Max, his face flickered with uncertainty.

Max stared back at him, pouring every ounce of sincerity he had into his expression. "I have one thing I need to say. Hear me out, or you might regret it for the rest of your life."

Oliver hesitated for a moment longer before sighing. "Mom, this won't take long. I promise."

She grumbled but didn't object, folding her arms across her chest and leaning against the car.

Oliver nodded at Max. "You have one minute."

Showtime. Don't fuck this up.

Max took a breath. "You're right. Things aren't perfect between me and Aiden. But you know what? They weren't perfect before. Not before we reunited with you. Not before we left for college. Never. And no matter how many heart-to-hearts we have, they won't be. You know why?"

Oliver shook his head.

"Because family isn't perfect. You know that better than anyone. This isn't the last fight Aiden and I will ever have. We're going to need more than a summer to work through our shit. It's gonna take a whole lifetime. You're not the reason we fought, but you are the reason we realized we'd been stuck in our weird twin box for far too long. So for that, thank you."

Oliver didn't react, so Max continued. "I get why you think you need to leave—and I get that it's stressful for you to be around conflict—but Aiden and I are all right now, I promise. If you're leaving because you don't want to be around our problems anymore, fine. I'll wish you well after I've done the big-brother thing and berated you for breaking Aiden's heart. But if you think you're the problem, I'm telling you that you're not. My mom called you a good influence recently, and I think she was right."

Oliver looked conflicted.

Max held his breath. He didn't want to say too much and ruin his argument.

To his surprise, Oliver's mom broke the silence. "I have to say, he makes some good points."

That seemed to snap Oliver out of whatever moral limbo he'd been caught in. "Yeah, he does." He glanced at the trunk, where his suitcase was stowed. "Can I really stay though? I was so dead set on going. I told myself a hundred times that nothing would stop me."

Max shrugged. "Going made sense before. It doesn't now. There's nothing wrong with that. You accomplished your goal: getting me and Aiden to talk. And Ollie, dude, you should have seen him. You know what a stubborn ass my brother can be. He apologized and admitted he was wrong and everything. I probably could've gotten him to cluck like a chicken if I'd wanted."

Oliver laughed. "But you didn't, right?"

"Of course not. I didn't think of it in time." He winked. "But seriously, when Aiden thought he was going to lose you, I saw a different side of him. I think you've played a big role in helping him figure out who he is, and you've done the same for me. I owe you thanks for that too."

"I don't deserve any thanks. It was all of us."

"So, you believe me? You'll stay?"

"Well . . ." Oliver scratched his head. "I have to ask. You're definitely Max, right?"

Max blinked. "Huh?"

"I got you two mixed up the last time I saw you. What if you're Aiden doing an admittedly perfect Max impersonation to get me to stay? How do I know for sure?"

"Search your feelings, Ollie. You know it to be true."

"I'm gonna need a little more than a Star Wars reference to go on."

Max thought back on the past fourteen years, searching for something that only he and Oliver knew. There wasn't much. He could hardly think of a time when the three of them weren't all together.

A much more recent event popped into his head. "When you crawled through Aiden's window, before the whole kiss fiasco, you said you did it because it was 'your thing.' I have no idea what that means."

Oliver laughed. "Aiden does. And since he wasn't in the room to hear me say that, I guess that means you're really Max."

"Of course." Max grinned. "I'm the handsome twin, remember?"

Oliver's mom cleared her throat, bringing their attention to her. "'Kiss fiasco'?"

Oliver turned red. "Oh, um. That was . . ."

"Nothing," Max finished. "Nothing that we ever need to talk about again. Oliver, if you're ready, I'd like to take you back with me. There's someone who's dying to see you."

The last of the hesitation melted off Oliver's face. "Aiden. I want to see him too." He turned to his mom. "Will you murder me if I change my mind?"

She spent a long moment studying her son's face before shrugging. "No. I mean, I did drive two hours in rush hour to come get you, so I expect one hell of a Mother's Day card. But you're an adult, and it seems like you're in good hands."

"I'm sorry I made you come all this way."

She patted him on the cheek and then popped the trunk again. "It's okay. I was in labor with you for twenty-eight hours. This is nothing in comparison. Although, every time I trek out here to the 'burbs, I feel like I'm in *The Stepford Wives*. You and your boyfriend had better live in the city when you grow up."

"Deal. I guess I'd better take my suitcase inside." He pulled it out and turned to Max. "You wanna give me a hand?"

"Hell yeah!" Max threw a fist in the air and whooped. "The Three Musketeers are back together! Now our ultimate party summer can resume."

Oliver kissed his mom on the cheek. "Ignore him. He doesn't get out enough."

"Will do." She gave him a quick hug. "Call me if you change your mind. I'm not looking forward to telling your father you decided to stay. I can hear the crowing now."

"You're the best mom ever. Drive safe."

They waited until she'd driven away before Max took Oliver's suitcase. "Come on. Let's throw this inside, and then I'll drive you to our place. Aiden is going to *flip*."

A few minutes later, they piled into the car. The drive back home seemed to go at double the speed of the drive there. Max swore it was only seconds later that he pulled into the driveway—which was now devoid of Mom and Dad's cars—and killed the engine.

He glanced over at Oliver. "You eager to see Aiden?"

Oliver answered by flinging the passenger door open and scrambling out of the car.

Laughing, Max chased after him. They jogged up to the front door. Right as Oliver grabbed the doorknob, Max caught him by the shoulder. "Wait."

Oliver glanced at him. "If you're going to give me a pep talk, I don't need it."

"No, it's not that. How many opportunities like this do you get in your life?"

"What do you mean?"

"You're about to be reunited with your childhood sweetheart for the second time. Don't you want to make a spectacle out of it?"

"Um. I guess? What did you have in mind?"

"I'll go in first and talk to Aiden. I'll act like I didn't make it in time, and you were already gone when I got there. Then, when the time is right, you can walk in and surprise him. Imagine the look on his face! He'll be even more thrilled to see you."

Oliver stared at him with wide, incredulous eyes. "You want me to toy with Aiden's emotions? That's deceitful. And cruel. And morally dubious." His face warped into a grin. "I love it. Let's do it. How will I know when to make my entrance?"

"If I know Aiden, he's watching the front door, waiting for us. When I go in, I'll leave it cracked so you can hear what we're saying. Then all you gotta do is choose your moment. Okay?"

"Okay." Oliver stood off to the side near some potted plants, out of view of the door. When he was in position, he gave Max a thumbs-up.

Max screwed up his best disappointed expression and walked inside. As he'd predicted, Aiden was sitting on the sofa in the living room beyond the entryway.

As soon as he saw Max, he sprang to his feet and bounded over to him. "Well? What happened?"

Max closed the door behind him, leaving an inch of space. Then, summoning up all the hammy overacting he'd learned from that one theater class he'd taken, he looked at his brother. "Aiden . . . I'm so sorry."

Aiden breathed out, making the smallest, most broken sound. "He wouldn't listen to you?"

"I never even got to talk to him. I was too late. By the time I got there, the house was empty. There weren't any cars in the driveway or anything." That last part wasn't a lie. Max paused for effect. "I knocked on the door and called his name, but he'd already left." He sucked in a breath and hung his head. "I'm so sorry, Aiden. I let you down."

His speech was followed by thunderous silence. It took everything he had not to peek up and ruin the illusion. Just as he started to get antsy, he heard a noise that sounded suspiciously like a sob.

He broke character and raised his head. "Aiden?" To Max's complete and utter shock, tears were rolling down Aiden's cheeks. Max dropped the act and took him by the shoulders. "Oh my God, Aiden. Are you okay?" *Now, Oliver. Now's your chance.*

Aiden sniffed. "I'm fine. But I'm also . . . sad and angry and heartbroken."

Max couldn't help but ask, "You're not angry with me, are you?"

"No, you tried your best. I'm angry at myself. This is all my fault."

"It's not, Aiden. We all played a part in—"

Aiden shook his head. "I drove him away. If I'd been smarter, or more mature, I could've fixed this. But I let my own pettiness get in the way, and now, I may never see Oliver again. I might never get the chance to tell him I love him."

Max's heart skipped a beat. *Oh shit.*

Right on cue, the front door burst open, and Oliver strode in. His green eyes were huge, and his mouth was slack as if someone had slapped him. "You love me?"

Aiden gasped and clapped both hands over his mouth. "Oliver?"

Max managed a clumsy smile. "Surprise."

But Aiden wasn't looking at him. He was staring at Oliver as if all his dreams had come true. They moved together like magnets, like planets that had abandoned the sun so they could orbit each other instead.

"Did you mean what you said?" Oliver reached out and touched Aiden's chin. "Do you love me?"

Aiden still had tears in his eyes. He swallowed. "I do. I love you, Oliver."

Oliver exhaled sharply before grabbing the back of Aiden's neck and kissing him. Against his lips, he mumbled, "I love you too, Aiden. I love you so much."

Max looked up at the ceiling. *Well, this is awkward.*

It occurred to him that he was officially intruding on a private moment, and he should probably leave. An odd emotion kept him frozen in place, however. He'd gotten very familiar with jealousy in the past week, but now he was encountering a new facet of it: no one had ever looked at him the way Aiden was looking at Oliver right now. And vice versa. It was like they could see something written on the other's face that no one else could read.

For the first time in his life, Max realized he wanted that. *Really* realized it. He wanted to love someone the way these two loved each other: in ways that were healing. Max thought that might be the truest expression of love he'd ever seen. If his unmovable brother and quiet best friend could find someone that made them want to grow, there was hope for them all.

Max almost said something to that affect, but he doubted they would hear him. They were too busy making out, and the kissing was getting . . . intense.

I think that's my cue.

"I'll, um, go hang out with some friends," he announced to no one in particular. "Leave you two lovebirds alone."

Keys in hand, he exited the house, shutting the door tightly behind him. He did *not* want to hear any stray sounds from inside.

What now? You're on your own, Max Kingsman. What's going to be your first official act without Aiden by your side?

Now that he thought about it, he'd never reached that girl from the arcade. What was her name? Danielle?

He pulled his phone out of his pocket. "If you want true love, you have to start somewhere." He found her name in his contacts and hit the Call button as he made his way to his car.

She answered on the third ring. "Hello?"

"Hey, Danielle? It's Max, from the arcade. Remember me?" He paused, listening to her response. "Yup, the guy with the gay twin. That's my baby brother all right. You wouldn't happen to be free for lunch would you?"

Chapter 14: Oliver

If it was possible to die from happiness, Oliver was about to flatline. It felt so good to have Aiden in his arms again. When he'd decided to leave, it was like the world had grayed around him, but now it was back to full color. The sunshine seemed brighter, and the warmth of Aiden's body set his nerve endings on fire. Even the soapy-sweet smell of his skin seemed sharper. Oliver buried his face in Aiden's curls and breathed deeply, trying to soak him in.

But Aiden was apparently too impatient to allow that for long. He found Oliver's mouth again and drew him into a deep kiss. The emotion behind it left Oliver breathless. He didn't care that they were making out in the middle of Aiden's living room. He wrapped his arms around Aiden and pulled Aiden firmly against him.

Aiden gasped and murmured something against his mouth.

Between kisses, Oliver asked, "What?"

"I said I'm so glad you didn't leave." Aiden leaned away and looked at him with eyes that were bright crystal blue in the morning light. "I love you. I never want to let you go."

Oliver cupped his face with one hand while the other settled on his waist. "I'm here. Do you want to talk about what happened?"

"Later." Aiden took both of Oliver's hands and stepped back, tugging him along. "Right now, I want you. I want to be as close to you as I can be. Is that okay?"

Oliver, who had been fighting back a rising tide of desire since he'd walked through the door, followed without complaint. "Your parents aren't home?"

"They're at work. We have the whole place to ourselves." Aiden led him to his bedroom. The curtains were drawn, letting sunlight spill over the furniture and bed.

Before Oliver could do more than take his shoes off, Aiden took him by the shoulders and guided him back, pushing him onto the bed. Oliver recognized that move: he'd done the same thing to Aiden the first time they'd had sex.

Oliver propped himself up on his elbows. "I like this assertiveness." Aiden's duvet had been heated by the sun. It felt amazing, as warm and welcoming as the man in front of him.

"Good." Aiden stood in front of him, their knees almost touching. With a grin, he fingered his belt. "Because you're going to be seeing a lot more of it." He undid the buckle in one smooth movement but didn't remove the whole thing. Instead, he opted to leave it hanging in the loops while he worked open his fly. The bulge between his legs was visible long before he unzipped.

Oliver's mirth melted away and was replaced with raw need. "Shit." His eyes roved over Aiden from head to toe. Aiden seemed content to let him look. He even hooked one of his thumbs into a front pocket, which pushed his jeans down farther and drew attention to his clothed erection.

Oliver swallowed. "That has no right to be as hot as it is. When did you become a sex god?"

"What can I say?" Aiden stepped between Oliver's spread legs. "You bring it out in me."

Suddenly, the amount of clothing Oliver was wearing seemed unacceptable. That needed to be fixed *now*. He whipped his shirt off and tossed it away like it was on fire. Aiden took the cue and did the same, only he made a spectacle of it. He moved slowly, peeling his shirt off his frame. Oliver nearly salivated. Aiden wasn't as broad as him, but lacrosse had made him rip-cord lean. Tight and compact, but still with a fair amount of muscle.

Oliver couldn't decide where to look. Luckily, Aiden made the decision for him. He pushed his pants down to his thighs, underwear and all. It occurred to Oliver, as Aiden's cock bobbed up and slapped his stomach, that he hadn't given it the attention it deserved last time.

Seeing it standing straight out from Aiden's groin, glistening at the ruddy head, made his mouth water.

He reached out to touch it, but Aiden pushed his hand away. "Not yet." He slipped his fingers down Oliver's bare stomach, pausing to swirl one around the ocean tattoo, and went for Oliver's jeans. It took everything Oliver had to not rut against Aiden's hand when it came close to his cock.

The zipper seemed to burst open, the pressure from Oliver's erection was so great. He lifted his hips so Aiden could slide his clothing down, leaving him bare. He expected Aiden to pull them all the way off, but as soon as his cock was free, Aiden eyed it in a hungry way that made Oliver's blood hot.

Before Oliver could react, Aiden lowered his head and licked a long, wet stripe up the underside of Oliver's cock. Oliver jolted like he'd been shocked. Fuck, he was more turned on than he'd thought. He actually felt his dick twitch against Aiden's tongue.

Aiden sucked in a breath and made like he was going to sink his mouth down on Oliver's cock.

Oliver collected the tattered remains of his self-restraint and waved him off. "No, wait. Don't."

Aiden froze, mouth hovering inches away. "Sorry. Was that not good?"

His breath tickled the head of Oliver's dick, making him shudder. "That's *phenomenal*. But I'm way too turned on for that. I don't want to come too soon, and we shouldn't do anything without a condom."

"Oh, okay." Aiden bit his lip sheepishly, but when he met Oliver's gaze, he was grinning. "Sorry about that. You looked so good, I couldn't resist."

Oliver groaned. "You're going to be the death of me. Get up here." He didn't wait for Aiden to comply. He sat up, grabbed him under each arm, and hauled him onto the bed. Aiden laughed but quickly grew serious once their faces got close. Oliver lay back, settling Aiden's weight on top of him, and stroked his sides.

"See?" Oliver breathed. "I don't always end up on top."

Aiden nodded, breath coming in pants. He kicked his clothing the rest of the way off, and Oliver followed suit. The skin-to-skin contact added a level of intimacy that made Oliver's head spin.

When he leaned in for another kiss, Aiden met him halfway. His bare chest felt so good on top of Oliver, not to mention how it felt when Aiden slotted their hips together and thrust gently. The motion was unhurried, as if they had all day, but Oliver wasn't in the mood to draw this out. He was naked in bed with the man he loved. He wanted to be as close to Aiden as he could get.

Aiden shifted, and his hard, leaking cock brushed up against Oliver's just right. Oliver officially ran out of patience. He grabbed Aiden by the ass and hauled him closer as if he were weightless. "Come here."

Aiden whimpered and straddled him, thighs spread wide on either side of Oliver's hips. "You're strong."

"Consider it payback for that time on the roof."

Chuckling, Aiden bent down and kissed along Oliver's jaw to his throat. One hand found its way into Oliver's hair and tugged gently, getting him to expose more of his neck. Oliver squeezed Aiden's ass in encouragement until Aiden sucked on a mouthful of skin.

Oliver moaned and wriggled under Aiden's body. "That's good. Do it again, but lower this time."

Aiden obeyed, kissing down Oliver's shoulder until he reached his collarbone. "I remember when you bit me here before. Like this?" He mouthed it once with soft lips before his teeth latched on.

"Ah, perfect." Oliver was fighting the urge to rock his hips against Aiden, desperate as he was for friction. "Keep going. Please."

Aiden kissed down his chest, and to Oliver's delight, he gave one of his nipples a tentative flick of his tongue. Oliver moaned encouragingly. Aiden rolled his tongue over it while his hand found the other one and brushed it with the pad of his thumb.

Oliver couldn't hold off any longer. He was rock-hard, trembling with pleasure, and he had a beautiful, naked man on top of him. If they didn't have sex soon, he was going to faint.

Which brought Oliver to a question he'd been meaning to ask.

Oliver wet his dry lips. "Do you want to top this time?"

Aiden looked up at him and popped off his nipple. "You mean it?"

"Yeah. I'm sure there are lots of things you want to try."

"Do you want me to top, or are you offering to be fair?"

Oliver shrugged. "I don't care how we have sex. I'll take you any way you like."

"In that case . . ." Aiden's mischievous grin was back. "I do want to top. But maybe not in the way you're thinking."

Frowning, Oliver was about to ask for clarification, when Aiden opened his nightstand drawer and pulled out a condom and a brand-new bottle of lube.

He tossed the condom to Oliver. "Mind putting this on?"

Oliver didn't need to be told twice. He tore it open and was about to roll it on when he happened to glance at Aiden. Aiden had coated his fingers with lube and reached behind himself. Oliver couldn't see his hand, but judging by the way his breathing quickened and his eyes clenched shut, it wasn't hard to guess what Aiden was doing.

A frisson of arousal ran the length of Oliver's body before settling between his legs. Shit, that was hot. "You want some help with that?"

Aiden made a soft, needy sound and shook his head. "Won't take long. Since we had sex the first time, I've been practicing."

Fuck. Oliver was going to *burst*. He didn't think it was possible to come from so little contact, but if it was, he was dangerously close to finding out. He had to take several deep breaths before he was willing to risk touching himself long enough to put the condom on. After that, he kept his eyes on the ceiling and did long division in his head, though nothing could drown out the small, pleasured noises Aiden was making as he worked himself open.

After a moment, Oliver heard a slick sound, and the moaning stopped. He chanced a glance at Aiden. "Need me to do anything?"

"Stay there." Aiden shuffled up his body until their cocks were flush. "You're right where I want you."

"Oh fuck." Oliver whimpered as he realized what Aiden had planned. "You're going to ride me, aren't you?"

"If it's all right with you."

"Fuck yeah." Oliver took the lube, added some to his hand, and slicked his cock before holding the base. "Go slow, okay? You have more control like this, but you shouldn't try to take me all at once."

Aiden nodded, raising onto his haunches. He lined himself up with Oliver's cock, and his hand joined Oliver's at the base. Together, they held Oliver steady as Aiden lowered himself. The head of

Oliver's cock met with some resistance, but after a second, it popped past the ring of muscles and into velvety heat.

Oliver groaned helplessly. He grabbed Aiden's thighs and squeezed, feeling his muscles. They were taut from the effort of holding him steady. "Fuck, Aiden, that's perfect."

Aiden's eyes were half-lidded, his lips kiss reddened and parted as he panted for breath. "I want more."

"Go slow. I mean it. You— *Ah*." Despite Oliver's warning, Aiden thrust his hips downward and took almost all of Oliver at once. Oliver couldn't find it in himself to be angry; it felt so incredible. His eyes slammed shut, and his head fell back. "Jesus. Don't move."

"I can take it."

"Maybe you can, but I need a minute." Oliver moved his hands to Aiden's hips and held him still in case he got any ideas about disobeying. Oliver couldn't believe how close he was to coming, and they were only getting started. "Good. So good. I—"

Aiden touched Oliver's face. "Look at me."

Oliver cracked an eye open.

He leaned down and kissed the corner of Oliver's mouth. "You're amazing."

"You too." He turned his face to catch Aiden's lips.

Smiling, Aiden ground his hips in a slow circle. "Can I move now?"

"Yeah, but *please*, go slow."

Aiden mercifully obeyed, sinking the rest of the way down on Oliver's cock and pausing to adjust before he made an experimental gyrating movement. He steadied himself with a hand on Oliver's chest and lifted up, thigh muscles flexing beautifully, only to cant down again.

Oliver watched his cock slide in and out of Aiden's body with nothing short of wonder. "That's perfect. You can go faster when you're ready. Figure out what feels good."

Aiden whimpered and rocked his hips shallowly. "Everything feels good. It's hard to concentrate. I dunno if I can make this last."

"Thank God, because I sure as hell can't."

Aiden started moving faster, working himself up and down on Oliver's dick. He switched rhythms every minute or so, trying to find what worked for him. Oliver, for the most part, was happy to lie back and let him experiment, but he kept his hands on Aiden's hips, guiding him when he faltered. Pleasure was clouding his brain with every thrust. He hoped Aiden really was close, because he was hanging on by a thread.

Almost as soon as he thought that, Oliver rolled his hips up without meaning to, and Aiden cried out as Oliver's cock slid deeply into him.

"Oh fuck." Oliver sat up a bit. "Did I hurt you? Was that too much?"

"No, it was good." Aiden grasped at his shoulders and trembled. "That angle . . . Do that again."

Oliver sucked in a breath. "Like this?" He rolled his hips, like he had before, setting a steady rhythm. When Aiden sank down on Oliver's cock, Oliver pushed up, fucking him hard.

Aiden let out a sound so loud and resonant Oliver felt it in his bones. "Fuck. Oliver, yes. Don't stop. That's feels— I'm so— *Oh God.*"

Now that they knew what to do, they set a furious pace. Soon they were both moaning, sweat dripping between their bodies. At some point, Oliver gripped Aiden's cock and pumped him sloppily.

After a particularly hard thrust, Aiden convulsed on top of him. Oliver thought he was coming and pulled his hand away, but Aiden merely shivered. "Oliver, I'm close. I'm so close. I need . . ." He made a frustrated sound. "I don't know what I need, but I'm right there."

Oliver sat up, bringing Aiden into his lap, and kissed him. Aiden was still moving, but it was more of a grind now. He was whimpering and shaking, his cock leaking freely. Oliver had never seen someone suspended this close to orgasm before. From his flushed skin to his damp curls, Aiden was lewd and beautiful.

"Whatever you want, Aiden." Oliver kissed as much of him as he could reach, speaking against his skin. "I'll do anything. Want me to suck you off? Or keep fucking you until you come?" He reached between their slick bodies and took hold of Aiden's cock again. This time, he stroked him in earnest.

Aiden made a helpless noise. "I want . . . I want . . ." He swallowed, and his eyes cleared. He picked up the rhythm again, fucking himself in Oliver's lap. "Say it. I want to hear it."

It took Oliver a moment to get what Aiden meant—he was a little distracted, after all—but as soon as he realized what Aiden wanted, fire swept through him. "I love you, Aiden. I love you so much."

Aiden cried out, sounding utterly shattered, and a second later, he came all over Oliver's stomach. His rhythm fell apart at the same time, and the noises that dripped from his lips were sweet as honey.

Oliver was convinced the sight of Aiden alone could have tipped him over the edge, but it helped that he'd been close for what felt like years. Whatever the cause, Oliver's orgasm *descended* on him. It hit so hard and fast, his vision blurred. He had a vague memory of thrusting up into Aiden one final time, and then his body stiffened. The pleasure that ripped through him blotted out all thought.

He had no idea how much time actually passed, but when he came back down, he'd fallen onto the mattress with Aiden on top of him. They were both breathing hard, their chests rising and falling in a pattern similar to their sex.

Oliver might have lain there for the rest of his life, but after a minute, Aiden stirred.

"Fuck," he said, seemingly to himself, before he slid carefully off Oliver and rolled to the side. "That was so intense."

Oliver grunted in agreement. "Getting you to curse is how I know I've done my job."

Aiden lay flat on his back, hands folded over his sweaty chest, and didn't respond.

Oliver summoned up the strength to remove the condom and throw it in Aiden's bedside trash can before he snuggled up to Aiden's side. "You all right?"

"Yeah. Better than all right."

"You look like you're thinking about something."

"Honestly?" Aiden wet his lips. "I don't want to be cliché, but I was thinking that I've never felt anything like that before."

Oliver kissed his cheek, heart fluttering. "You liked being on top, huh?"

"That's not what I mean." Aiden rolled onto his side to face him. "Obviously, I haven't slept with anyone but you, but even I can tell what we have is different. I've masturbated before. I've given myself *really* good orgasms. But *that*. That was . . ." He trailed off like he couldn't find the words.

"Yeah." Oliver closed his eyes and pressed their sweaty brows together. "I'd heard before that sex is better when you're in love, but I thought that was a myth. A fairy tale."

"So—" Aiden trailed a finger down his chest "—I take it you've never been in love before?"

Oliver opened his eyes. "Not like this. Feels like a dream. Aiden Kingsman is finally mine."

"I know exactly what you mean."

For a moment that seemed to stretch on forever, they lay together, quiet and satiated.

Eventually, Aiden yawned, his dark eyelashes drooping over his eyes. "I could sleep for a year."

"Same, but we can't. This is what we get for always having day sex. What if your mom decides to surprise us with lunch again?"

Aiden's eyes flew open. "I'm awake."

Oliver laughed. "We should talk about what happened. But first, come here." He slipped a hand under Aiden and pulled him against his chest, wrapping his arms around him. "Much better."

"Did I mention it's really hot how you can move me around like that?" Aiden wriggled against Oliver. "I might return the favor later."

"I know you can." Oliver skimmed a hand down Aiden's back. "I still remember you doing that to me on the roof, the first time we kissed. You inspired me."

Aiden made a small sound. "Keep touching me like that, and there's going to be a round two."

"Tempting. We really should talk, though. What happened with you and Max this morning?"

"We talked everything out. It's not all fixed, but we'll get there. What about you? What did he say when he showed up to stop you from leaving? Was your mom mad?"

"Max gave a stirring speech. I was actually impressed. And Mom was more irritated than mad. She'll get over it when I tell her the good news."

"News?"

"Yeah, that I have a boyfriend I'm crazy about." He kissed Aiden's cheek. "Unless you're not ready to make it official?"

"Oh, I'm ready. I want to skywrite it over New York City. My parents will be thrilled too, you know. They love you."

"And I love your whole family. That's why I was so scared when I thought I was causing problems."

Aiden shook his head. "You weren't. You were a huge help, actually. And on a personal note, I'm glad we went through all those ups and downs, because it helped me grow into someone who can be in a real relationship."

"Same. I didn't realize how much baggage from my parents I was holding on to." Oliver chewed on his bottom lip, thinking. "It's funny: I always kind of thought they gave me warped ideas of what love and marriage are, but now I see they taught me how to tell when something is real. When it's worth fighting for."

Aiden made a contented humming sound. "Looks like we all learned something. I dunno about you, but I'm excited for the rest of summer."

"Absolutely. It's gonna be a whole different ball game now that we're no longer split into teams. It's not the Kingsman twins and Oliver anymore, or us as a couple and then Max. We're Oliver, Aiden, and Max. Three separate people."

"If I had a drink, I'd say cheers to that. There's one more thing to consider, though."

"What's that?"

Aiden turned his head to look at him. "What are we going to do when the summer ends? Max and I will be heading back to Westchester, and you'll be in the city. We aren't going to be able to see each other easily."

Oliver shrugged. "I'm willing to make it work if you are."

"I'm willing. It just kinda feels like yet another roadblock in our way."

"It's a temporary one, though. I can see it now. We can visit each other on weekends when we're free, and we'll have time off for Thanksgiving. Same for winter break and then spring break. After that, it'll be summer again. We'll only have to go a month at a time max without seeing each other, and in the meantime, there's Skype." He grinned. "And phone sex."

Aiden laughed. "That does have a certain ring to it."

"Plus, after next year, you're transferring, right? Brooklyn and Queens aren't that far away. We'll be able to see each other whenever we want."

"That's true. I'll finally learn to take the subway without getting lost."

Oliver hesitated, drawing little soothing patterns on Aiden's skin with his fingers. "You know, since we're talking about the future . . ."

Aiden quirked a brow. "Yes?"

"I live with my mom right now. The city's too expensive for me to get my own place. I was thinking . . . if we're still going strong in a year, we could get a place together. Somewhere between our schools, maybe."

Aiden inhaled sharply. "You mean it?"

"Only if you're not freaked out. If you're freaked, then I'm totally joking."

"I think it sounds like a great idea." Aiden put one of his hands over Oliver's. "It might be a bit soon to think about that, but a year from now? Absolutely. If we can survive long-distance, then I bet we can survive anything. Do you suppose the time will fly or drag?"

Oliver thought about it for a second. "Both. The times we're apart will be agonizing, but that will make the reunions all the sweeter. And hey, we've waited this long. What's one more year?"

A smile spread across Aiden's face, warm and golden as a new day. "You're worth waiting for."

In that moment, Oliver felt such perfect, complete happiness, he could scarcely breathe.

epilogue: Aiden

Three Years Later

On a sunny afternoon in mid-October—when the sky was clear, autumnal blue, and crunchy leaves littered the ground—Aiden Kingsman got married.

Granted, he would have been fine going to a courthouse, and the big church ceremony was really for the benefit of their families. But it was still a momentous occasion.

Standing in one of the back rooms of St. Peter's Chelsea, mere steps from where he'd soon stand before a priest and almost everyone he knew, Aiden studied himself in an antique full-length mirror. Light streamed through the white curtains undulating by the windows, bathing his features in a warm glow.

He looked good. Maybe a little pale, but there was excitement sparking in his eyes, and as he slid a blue silk tie around his neck, his fingers were steady. His three-piece tux was a navy affair that brought out the color of his eyes, and his curls had been tamed with product, courtesy of his mother.

There were times when he glanced in mirrors and couldn't quite see himself. Sometimes, he saw flashes of Max instead, or he saw one of the younger versions of himself he'd left behind as childhood had melted into adulthood. But today, when he studied his reflection, he saw himself as he was right now. A man who was not just ready, but eager to take one of life's biggest steps.

His phone buzzed in the pocket of his suit jacket, dragging him from his reverie. He pulled it out.

Nervous?

Aiden smiled at the message from his husband-to-be and typed back, *Maybe a little. But that's because of the crowd, not because of what we're about to do.*

It's not too late for us to sneak out the back and elope. I hear Vegas is lovely this time of year.

Aiden snorted. All these years later, Oliver could still get a laugh out of him no matter what.

My mother would hold us down, and yours would murder us.

Touché. Can't wait to see you out there, love. In a few short hours, you're going to be stuck with me forever.

Aiden's heart fluttered. *Can't wait.*

He put his phone away, walked over to the heavy door, and pushed it open so he could peek out at the church. It was a lot fuller than it'd been ten minutes ago, when he'd last sneaked a look. Throngs of people were gathering at the pews, chatting and laughing. The dull cacophony rose all the way up to the large wooden ceiling beams.

A wave of nervousness hit him. He let the door fall shut and glanced back at the mirror, checking himself for flaws. His tie was straight, he had his father's old, blue, and borrowed handkerchief folded neatly in his pocket, and a delicate white rose had been pinned to his lapel. Basically, all that was left for him to do was show up, stumble through his vows, and sign a piece of paper that would change his life forever.

For the better.

Even his nervousness couldn't drown out the effusive excitement coursing through him.

The door creaked open. Aiden whirled around, hoping irrationally that it was Oliver, but Max's head popped into view. He had on a blue tie, same as Aiden's, but his suit was gray. Though they were identical, he pulled off the dove color and faint black pinstripe in a way Aiden never could.

"You ready, buddy?" Max grinned. "It's showtime."

Aiden blew out a breath and nodded. "I'm ready."

Max slung an arm around Aiden's shoulders and led him out. The church was bursting with white roses. Garlands of them lined the pews, and a huge arrangement had been placed on the altar. Dozens of lit candles adorned the alcoves. A rainbow of colored sunlight streamed through the stained-glass windows. Everywhere Aiden looked, people were smiling.

Max led him to the start of the aisle, where their parents awaited them. As soon as he appeared, the string quartet in the corner kicked up the soft music they'd been playing. People turned to look. Familiar heat took up residence in Aiden's face.

"I have to join the processional." Max squeezed Aiden's arm. "But when the time comes, I'll be right by your side."

"You memorized my vows, right?"

"Yup. I'm ready to feed them to you from the wings like an overeager understudy. Don't worry, though. You're going to do great."

Aiden nodded, though as soon as Max released him, he clasped onto his parents for dear life. They took up spots on either side of him like sentinels.

"Don't be nervous, honey," Mom whispered to him. "You're going to do great."

"Could you ease up on your grip a bit, though?" Dad shifted his arm. "You're gonna snap something."

Aiden took a breath and tried to relax. To no one, he said again with confidence, "I'm ready."

Mom and Dad walked him down the aisle while eighty guests looked on. Oliver's side of the church was packed with family members—judging by the sea of dark hair and tan skin—but Aiden's side was plenty full as well. He spotted distant family, old friends from college, and a dozen of his new coworkers. As it turned out, engineers loved to party, and when they'd heard quiet Aiden Kingsman was tying the knot, half his department had turned up for the occasion.

He made it to the end of the aisle without falling on his face, thanks to his parents' literal support. But they had to let go eventually. They murmured some final words of encouragement before patting him on the back and taking the seats reserved for them in the first pew.

Breathing unsteadily, Aiden climbed the three steps up to the rose-adorned altar. The priest flashed him an encouraging smile as he stumbled into place. "You're gonna do great. Love the suit."

"Thanks." *At least everyone seems to know I'm nervous about public speaking, not getting married. I bet that's Max's doing, somehow.*

To curtail his nerves, Aiden focused on the church itself. They'd selected a same-sex-friendly Episcopalian church. The towerlike exterior had all the regality expected of a wedding while the interior was warm and inviting. Through the decorative windows, Aiden caught glimpses of trees loaded with gold and red-brick buildings. It gave Aiden a sense of peace in the middle of the bustling city.

The music swelled again, gripping Aiden's attention with viselike fingers. With a rustle of fabric, the guests stood and faced the back of the church. Aiden straightened his posture and reminded himself to breathe.

The processional was short: there were no bridesmaids or groomsmen. Instead, Aiden had chosen Max to be his best man— big surprise there—while Oliver had picked a college friend, a blond twentysomething named Adam who resembled a dog, from his shaggy hair to his playful energy.

Max and Adam marched down the aisle together, arm in arm. They wore nigh-identical big grins on their faces that made Aiden's lips twitch in response. When they reached the end of the aisle, they split off to stand on their respective sides. Max paused long enough to touch Aiden's shoulder and shoot him a wink before he took up his spot beside him.

The warmth of his hand lingered on Aiden's shoulder, giving him an unexpected boost of confidence. The ring bearer appeared next: a cousin's child who'd inherited the Kingsman curls and looked like an actual cherub. He giggled his way down the aisle while the audience oohed and aahed. The flower girl—another child of a cousin, but from Oliver's side this time—appeared next in a white dress that offset her silky black hair.

And then finally . . . there was Oliver.

He appeared beneath the arch at the entrance to the church with his parents on either arm. Though Aiden had already seen him in his beautiful jet-black tux and green tie, there was no comparison to how he looked now. He wasn't simply beaming. He was *radiant* as his eyes swept over the crowd before landing unerringly on Aiden. As soon as they did, he perked up like a sunflower who'd found its own personal sun.

A shiver danced up Aiden's spine when their eyes locked, as it had a hundred times before on smaller occasions. Oliver started down the aisle—parents in tow—and Aiden prayed their photographers were getting him from all angles, because *that* was one for his work desk.

Oliver walked with confidence, gliding down the aisle like he'd done it a hundred times before. It was all in his gait, the set of his shoulders, and the relaxed smile on his face that said he was exactly where he wanted to be.

Aiden was mesmerized just watching him. As Oliver got closer, Aiden's eyes prickled, and he started chanting a mantra in his head: *don't cry, don't cry, don't cry.*

The flower girl walked too slowly, intent as she was on scattering rose petals with the tongue-between-teeth concentration of a six-year-old. Oliver's party soon caught up with her.

Rather than ignore her or try to walk behind, Oliver released his parents and scooped her into his arms. He carried her the rest of the way down the aisle while she squealed with delight and the onlookers cooed. Aiden damn near joined them.

When Oliver reached the steps, he set the flower girl down again, kissed both of his parents on the cheek, and walked up to join Aiden. As the distance between them closed, Aiden felt like he was going to float into the air, he was filled with such incandescent happiness.

Oliver took his place before the priest, a step or two away from Aiden. His smile was brilliant in every sense of the word. "Hi."

"Hi." Aiden was barely audible.

The priest seemed like he was fighting a smile himself. "Are you ready, gentlemen?"

After a quick exchanged glance, they nodded in unison.

The priest looked out over the assembly. "Friends and family, we are gathered here today in the name of commitment and love, to join these men in matrimony . . ."

The ceremony passed in a blur. Before their gathered loved ones, they swore to be honest and supportive, and to love each other beyond their last breaths. The sound of Oliver's earnest, "I do," when the priest asked if he would take Aiden as his husband finally broke Aiden's resolve not to cry.

Apparently, Aiden got through his vows just fine, but if he said a single word of English during the ceremony, it was news to him. They exchanged simple gold wedding bands, signed their marriage certificate with shaking hands, and shared their first kiss as a married couple.

The applause was deafening. Aiden had never guessed a small group of people could make so much noise. It only got louder when they strode hand in hand down the aisle. More people awaited them outside. When they appeared, they were showered with rose petals and cheers. Someone put a garland around Aiden's neck with a sign that read *Just* while Oliver got *Married*.

Laughing, they jogged down the sunlit street, shouting for the people pouring out of the church to join them at the reception. It was a few blocks away, and they took it at a dead sprint, never letting go of each other's hand. People on the street clapped and shouted congratulations as they passed, but Aiden could barely hear them over the sound of his own heart.

They didn't stop running until they reached the riverside restaurant they'd chosen for the reception. It had a huge dance floor and an outdoor deck that led right up to the water. Inside, mahogany tables had been decorated with blue-and-green centerpieces, and a swing band was setting up on the makeshift stage. Candles crowded every available surface, bathing the restaurant in flickering light. When the sun set in a couple of hours, it was going to be magical.

As soon as they entered, the maître d' greeted them and directed them to a back room where they would await their announcement.

Once there, Oliver squeezed his hand. "We did it, Mr. Kingsman. We're married. That went by so fast."

"I think so too, Mr. Kingsman." He leaned his head on Oliver's shoulder. "In a good way, though. Now we can get to the fun part."

"The reception?"

"The rest of our lives together."

Oliver kissed his brow. "Is there anything you would have done differently?"

"No. I could have been less nervous, but I wouldn't change a thing. What about you? Any regrets? We can still hyphenate if you've changed your mind about taking my name."

"Definitely not." Oliver held up his hand, and the ring on his finger glinted. "I'm a Kingsman now. The name Jones belonged to my parents, and it meant fighting and divorce. I was ready to leave that name behind. Besides"—he winked—"I've wanted to become one of the Kingsman brothers since we were kids."

Aiden reached around him and laced their fingers together so their rings lined up. "It seems we both got our wish."

They only had a moment to enjoy the privacy before they heard the sound of their friends and family filing into the hall. Not long after that, the MC's voice came over the speakers.

"Ladies and gentlemen, please join me in welcoming the newlyweds for the first time: Mr. and Mr. Kingsman!"

"That's us." Oliver had a huge grin on his face. Aiden was about to ask what was so funny when Oliver repeated, "That's *us*."

With their arms around each other, they exited the back room and walked out onto the dance floor. The crowd had gathered around the edges and was cheering them on. They took up a spot in the center and fell into a familiar embrace: one hand on the other's waist while they clasped their free hands together, like they'd practiced in rehearsal.

"And now," the MC continued, "the grooms will enjoy their first dance as a married couple."

The swing band struck up a slow but upbeat Frank Sinatra song. A handful of people waved at Aiden from the crowd, but he kept his attention on his husband.

"My face hurts from smiling so much," Oliver said. He stretched his mouth like he was trying to stop, but his lips slid right back up into a grin.

"You know, I never liked dancing before I met you." Aiden squeezed his waist. "It was those lessons you signed us up for that changed my mind. No matter how much I stumbled, you always caught me."

"And *you*, my rock, you never gave up." Oliver led him through an easy spin. "I expected you to go to one lesson to humor me. Imagine my surprise when you started waking me up on Sundays for dance class."

Aiden glided through a series of steps and then led Oliver through his own spin. It was impossible to tell which of them was leading, just as they'd planned. "It was more fun than I'd expected, like everything you've introduced me to over the years."

Oliver laughed. "That's sweet, but let's not forget about the oyster incident."

Aiden made a face. "Okay, maybe not *everything*. But most things."

The lead singer of the band—a beautiful blond woman with dark-brown skin—took to a Billie Holiday–style microphone and started singing.

Oliver pulled Aiden closer and sang the lyrics along with her softly, so only he could hear. His breath tickled Aiden's ear, soft and sweet. Aiden was suddenly in danger of crying again. Luckily, at the MC's behest, the rest of the wedding party joined them on the floor: both sets of parents and the best men, who brought the flower girl and ring bearer with them.

Max caught Aiden's eye and mouthed, *Nice moves.*

Thanks, bro, Aiden mouthed back.

"Oh, hey, there's the photographer." Oliver whirled Aiden around. "Smile!"

The photographer snapped at least a dozen photos of them. Then Oliver dipped him, which prompted another round of furious camera clicks.

"You are so theatrical," Aiden groaned when Oliver pulled him back up and the photographer drifted away.

"You're the one who insisted we learn how to do dips." Oliver nuzzled his cheek. "Did you really think I wouldn't seize the opportunity?"

The wedding party danced together until the song ended and the singer signaled to the crowd. They spilled onto the floor as well, some breaking into pairs, some hovering near the grooms, clearly eager to speak with them.

The next song started, and Aiden's mom decided hovering wasn't good enough. She dragged Dad over and danced right next to them, smiling from ear to ear. "How are my boys?"

Oliver smiled back. "We're wonderful, Kim."

"It's Mom now." She winked. "I always had a funny feeling you'd be a part of our family someday. Though I will admit, I didn't expect for Aiden to be the one to propose, and during Christmas dinner at our house."

"Mom," Aiden whined. "We know the story. We were there."

"I know, but I'm your mother. It's my job to embarrass you."

"I like hearing the story," Oliver said. "Especially the part where you were so panicked you fell over the second you got down on one knee."

Aiden looked heavenward and groaned. "This is what I get for marrying a family friend. I'll never be able to escape the embarrassing stories now."

"Wait until you have kids of your own," Dad said. "Then you'll get to embarrass them instead."

"Dad," Aiden whined again. "We've been married for fifteen minutes. Can we save the kid talk for after the honeymoon?"

Mom laughed. "Fine, we can take a hint. But just so you know, I've done a lot of research on gay adoption laws in the state of New York, and I'm ready to—"

"*Mom*, I swear. I will die, right here, on my wedding day."

"All right, sweetie. We'll talk later." She said that last part like it was a threat. "Congratulations again. Love you both."

They danced off, leaving Aiden and Oliver alone. Aiden was frowning, but Oliver was trying and failing not to laugh.

Aiden glowered. "It's not funny."

"It really is, love."

The song ended, and everyone applauded. The band struck up another one.

Oliver turned to him. "You want to keep dancing?"

"Yeah, but the crowd looks impatient." It was no joke. People were eyeing them like they were choice cuts of meat. "We can't put off greeting them forever."

"You're right." Oliver took his hand and kissed it. "If we split up, we can cover them in half the time."

Aiden paused before taking Oliver's face in his hands and kissing him square on the lips. "This is one of the many reasons why I married you. Because you're a *genius*."

They parted ways, each posting up to one side of the dance floor. Immediately, throngs of people flocked to them. Anxiety spiked through Aiden, but anytime he needed to, he glanced across the room at Oliver. Seeing the ever-present smile on Oliver's face was enough to quiet his nerves.

He mostly received Oliver's guests, and there were a *lot* of them. Aiden had thought he'd met a good chunk of Oliver's family over the years, but he was mistaken. They were a curious bunch too. They asked him everything from what he did for a living to his medical history.

What felt like fifty thousand handshakes later, the band announced that dinner was about to be served, and the crowd finally thinned.

Oliver appeared by his side as if by magic. "How was it?"

"Your family is . . . interesting." He paused. "I mean that in a positive way. They're very direct. And fast. I can handle embarrassing conversation, so long as it doesn't last. I think I'm going to get on with them just fine."

"Good. Your family was polite and charming, like you."

"Thank you. I think we handled that well, considering neither of us are extroverted. You ready to eat?"

"*Hell* yeah." Oliver held out his arm.

Aiden linked their elbows, and they made their way to a long table that was set up at the head of the room. They were facing the dance floor with their backs to the view of the water. Max had already taken his seat next to Oliver's place and was talking to Mom.

When they arrived, the MC announced it was time for the toasts. The guests quickly found their tables and quieted down. The waiters began handing out flutes of champagne.

As soon as everyone had one, Max stood up and clinked his glass with a knife. A hush fell over the assembly.

Max waited until all eyes were on him before flashing a wide grin. His voice carried easily over the crowd. "When Aiden asked me to be his best man, I knew I needed to write one hell of a speech. It was suggested to me that I start by saying how I know the grooms. Well, in Aiden's case, that much should be obvious."

The crowd laughed right on cue. Max waited for them to quiet again before he continued. "As for Oliver, I've known him since childhood, and it's been a pleasure watching him become the man he is today. Loving, kind, and willing to put others first, even at his own expense. Over the years, we've been through a lot, and now I have the privilege of calling him one of my closest friends. I couldn't imagine trusting Aiden's happiness to anyone else. Words can't describe how thrilled I am to welcome my new brother into the family."

There was awwing and scattered applause.

Max waited for silence once more. "Aiden and Oliver are a phenomenal couple for more reasons than I can name. They've known each other most of their lives. They complement each other. And they're the only two people I know who have strong opinions about the Oxford comma. But the main reason they work is this: when tough times inevitably come, they have a solid foundation of friendship to help them weather the storm.

"As some of you may know, they were in a long-distance relationship for a year during college. Hard as it was at times for them to be separated, they always found their way home. Every time classes let out for any length of time, I could expect to find Oliver waiting at our house. Eating our food, if I recall correctly."

More laughter. Max had the audience enraptured.

"When graduation rolled around, I had no idea what to do with my life, but these two had it all planned out. They got an apartment together in the city and settled down as if they'd been ready to spend their lives together from day one. I remember visiting their dinky place in Brooklyn and listening to Oliver talk about their new dishes while Aiden went on and on about the throw pillows they'd picked out. It was like they were talking about baby names.

"I'd never seen two people so thrilled to do mundane things, so long as they did them together. That was the first time I thought to myself, 'Not only are these guys going to get married, but they're going to be *so* happy.' I believe that with everything I have. Whether they have countless adventures or a quiet life together, they'll be happy."

The crowd applauded, and this time Aiden joined in. He peeked at Oliver for his reaction: he was dabbing his eyes with a napkin.

Aiden was about to stand up and hug his brother, when he realized Max hadn't raised his glass. His speech must not be over yet.

Sure enough, Max reached into his suit jacket and pulled out a crumbled piece of paper. It looked old, and it'd been folded and refolded so many times it was practically falling apart.

Max held it up for everyone to see. "A million years ago, my brother wrote these vows. This is authentic Aiden Kingsman crayon work right here." He pointed to the sloppy scrawl on the page while everyone laughed.

Aiden gasped and leaned toward Oliver. "Is that . . . Are those the vows I wrote for when we used to play marriage?"

Oliver grinned. "They sure are. Your brother asked me if I still had them when he started writing his speech."

"You really kept them all these years?"

Oliver winked and put a finger to his lips.

Max gently took the paper in both hands. "Even back when we were children, we wanted Oliver to become a part of our family. We held no fewer than a dozen fake weddings in which we welcomed him into our clan. Although, back then it was *me* who married Oliver. Needless to say, things didn't work out between us."

Aiden and Oliver chuckled along with the crowd.

"I'd like to read these vows to the newlyweds now and see if they still hold up." He turned to Oliver and read from the paper. "Do you, Oliver Jones—now Oliver Kingsman—promise to be a good new brother and to play with us every day forever?"

Oliver forced his face into a serious expression. "I do."

"And do you, Aiden Kingsman, promise to never hog the remote?"

Aiden feigned indignation and called back, "That was one time."

Max grinned. "Fair enough. This last vow is for both of you. Do you both swear—cross your hearts and hope to die—that you will always, *always* be the very best of friends?"

They looked at each other. In unison, they said, "We do."

"Then I'd like to raise a glass to the happy couple." Max held up his champagne. "Congrats, you two!"

The applause was deafening, almost as loud as when they'd gotten married.

Aiden tried to discreetly wipe tears from his eyes, but they rolled down his cheeks. He stood up and wrapped his brother in a tight hug.

A moment later, he felt another pair of arms join them. He heard Oliver whisper, "That was perfect, Max."

"Yeah, well." Max pulled back with a sniff and noticeably dewy eyes. "How often do you get to deliver a speech at the wedding of both your brother and your best friend?"

They retook their seats. Adam stood up and gave a stirring speech as well, but he kept it short and sweet, probably sensing that there was no following Max's act.

After that came food, alcohol, and all the congratulations they could stomach. As the evening wound down, Aiden found himself standing on the edge of the dance floor with Oliver on one side and Max on the other.

He surveyed the guests. "Looks like everyone's having a good time."

"Even my parents." Oliver waved at where they were dancing near the bar. "I can't believe they came as each other's dates. That might be the biggest show of solidarity they've ever put on for me."

They waved back, and Aiden blew Oliver's mom a kiss. She pretended to catch it and slap it onto Oliver's dad's cheek. He accepted it good-naturedly before twirling her away.

"It's amazing how a wedding can make everyone come together." Aiden turned to his brother. "Wonderful speech, Max. Thank you so much."

"I meant every word. It was easy to write, considering I practically had a fairy-tale romance to inspire me."

"I don't know about the fairy-tale part." Oliver took Aiden's hand. "It feels plenty real to me."

"Yeah, and that whole 'perfect' thing isn't true." Aiden gave his fingers a squeeze. "The other day we had a thirty-minute long fight about china patterns. But if that's our biggest problem, I think we'll be fine."

"I think you will too." Max looked wistfully up at the ceiling. "I have to admit, I'm jealous."

Aiden blanched. "Dude, no. We know what happens when you get jealous."

"Don't worry, I'm not gonna spike the punch or get drunk and make a second speech that totally ruins my first one. I meant that as a compliment. What you guys have . . . it's what we all want, you know? Some people spend their whole lives looking for that and never find it."

Oliver slung an arm around Max's shoulders. "You'll find it. You and your brother have so much love to give, someone is bound to fall head over heels. Trust me, it happened to me." He planted a kiss on Aiden's cheek.

Max crinkled his nose. "I'm gonna get cavities from how sugary sweet this whole day has been. Though I do wish there was a single bridesmaid at this wedding. Who am I supposed to dance with?"

Adam appeared as if summoned, brown eyes bright with excitement. "I *love* this song."

"Hey, Adam." Aiden let go of his husband long enough to point at his brother. "You want to dance with Max? Traditionally, the best man and maid of honor are supposed to pair up, but I think in this instance we can flout tradition."

Aiden was expecting Max to protest, but to his surprise, Max held out his hand. "Shall we?"

Adam took it. "It'd be my pleasure!"

Max started for the dance floor only to turn back. "Can I tempt you guys to come with us?"

Aiden looked to Oliver.

Oliver shook his head. "We're going to sit this one out. But thanks for the invite."

"Your loss." Max pulled Adam out onto the dance floor, and soon they disappeared into the sea of people.

Oliver indicated the outdoor deck with a nod of his head. "Wanna get some air?"

"I'd love to."

They opened the doors and made their way outside. The sun was setting over the water. Cool October air ruffled their hair, carrying the smell of autumn and the sea. There were a handful of other people around, but when they saw the grooms approach the wooden banister, they scurried back inside. Aiden made a mental note to write each of them a special thank-you card.

Oliver leaned on the railing and closed his eyes, as if he were soaking up the breeze. "I didn't think it was possible to be this happy."

Aiden sidled up next to him until he could feel heat against his side. "I did. I was almost this happy the first time we kissed. And the day you agreed to marry me."

Oliver stood up and wrapped his arms around Aiden's shoulders. "Today definitely takes the number-one spot, though."

"Do you suppose it'll hold that title for long?"

"At least until we adopt those kids your mom was talking about."

Aiden laughed. "You're as bad as she is." He pressed their foreheads together. "I love you, Oliver Kingsman. More than I can say."

"I love you too, Aiden Kingsman." Oliver brought their mouths close. "You know, I think our childhood vows were better than the ones we said in the church. How did that last part go again?"

"We will always," Aiden began.

"*Always,*" Oliver echoed.

Together, they said, "Be the very best of friends."

As the sun cast ribbons of gold onto the water, and a room full of their friends and family danced nearby, they shared a kiss that held the promise of a happy ever after.

Dear Reader,

Thank you for reading Quinn Anderson's *Fourteen Summers*!

We know your time is precious and you have many, many entertainment options, so it means a lot that you've chosen to spend your time reading. We really hope you enjoyed it.

We'd be honored if you'd consider posting a review—good or bad—on sites like **Amazon, Barnes & Noble, Kobo, Goodreads, Twitter, Facebook, Tumblr,** and your blog or website. We'd also be honored if you told your friends and family about this book. Word of mouth is a book's lifeblood!

For more information on upcoming releases, author interviews, blog tours, contests, giveaways, and more, please sign up for our weekly, spam-free newsletter and visit us around the web:

Newsletter: tinyurl.com/RiptideSignup
Twitter: twitter.com/RiptideBooks
Facebook: facebook.com/RiptidePublishing
Goodreads: tinyurl.com/RiptideOnGoodreads
Tumblr: riptidepublishing.tumblr.com

Thank you so much for Reading the Rainbow!

RiptidePublishing.com

Also by
Quinn
anderson

Murmur Inc. series
Hotline
Action
Cam Boy

New Heights
On Solid Ground
All of the Above
The Other Five Percent
In Excess

about
the author

Quinn Anderson is an alumna of the University of Dublin in Ireland and has a master's degree in psychology. She wrote her dissertation on sexuality in popular literature and continues to explore evolving themes in erotica in her professional life.

A nerd extraordinaire, she was raised on an unhealthy diet of video games, anime, pop culture, and comics from infancy. Her girlfriend swears her sense of humor is just one big Buffy reference. She stays true to her nerd roots in writing and in life, and frequently draws inspiration from her many fandoms, which include *Yuri on Ice*, Harry Potter, Star Wars, *Buffy*, and more. Growing up, while most of her friends were fighting evil by moonlight, Anderson was kamehameha-ing her way through all the shounen anime she could get her hands on. You will often find her interacting with fellow fans online and offline via conventions and Tumblr, and she is happy to talk about anything from nerd life to writing tips. She has attended conventions on three separate continents and now considers herself a career geek. She advises anyone who attends pop culture events in the UK to watch out for Weeping Angels, as they are everywhere. If you're at an event, and you see a 6'2" redhead wandering around with a vague look on her face, that's probably her.

Her favorite authors include J.K. Rowling, Gail Carson Levine, Libba Bray, and Tamora Pierce. When she's not writing, she enjoys traveling, cooking, spending too much time on the internet, playing fetch with her cat, screwing the rules, watching Markiplier play games she's too scared to play herself, and catching 'em all.

Connect with Quinn:
Facebook: facebook.com/AuthorQuinnAnderson
Twitter: @QuinnAndersonXO
Tumblr: QuinnAndersonWrites.tumblr.com
Email: quinnandersonwrites@gmail.com

Enjoy more stories like
Fourteen Summers
at RiptidePublishing.com!

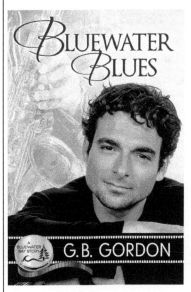

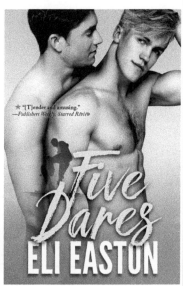

★ "[T]ender and amusing."
—*Publishers Weekly, Starred Review*

Bluewater Blues

Five Dares

Bonding over the blues is just the start—if they can learn to trust each other.

ISBN: 978-1-62649-458-9

To fix things, he'll have to face the greatest dare of all.

ISBN: 978-1-62649-651-4